Praise for C

"Witty, startlingly astute."   —People (Book of the Week)

"I can't remember the last time I was as completely bewitched by a fictional character as I was by Bea Seger. What a treat to view life through the eyes of this funny, smart, gutsy woman who has suffered its outrageous slings and arrows and just keeps coming back for more."

—Richard Russo, author of *Empire Falls*
and *Chances Are . . .*

"Stephanie Gangi's *Carry the Dog* is powered by insight and true wit as it explores families and their aftershocks, as well as art, regret, and the state of being an older, desiring female in a world that too often looks away. I enjoyed it immensely."

—Meg Wolitzer, *New York Times* bestselling
author of *The Female Persuasion*

"*Carry the Dog* . . . takes up critiques of visual culture within a very personal context: a novel about aging and coming to terms with childhood trauma. By placing these conundrums inside the body of a sixty-year-old woman experiencing a long-delayed coming of age, she speaks to the many women . . . who are going through this transition. It's a deeply ironic moment . . . to perceive themselves, finally, *as* themselves, even as they are becoming invisible to the world that has fetishized them . . . When such a change is touched on in books or film, too often it's a source of tragedy, even madness. Gangi, in refreshing contrast, argues that invisibility is freeing."

—*Los Angeles Times*

"Memorable . . . Worth reading . . . Most endearing is the character of Bea, who deals with the physical, psychological, economic, and romantic challenges of aging with humor and attitude."

—*Publishers Weekly*

"*Carry the Dog* is a fantastic novel about art, fame, aging, and the unfathomable mystery of family. Stephanie Gangi writes with a rare mix of grace and urgency."

—Jess Walter, author of *Beautiful Ruins*
and *The Cold Millions*

"With the rambunctious and moving *Carry the Dog*, Stephanie Gangi shows us how uncovering the truth to our past can push us to live better lives in the present . . . She narrates all this with a light tone that is often humorous and, frankly, very entertaining; her characters are ruthless and utterly relatable every step of the way . . . Bea deals with the aging process with wit, intelligence, humor, and a feistiness that never grows old."

—*The Brooklyn Rail*

"A keenly observed and devastating novel. Though Bea's is a voice that, at times, made me laugh with recognition, her story is so dark and compelling that I woke before dawn to finish reading."

—Polly Samson, author of *A Theater for Dreamers*

"Beautiful . . . Haunting and fantastic. I was so captivated by this novel. I loved it!"

—Zibby Owens, *Moms Don't Have Time to Read Books*

"Funny and humane . . . Gangi's heroine, Bea Seger, is warm and complex, engaging and brave and messed up, but the book is deceptively likable; it also takes on big subjects: aging and sexuality, agency and consent, and who gets to say what, exactly, gets to happen in the name of art."   —*Bloom*

"[Bea is] one of my favorite protagonists of the year, an indefatigable older woman facing crises with great doses of wit, determination, and vulnerability."   —*Largehearted Boy*

"Extraordinary . . . A fun, interesting read that deals with aging in a funny and sarcastic way."   —*Revel*

"[*Carry the Dog*] brings a great amount of insight into the life of a child brought up as a muse to her mother's art . . . Heartbreaking and gripping."   —*Campus Circle* (Best Books of 2021)

"Remarkable . . . Brims with wit, warmth, and compassion."
                                        —*My Prime Time News* (Denver)

"Fiercely funny . . . A story of possibilities."   —*New Pages*

CARRY THE DOG

Also by Stephanie Gangi
The Next

CARRY THE DOG

a novel

Stephanie Gangi

ALGONQUIN BOOKS OF CHAPEL HILL   2022

Published by

Algonquin Books of Chapel Hill

Post Office Box 2225

Chapel Hill, North Carolina 27515-2225

an imprint of Workman Publishing Co., Inc., a subsidiary of

Hachette Book Group, Inc.

1290 Avenue of the Americas

New York, New York 10104

LIBRARY OF CONGRESS CATALOGING-IN-PUBLICATION DATA

Names: Gangi, Stephanie, author.
Title: Carry the dog : a novel / Stephanie Gangi.
Description: First Edition. | Chapel Hill, North Carolina : Algonquin Books of
  Chapel Hill, 2021. | Summary: "A woman looks back at the events that shaped
  her life, especially the scandals and family secrets that stand in the way of her
  making peace with her past"— Provided by publisher.
Identifiers: LCCN 2021019227 | ISBN 9781643751276 (hardcover) |
  ISBN 9781643752242 (ebook)
Subjects: GSAFD: Mystery fiction.
Classification: LCC PS3607.A465 C37 2021 | DDC 813/.6—dc23
LC record available at https://lccn.loc.gov/2021019227

ISBN 978-1-64375-327-0 (PB)

10 9 8 7 6 5 4 3 2 1
First Paperback Edition

for Sophie
for Grace

The Uses of Sorrow

(In my sleep I dreamed this poem)

Someone I loved once gave me
a box full of darkness.

It took me years to understand
that this, too, was a gift.

—Mary Oliver

CARRY THE DOG

Chapter One

I'M IN THE dark, I can't see.

The glow of electronics in the bedroom messes with my mela-
tonin so I've shut down the computer, unplugged the printer, there's
no phone or tablet charging nearby, no LED clock numbers. It must
be two or three a.m., a winter night. City noise outside is sporadic,
but bus brakes and sirens still shriek, and random humans and cats
do too, and dogs bark, and the traffic on the highway rumbles, tidal.
Under everything is the constant night hum peculiar to Manhattan. It
sounds like the whir of the Vornado standing fans in the house where
I grew up.

I once read that if you can't sleep, don't force your eyes closed,
keep them open. To tire them out. So I search the dark for what I
know is there—armoire, desk, big chair, Dory the dog—but can't see.

I feel-think around the rims and detect a slight burn and heaviness, like my eyes want to close so I close them.

Here we go. My brain is like a tourist clicking through souvenir scenes on an old View-Master with faded slides and old-fashioned darkroom prints. *Click,* a photograph emerges doubled behind each eyelid. *Click,* the two merge into one. A boy and a girl nap together. Nine and six, brother and sister, it's in the faces and the geometry of the limbs. The sheet's folds and wrinkles fit and draw the eye. Our shoulders are bare. My brother is on his back, arms wide, one leg flung off the side of the bed. His face is in shadow, obscured, but the way his curls cling to his neck, it is hot despite the fan. Summer. I am on my side turned away from him but close in the big bed, and my hands are held together under my cheek, like praying. My hair obscures my face too, except for my mouth, a slack bow. My brother's mouth is a slack bow, too.

My mother took the photograph. She shot us while we slept, and *Nap* is the only candid included in the series that came to be known in the newspapers as the Marx Nudes.

Don't move. Stay still.

Miri shot *Nap* with a Leica, but for the staged photo shoots she used an old-fashioned large-format view camera because she wanted to make big pictures. That camera was cumbersome outdoors, hard to move once set up, completely manual and labor-intensive. She would pose us, disappear under a canvas hood, managing exposure and composition, and wait for the light. We three—Ansel, Henry and I—would forget Miri was shooting and we'd wrestle and bicker or outright fight while she worked.

The hours we spent in the woods as subjects of our mother's work were our chores, and we got an allowance which she called "pocket money." I tell myself I was just a kid, that I didn't know any better. I obeyed, I complied, I followed along with Ansel and Henry although I hated chores. Our bodies were arranged by my mother, shot, developed, printed, and hung on gallery walls by my mother. If we resisted, Miri used her arsenal to get us back up into the woods: our competitive natures, her artistic calling, and, of course, the threat of withholding the pocket money. If one of us complained (me), slammed a door (Ansel), disappeared at the appointed hour (Henry), our avoidance tactics would earn us days of silent treatment, no eye contact, and messages relayed through whoever had been most cooperative or our father, Albert.

Dory dream-growls and deep-breathes and dog-paddles in her sleep, curled in the curve between my ass and my thighs. I punch the pillows. I try another insomnia cure, a little movie of the mind, starring me. I am in the cast-off T-shirt and jeans of my brothers, I am barefoot with my black hair in a braid, I am sweeping each room of the Grand View house. I sweep, sweep my way to the darkroom at the back, and there is Miri in a denim apron with leather ties, photos pinned to a line above her head. Her hair falls, hiding her face. She's smoking and stirring prints in development trays. She uses tongs, grips an edge, pulls me out, dripping. She frowns. I have not developed to her satisfaction. I am not who she saw through her lens.

Miriam Marx is long dead, and yet she's inside me, where she has been my whole life, from before my life, from when I was cells inside her trying to gang up and become a person. She seeped in, with her low murmur and cigarette smoke and darkroom chemicals. She's dead and yet when I catch a whiff of sour wine in last night's glass, or the stubbed butts from my ashtray on the fire escape, it's like smelling salts. She's revived. Just the thought of green beans makes me gag, remembering how she would dump them from a can into a pot and heat them in their tinged water to show Albert she'd put something green on our plates. I would push them around with my fork, try to relax my throat, try to swallow to keep peace at the dinner table. Miri sat back with her wine, her cigarette, the squint that meant she was killing time until she could retreat to the darkroom with the day's film.

On a night like tonight I think, *Where was Albert?*

I grope the bedside table for my notebook, my pen. I can't see but I scrawl *Albert* with a question mark across the page, a note for the memoir I'm trying to write. The title is *Exposed*. Or *Exposure*. I can't decide. It's a work in progress, glacial progress. My idea is to look back from the brink of sixty and tell my story. The brink of sixty, it's rough terrain for anybody, time to take stock of your life even if you didn't have Miriam Marx as a mother.

I was born Berenice Marx-Seger. We were hyphenated before it was common but I dropped Marx a long time ago. I go by Bea, a nickname my mother hated. My brothers and I were each named for a photographer Miri idolized: Berenice Abbott, Ansel Adams, Henri Cartier-Bresson. Miri called Henri "Ahn-ree," with a Parisian spin. She teased Ansel that he was lucky, she wanted to name him Weegee but Albert put his foot down for once. Albert is still alive, parked and idling at the Sandy Edge assisted living facility in Delray Beach, Florida. Ansel is dead. I haven't spoken with Henri—he's Henry to me, the regular way—in decades. So much has kept us apart.

Every few years there's an article about my mother and then a rapid round of attention to Miriam Marx and her work. Culture vultures pick through everything old, everything "vintage," especially art, especially controversial. People with a dark interest in naked kids explore my mother's work from the anonymity of their devices. The backstory increases the buzz. I ignore the calls and the emails and the notifications and hide out until it all passes, but recently high culture, in the person of the associate curator of photography at the Museum of Modern Art, has found me.

Violet Yeun has been trying to contact me for months. *Ms. Marx, on behalf of the Museum of Modern Art . . . Ms. Marx, as Associate Curator of the Photography Department of the Museum of Modern Art . . . Ms. Marx, if I may request an hour of your time . . .* She is the foremost authority on my mother, besides me. She thinks my mother was a feminist visionary. She thinks the Marx Nudes represented a radical departure from the traditional family values of that era. She thinks Miri's photographs showed that childhood is dark, innocence is a myth, motherhood is a trap, and art—Art—will set you free. Dr. Yeun wants to restore my mother's reputation.

I get it, I do. And yet. That's me in the photographs, with my brothers, posed by our mother. Nude seems different than naked, nude means on display. A generation after Miri, Sally Mann got famous for photographs she took of her children, and there was a rush to compare us. At some point I got brave and read everything and zoomed in and the thing is, her kids look like themselves, except naked. We don't. We're on display. We're nude.

I wonder what Henry would say.

The black room has blurred to dark gray. It must be predawn—four-thirty? Five? I can almost see the armoire, the desk, the books, shapes that loom. I can feel Dory breathing and I pace my breath to hers, the rise and fall, and that helps me sleep, almost. In old movies, magical spiritual types—Aborigines or Native Americans or the Amish—recoiled from cameras. They worried the camera would steal their souls, that the image would be cursed and the person in the photograph would suffer. From my own experience, the magical movie types had a point. I do feel like part of my soul was stolen by my mother's camera. I do feel cursed.

Also, I'm waiting for some test results.

I go by Seger but inside, I am still part Marx. I can't help it—I blister with something like pride when I read about my mother, the groundbreaking female photographer. I despised chores, but Miri stood me on a box and helped me fit my head under her canvas hood. She told me what to look for through the lens. She taught me how to look wide and change my perspective to see close. She showed me that far away is one place and near is another, even though they are both aspects of the same landscape. How the light will tell you what to see, if you wait. How if you wait, the right light will light the dark.

My brain hurts like a warehouse. I've always loved that Bowie lyric. There's a storage unit north of the city with all of Miriam Marx's work. I've never been there. I imagine it's packed to the rafters with her cameras, equipment, undeveloped negatives, original prints, all the versions, rejected work, slides, videos, journals. All the images of me and my brothers. The Marx Nudes. I assume. I don't know.

Chapter Two

IT'S ALL A great debate between Gary and me.

Gary is my ex-husband. Twice. We've been together in various configurations since I was seventeen years old. He's invited me to dinner tonight at Balthazar, and a money talk will surely be on the menu. He believes there are Miriam Marx licensing opportunities, maybe tastefully rendered cards and little notebooks, postcards and calendars, to generate income I could certainly use. Gary sent me a link recently where you could buy T-shirts printed with Diane Arbus holding her Rolleiflex, fifty dollars apiece.

"Bean," he is fond of saying, repeatedly, "it comes down to retirement. You have to leverage the past to secure the future." We have a complicated financial history built on calcified guilt and resentments, traversed by crumbling bridge loans and a trickling cash flow, all muddied by who earned what and who squandered it during our years together. Gary helped me buy my apartment and Gary's guy pays the mortgage every month, what Gary and the accountant call "Bea's subsidy." Naturally he has a vested interest in seeing me financially secure. I have dwindling savings, a sad IRA, a few resilient stocks from the olden days, gifted to us kids by Albert when we were little: a tractor manufacturer, American Airlines, some Coca-Cola. I make a little freelance money, enough to subsidize the subsidy, from interviews I conduct with corporate executives, mostly men. I ask question after question and record them droning on, saying the same thing: revenue, shareholders, markets, and projections. I transcribe their words and turn them into articles or biographies or content for annual reports or websites. Nobody's looking to be original, they stick to a script, but I do try to listen for one thing I can use to make these guys interesting. It makes me feel like I am a writer, although not the way I imagined it. The truth is, all I ever did was *imagine* being a writer. The next step was never clear to me.

Anyway, at fifty-nine, with the postmenopausal attention span of, well, a fifty-nine-year-old woman, it takes me twice as long to transcribe the corporate guys as it used to. Lately my mind wanders as soon as the men start talking in my earbuds. I stab and swipe at my smartphone to start over, and then over again. I try to concentrate and then I *really* can't concentrate. Writing the memoir, that struggle, started with me trying to remember dates, figure out how old I was when certain things happened. Not having family means there is no one to ask, no one to set you straight. I talk to Albert down at Sandy Edge once a month, and I have a list of questions to help with my project, but he's either too spaced out or I lose my nerve.

I have to get ready for dinner. I have to look good. Gary might bring a date, someone young. He's pushing seventy and craves the reflected shine of youth, which he thinks buys him a decade off his own age. He's a man, he may be right. He's showed up with young women in the past, as if I'm the amicable ex-wife and we're a cool, evolved divorced couple. I don't feel that way, but I know how he thinks. He can get away with it, a little tax on "the subsidy," a little uptick on the interest rate.

I need bright light so I'm up on a stepladder to change one of three awkwardly situated, very delicate light bulbs in the fixture above the bathroom sink. I can't remember the last time I climbed a stepladder without fearing for my life. My fingers are fat from Thai at lunch, my glasses are in the other room, my arms ache from reaching, and I have a cramp in abdomen muscles I don't have.

"Echo! I need help! In the bathroom!"

Echo lives here now. A couple of months back, I got an email from her telling me she was moving to the city, wondering if I could help her find a job waiting tables. On impulse I invited her to stay in the second bedroom until she sorts herself out. She's my father's step-daughter. I mean daughter. He adopted her. She was born Hannah but rechristened herself when she left Florida. She's trying Echo on. I say, Go for it, that's what New York is for. She scours "Roommate Wanted" on Craigslist for a hipper living arrangement, downtown or Brooklyn, but I offer meals, the complete cable package, and a closet full of clothes she considers vintage. I like the company. She helps with Dory. Dory loves Echo.

I hear her laugh from her room. "Damn, Bea! I didn't sign up for senior bathroom assistance." She comes and offers me an arm and eases me down and goes up and gets the job done. "Maybe it's time for a Life Alert necklace?"

"Hilarious. You are on Dory duty. I'm going out."

"With your rock star?"

"He's not my rock star, not anymore. He's just my old ex. Walk the dog!"

Gary *is* a rock star. An actual rock star. He's Gary Going. He was never a rock god, never hit the stratosphere, but he's in a substratosphere, for sure—Lou Reed level, still playing out. He can walk the city without being harassed like a Mick or a Sir Paul, but there are a lot of guys who fell in love with Gary's band Chalk Outline in the seventies. He was their guitar hero, with a voice he worked from croon to yelp.

Gary knows about leveraging the past. Old rock and roll is good business. He's always hustling with the reunion tours, the remastered this, the reissued that. Now and then he sits in when a producer wants to add an artsy-punk cred to an up-and-comer in the studio. He's had some throat problems, nodules, and when he's onstage they cover his old-man croak with backup singers. His fingers are gnarled with arthritis, they hurt him, so he plays what amounts to convincing air guitar while a younger band member does the shredding. Young men discover him anew all the time because of their dads, their granddads. He gets adulation but he needs more than that. He needs the girls and the money too, even though he's a septuagenarian. It's all part of the rock-and-roll job description. Except his stash these days includes statins for the cholesterol, insulin for his sugar, Zoloft for impending doom, the purple pill for the GERD, and the blue one for the exhausted penis. He was on an oxy binge a couple of years ago when he had his hip replaced but was taking it more to blunt the shame of using a cane than for the pain.

I check my phone. I have missed call notifications from two old-school 212 numbers. One is Dr. Keswani. The other is from MoMA. I ignore both. There's a text from Gary: **See you at.** He doesn't text properly. It drives me crazy. He rants about texting, that it's the final nail in the coffin of our soul-dead society. I've pointed out that he made a career screaming into a microphone about our soul-dead society but he waves me off. Texting is an ordeal for him. He has to locate his glasses, manage the tiny touchpad, and stop taking autocorrect so personally. It's a lot at his age.

Dory snores at the foot of my bed, which I recently vacated. Of course I napped. I don't sleep well and I need to look rested for Balthazar. I've got temporary wrinkles from the pillowcase. I keep meaning to buy satin. The wrinkles take longer to recede every month. I wash with the anti-everything cleanser, apply pro-everything serum, *pat, pat, pat* and wait for my face to un-crevice. One good thing about being an older woman is you can be vain and not hide it anymore. People find it amusing. My black hair is still magnificent, if I do say so myself. It's thick and threaded with silver and I have a white streak at my widow's peak—pretty dramatic. I don't do much, just fluff it up, encourage the wild. I like to look like I have bed hair, something men find sexy. Found sexy. My mother had hair like mine; I mean, I have hair like hers. I resemble her, same mane, same size, same bone structure. I think I look how she would have looked if she had lived. Which she didn't.

I press my fingers where frown lines would be. Those I take care of. I started with Botox years ago, almost by accident, before it was a grooming essential. I was writing luncheon speeches for a makeup mogul, and she offered to pay me in botulism injections to eradicate the parallel lines between my eyes, the "elevens," which gave me a look of being mildly angry all the time. I *am* mildly angry all the time, but I don't need everyone to see it coming. I was panicked when she stuck me eight times in the forehead. I went home and waited to die. But I was fine and the lines were gone and now I'm a regular.

I do my eyebrows. I tap nude shadow across the lids with a fingertip. I can't drag a brush across them; they would crepe. Mascara, of course—it's the only thing I haven't had to change from when I was young: strokes and strokes of black mascara, very Chrissie Hynde. A swirl of blush, and Rouge Dior 999 on my lips.

I am not Gary's first love. There was an Italian babysitter, Angela; this was up in the Bronx. He was a freshman in high school. She was experienced. He searched for her on Facebook a few years ago and she looked pretty good for an old lady, which Gary took as confirmation of his own enduring sex appeal.

I'm not even his big love. That was his first wife, Margaux, child of an English acting dynasty crossed with musty-money royalty. Margaux flew around the globe with her flock of British birds chasing rock stars, embarrassing her family. Chalk Outline was the opening act for the Rolling Stones for one infamous tour, '65 or '66, and that's where Gary and Margaux met, backstage at the Albert Hall. Eventually she fell off her platforms, hit her head on a curb outside a club, and tabloid photos show them in lurid black and white, with black blood dripping onto white mink, and Gary, a cigarette dangling from his lips, bleary, dragging her up from the gutter. Her family stepped in; a divorce materialized. Sometimes I peruse the internet and Margaux is in all the best swinging sixties pictures, outside Annabel's in a long coat over a short skirt, high white boots, with porcelain skin, crosswise teeth, giant eyes fringed by black lashes that meet the edges of her long blond bangs.

Margaux was with Gary at the moment he was poised to launch, before he knew he'd never make it Mick big. She was his muse when everything was possible. Naturally he mythologizes that time, that girl. When they met, he was only twenty or so, and he'd recently been just Gary Goldbaum from the Bronx. I was still a child, posing with my brothers for Miri.

I'm not his first love or the big one, but I do know how to wait him out. I give my hair a final fluff. I see behind myself in the mirror, where *Carry the Dog* hangs on the wall. It's an early Miriam Marx photograph, from before she met Albert. If it weren't my mother's photograph, I would love it unreservedly. A girl and boy, sister and brother, carry a long dog. Each holds an end. They march through what looks like a rush-hour crowd in Times Square. The children wear limp T-shirts, baggy dungarees and no shoes. The girl is smaller but she leads, chin like a prow, tight-lipped with determination. They look as though they stepped out of a Walker Evans photograph from the thirties. They are touched by the sun in a way that no other people in the photograph are. Miri caught the light, and the children, precisely.

Carry the Dog was featured in the Speaking of Pictures section of *Life* magazine when Miri was just eighteen years old, a girl. Family legend has it that it was chosen by Margaret Bourke-White herself. I've seen Echo linger and study it. I imagine a future conversation with her where I am magnanimous, telling her the photograph is a gift, sister to sister, to celebrate some accomplishment of hers. Or maybe I will keep it. I do love that photograph, so I don't know.

Chapter Three

"WHAT HAPPENED TO your hair?"

"Is that how you say hello? Come meet Malcolm Bix. Malcolm, Berenice Marx-Seger."

Gary parades all my names. His hair is newly shoe-polish black. He's wearing a too-tight black leather jacket that matches the hair, and both work against his senior skin. He looks like a deflated Goth. I don't pull my skeptical eyebrows down fast enough, which Gary catches, and his upper lip retreats in embarrassment. He presents me to a standing, smiling man who is extending his hand. A good-looking man. The rose-gold lighting in Balthazar is advantageous and it sets off the man's tan, the silver bristle along his jaw and chin, and makes his steel blue eyes and his steel gray hair gleam.

"Ms. Marx. Malcolm Bix. Happy to meet you."

Bix guides me to my chair as waiters pour water and shake napkins onto laps and Gary pours pink bubbles into my glass and I get my reading glasses tangled up with my necklaces. I say, "Not Marx. Just Seger."

"Pardon?"

"Just Seger." I work to free my glasses.

"Berenice dropped the Marx years ago. For privacy reasons."

He never calls me that. "What's with the 'Berenice'? What's going on?"

Gary laughs his fake laugh, as if I'm adorable when confused.

Bix says, "Berenice, as in Abbott, right? The New York photographer?"

Anybody with Wikipedia access would know that. I curve my mouth into a polite smile. "I don't go by Berenice either." I slice a look into Gary and use the wife voice that is especially tuned to his frequency. "Can you tell me what's going on? What's up?"

Gary busies himself with his water. Bix puts a hand on my shoulder. He looks at me from under his brow. "Can I call you Bea? Does that work?"

"I'm sorry, who are you again?" I turn to Gary. "Who is he?"

Gary mumbles, "Why don't we let Bix explain himself?"

I am unaccustomed to Gary taking a back seat. The atmosphere is deionized of Gary, who looks even sillier in his aging rocker garb next to Bix. Bix is around fifty, a very good age for a man. He looks like the lumberjack-gentleman who appears on all my devices, his stock photo baiting me to click on senior dating sites, except without the plaid flannel shirt. I'm on guard but I want to stroke his sweater, a color between gray and lavender. I can't decide if his hair is an untended mess or artfully arrayed to look like one. There is man scent on my hand from when I shook his. I can't help myself, I raise it to my nose as if I'm doing a quick rub of an itch. Spicy forest, amber below and lime above, distant, alluring. My bottom buzzes a bit. I sniff and rub to inhale Bix again.

"Do you have allergies?" Before I have a chance to answer him, Bix says to a waiter, "Would you mind removing these?" and hands off the vase of flowers from the center of the table. It's both presumptuous and refreshingly man-of-action. Gary would not in a million years think to have the centerpiece exiled for my greater comfort.

"Here, Bea." Bix hands me an oxford blue cotton handkerchief with a monogram and the same waft of woodsy tang. "Keep that."

"What's going on? Am I about to be deposed or something?" I'm funnier now that I'm of a certain age. I'm not allowed to flirt overtly anymore—that reads desperate—but a smart mouth on an older woman, that's sitcom approved. Gary forces another laugh.

"Bea, first, I want to tell you how honored I am to meet you."

Honored? He is trying to butter me up. This is not the first time I've been the object of someone's questionable interest in the little girl in the photographs. Gary knows I get nervous around new people. I'm always leery. I'm leery now. I feel cornered. Bix is smooth, with an open face, a sincere tone, direct eye contact, very L.A.

I take tiny sips of the effervescent rosé. Gary says, "Bea, Bix is a producer. From the coast. We worked together on our little movie. *Opening Act*. Which did pretty well. You remember."

Gary is performing for Bix and is expecting me to perform with him. "Yes, Gary, I remember. I know *Opening Act*. If *you* remember, my song is in your little movie."

I tried to be a lyricist after Gary and I met. I wrote songs with his encouragement and the promise of his connections. One of my songs charted impressively. That was "*I, Alive,*" and that's when our money conflicts began. I was paid a flat fee for my work, having relied completely on Gary's advice, Gary's lawyer and Gary's accountant. There was no contract, no paperwork. We had a falling out over "*I, Alive*" royalties—he got a lot, I got none. He got recognition, I was still just the wife. It never occurred to me to sit across a table in a midtown office with my own guy and hammer it out, the way Gary did with any other cowriter. Instead I went sullen. I brought up the issue again and again at the worst times, which Gary considered nagging. To nag, to be a nag, that's a deal breaker, that's not sexy. Over the course of a year or so, Gary toured with my song. He hit the road with all its temptations, and that was that for our first marriage go-round. He divorced me, we split up, I got the famous subsidy he's always reminding me of.

When *Opening Act* was released, "*I, Alive*" got a big boost. Chalk Outline has been rediscovered by the kids, and "*I, Alive*" has been YouTubed and downloaded millions of times, and it's given Gary's career and his finances new life. Every time that song is played, people get paid—except me. Young music wants him. He tours again. He probably still gets laid off my song. Meanwhile, I had to beg to get my name added to the Wikipedia page as cowriter.

Bix redirects us like a pro. "Bea, I have something else in mind. Something I think you will appreciate. And benefit from. Financially. I think we all will. I *know* we all will."

I hand Bix back his handkerchief for dramatic, dismissive effect, now smudged with Rouge Dior 999. Gary puts a hand on my forearm. "Hang on, Bean. Just listen to Bix, will you? This is good. For you."

The underlying subject is money, so I am outnumbered, over-matched, outflanked, and about to be handled. These two know how to get it, how to keep it, how to make it multiply. They've talked. You could say they've plotted. A distinctive girly powerlessness flushes my ears, tightens my throat, burns my eyes, and affects my ability to hear, speak, or see clearly. I'm struck by a paralysis when the topic is money. I drain my drink to loosen up. My impulse is to shake Gary's hand off my arm, but instead I say, "Is this why you dyed your hair? For Hollywood?"

Gary is stung, as intended. I feel stung, too, by how mean I can be. Who knows? Whatever pitch is coming my way might actually be good for me, as he says. I flash on Malcolm Bix holding a giant check. On the other hand, it's my family, my childhood, my trauma locked away in that storage unit. I lift my chin. "I am not doing a sleazy movie about my mother. I'm not doing a documentary or a thinly veiled thing or a changed-names thing. It's not happening. I'm sorry." I don't know why I'm apologizing.

Malcolm Bix magically ordered because beautiful plates are set before us. Once again, he's both presumptuous and manly. I hate-love it. I'm starving. A glowing pile of pommes frites is set just under my nose. I pluck one with what I hope is disdain and touch it to the mayonnaise in a ramekin. New crystal appears and is filled all around with a Côtes du Rhône, bien sûr. There's asparagus and hanger steak, cooked to rare perfection.

Balthazar diners chat and lean toward one another. The bar is three deep, the little tables near the window are full. The waiters, in white shirts and black ties and long white aprons, weave and dip and bow. I am sitting between two men with what used to be called "presence." It's New York so other people don't look-look, they glance. Bix gives off a can't-place-him vibe. Gary is downtown famous. Nobody knows me, but they are glancing the hell out of the three of us. I dressed for it, black silk shirt, Darryl K leather pants, black boots—my uniform, my best clothes, bought for me a long time ago by Gary, clothes I baby so they last because I could never afford to replace them. I'm drinking now, I'm hell-bent on enjoying myself. I want some old-fashioned attention, my hair, my outfit, my undead female desire lurching like a zombie in Bix's direction. Who cares that the men are jockeying for position, what else is new?

Bix raises his glass. The wine sways as he gestures toward the table. "I understand. You've made yourself clear. But look at this beautiful meal. I'm a man, right? I want to give you my idea. Show off for a beautiful woman a little bit. Can you indulge me?"

Sometimes it's nice to be buttered up. It's exhausting to be suspicious all the time. I don't look at Bix, but I set my glass down, cut into my steak, and give the tiniest possible shrug with a soupçon of side-eye.

He locks ice eyes on me. "By the way." He leans and speaks as though it's just the two of us. "You have amazing hair."

I toss it. "Yours is pretty good, too. Very Clooney."

Bix nods his acknowledgment and says, "At least we've all still got hair, some better than others." He winks at me, at Gary's expense. I laugh with him because I am still mad at Gary for not warning me that a Hollywood producer would be here to try to sweet talk me into turning my family trauma into a biopic. Also I am intoxicated and I've just been winked at across candlelight by a good-looking man.

Gary touches his hair and mutters, "They overdid it."

I turn to Bix and lean my chin on my hand. I bat the black eyelashes. "Okay, consider yourself indulged. Show off."

"Think, *A Beautiful Mind*. Think, *I'm Not There*."

"So, not a documentary?"

"No, no. A biopic. A biopic with a budget. A name writer. A woman director. Possibly. A serious cast. Oscar-caliber. Classy." He's fallen into sales-y producer patter. It's kind of hypnotic.

Gary says, "*Almost Famous*. That guy. For the writer. He worked for *Rolling Stone* as a kid. He gets the time period. Somebody intense for your mother. The vampire girl. Kristen Stewart."

Bix shuts him down. "We could play the casting game all night. Let's not get ahead of ourselves. I want Bea to be comfortable."

"I'm comfortable. I'm very comfortable." I sip ruby wine from a crystal globe. "But why do you need me? Why not just make it all up, a fictionalized version of Miriam?"

"You ask a good question, Bea." Bix turns to Gary. "Smart. Very smart." Gary gives a smug *I told you* nod to confirm their condescending, secret man-findings right in front of me. Am I always ready to be offended, or are they always offensive? What can I do? I can't spend every minute calling men out for being men.

"I want the stars aligned on this, Bea. It has some tricky themes. Living subjects. I need the family—that's you, Bea—to sign off. Honestly, Bea, we need your participation. That's important to the success of this project."

As much as I want to stay open, I get even more suspicious when people use my name a lot. "Tricky themes. That's an understatement."

"Believe me. The events of your past will be treated with respect. Have you seen *Frances*? Jessica Lange? Neurotic woman artist kind of thing. Lobotomy. But well done. We understand that there are . . . challenges with the material."

Frances happens to be in my movie pantheon. I wonder if Gary offered this bit of intel in a predinner briefing with Bix. I can't hold back. "'Neurotic woman artist kind of thing'? You make lobotomy sound like a genre."

Gary adds, "Those challenges will make it a hit." I glare without looking at him to get him to back off, another wifely skill I have developed over years with Gary.

"Also, Bea, you are the gatekeeper of your mother's work. Is that accurate? Is that a fair statement?"

"I guess so, yes."

Bix says, "Tell me about ownership."

I spend a nanosecond too long thinking how I want to answer because of MoMA's interest, so of course, Gary answers for me. "The brother, Henry, not a factor. He's been gone a long time. No interest in the work."

I am tempted to clarify, but I don't want to keep jumping down Gary's throat. I expend so much effort reframing for Gary, translating for Gary, translating Gary to others. The truth is, I don't know that Henry is not a factor, that Henry has no interest in our mother's work. How could I?

"And what about your father? Albert?"

"My father is in assisted living in Florida. He's in and out. Mentally. Physically. He has a wife. An adopted daughter. My sister, Echo. She lives with me. But what does that have to do with anything?"

Gary says, "Sister? I thought she was your stepsister? She lives with you permanently? Did you tell me that?"

Bix ignores Gary. "I'm interested in the archives. In who has access."

"The archives are a storage unit in Rockland County, and me, I have access. Since recently. My father stored everything years ago and forgot about it, but when he went into assisted living, his wife took over. She doesn't want to deal with it anymore. She transferred the unit to me. Albert is ninety-one. One less thing, when the time comes. I pay the monthly charge and at some point I have to deal with the contents."

Gary puts his hand over my hand, to confirm the pecking order. "Yes, the archive costs are taken care of."

I can't help myself. "It's not an archive, Gary. It's a storage place in Congers. I have no idea what's in there and neither do you."

Bix says, "Okay. Okay. The idea is to integrate the actual images and ephemera. To bring as much authenticity as we can to the script. To the production. So we would need access too. Soon. That's it? There's nothing else?"

I haven't mentioned MoMA to Gary, and by not mentioning it right now, I am compounding the omission. Turning it into a lie. MoMA's interest in my mother is a very big deal, and yet I've kept it to myself. I don't usually lie or hide, not because I'm morally superior, but because I have a terrible memory. I choose my words carefully. "There are prints out in the world. I have no idea what's on the internet, or the auction sites. Miri was locked down by Stoffel Gallery when she was alive, and all those prints were sold at her last show. She died before the European shows. That's the public stuff. I don't know what's in storage."

"The less out there, the better. That means we—the production team, which would include you, you'd get a producing credit—will have the most authentic take on Miriam Marx."

I say to Gary, "And you? Would you get a producing credit too?" He twitches a smile like a guilty boy.

"Again, let's not get ahead of ourselves . . ." Bix waves for more wine.

"You both seem way ahead of me." They laugh the guilty-boy laugh times two. "And what's the title of this movie? Have you gotten that far?"

"Working title, *Exposed*. Or *Exposure*. We go back and forth. What do you think?" Bix and Gary beam at me.

My title! I almost whip around and blame Gary for sharing it— along with telling Bix how I like my steak cooked and how much I love the movie *Frances*—but Gary doesn't even know I'm writing a memoir. He refers to the notebook I carry as my "diary." I cringe a little hearing *Exposed/Exposure* said out loud. It sounds too obvious for a photography memoir, too cheesy, and then I think, *So what, I'm not actually writing it anyway.*

I've lain in bed and searched the dark corners, I've sat at my desk and stared at the screen trying to work it out, the story of the family, and my story, too, and I don't know. I can't see it. The past is like an optical illusion. The closer I get, the farther away it is. Why not just let these guys do all the work? Who cares what they call it? I shrug and nod.

I hate being cynical. I hate being suspicious. I love Gary and I trust him. He took me from bar to bed to breakfast with rock and roll and booze and weed when I was just a kid. I knew him for ten hours before I jumped into his chrome blue Karmann Ghia with a backpack and urged, "Go! Go!" He hit the gas and raced me away from my childhood home.

I trust him, or maybe I just know all his moves by now—my version of trust. It's work I've always done, anticipating and navigating and course correcting around Gary's moves. I doubt he's even aware of mine. But he has a point about using the past to secure my future. I've spent a long time not doing that. I've spent a long time keeping the past locked away.

Maybe I am withholding forgiveness. Maybe I don't understand closure. Maybe I am—have always been—stopped in time, the little sister in the photographs. Maybe I got trapped up there in the woods, and now the path is so overgrown I can't see how to get out. Maybe if I follow the directions offered by Malcolm Bix or Violet Yeun, I can move on.

Dinner has concluded. I use the signing pen that came with the dinner check and one of the extra receipts to make a note for the memoir. I write *Henry*, with a question mark, like the sleepless night note about Albert, and then I write *Ansel*, underlined so emphatically that I score the paper. I'm not sure I know why.

Chapter Four

WE LEFT BIX on Broadway and the topic of Hollywood Miri tabled at Balthazar.

Gary doesn't push it. It's a lot to think about. I have things on my mind he doesn't know about. MoMA. Dr. Keswani's voicemail with mammogram results. I had a scare years ago. It ended up being fine. I avoid her annually and she patiently leaves messages and I eventually listen and do what I must, get the mammogram. That's always Dr. Keswani's message: *You're fine.*

"Come over," he says into my neck in the cab. What interesting animals we are. I have inhaled Gary's breath when it's foul, I've heard it sputter and wheeze and gasp, I've written our initials in it as it condensed on a window pane, I have paced mine to his thousands of times and now, here we are, old marrieds, old friends, just plain old

"old," but first we were lovers, and his tone and his breath are still flint for my desire.

I take his rough hand, his calloused fingertips, and I hold it between my knees. Not too high up. Not yet. I am wearing the black leather pants, something sexy that I can still pull off. Gary says, "Mmm, leather," and I relax my knees and bring his hand farther up my inner thigh. He kneads one thigh and the other, which he knows I like. I put my hand under his sweater, and pass it across his belly, and up, across his chest, the fur there thinner and more wiry as he's gotten older; and there's his heart under my hand, and he's breathing deep with a tremor at the top. I press his hand against me and push against it. Gary says, "You're burning," and little miracle, I am and I whisper yes and we kiss. I peek at the driver in his rearview mirror, and he peeks back and shakes his head, either in disgust because we are old, or because he can't get one night without folks going at it in his back seat.

Gary says, "Let me take a pill."

Oh no, not the pill. "Not yet. Maybe we don't need it." I say *we* to make him feel less self-conscious. I pull at his belt and he pushes my hand away. He pops the pill with a swig from his ever-present water bottle and we come apart and wait in respectful silence for the erection, timed to coincide with our arrival at the loft.

Gary considers Viagra to be the greatest invention of the twentieth century, tied only with air-conditioning. He's an old guy, one of millions who want to solve time. I've read the erectile dysfunction brochure. I want to be supportive. I want to protect his ego. Hell, I want to solve time too. I mentally catalog my own issues—the dryness, the loose grip, the slice of pain, the rogue peeing—but I would never discuss my broken-down vagina with Gary. Never! A fundamental right for men, virility into old age, reads as pathetic for women. It occurs to me, maybe Gary doesn't need the pill with his younger women.

Maybe his dick remembers what to do when the body of the woman in hand is supple, when the lady parts are not postmenopausal.

We're motoring south slow in traffic to Tribeca. We stop and go, the meter on its roll, the driver's bad mood like a climate in the small cab. I look out the window, watch New Yorkers push through to the end of the day. Gary is in his "monitoring the effect" state, trying to feel the tingle, the pulse.

We ride the industrial elevator. We start up again. He peels off my pants, I lift his sweater over his head. We are undressing each other, kissing, both of us earnestly trying to get back to that rare hot spot we managed to occupy in the cab. His fingers probe. "Huh," he says.

I go looking for lube. I call from the bathroom, "Do you have any aloe?" and he calls back, "Aloe?" as if I've asked for baby elephant earwax. I walk across the loft to the kitchen zone. I take an egg from the refrigerator, impressed that the king of takeout has eggs. I crack it and separate the white into a small dish and bring that back to bed. I've read about this. It's a good lube alternative in a pinch, viscous and slimy. I say, "Put this on me," but Gary says, "What is that, eggs?" so I do it myself.

"Maybe with your sperm and my egg we will finally get a baby." It flies out of my mouth, a bad joke with a dark history. I'm nobody's mother but I almost was, a few times. I pretend it's ancient history, for Gary's sake. We've never really discussed it. Gary is not wired for the conversation.

For his sake, I act like it's not still so sad.

By now the mood is heavier. The moves are rote. He squeezes a thigh, he squeezes a breast. My desire has flickered out and Gary is hard. There's no getting away from the erection. I try to keep it going, but trying is *trying*. We are obliged, for what seems like hours. Hours of sex is no longer interesting to me, unless we're doing some druggy tantric thing I've read about with candles and lotion that's all about the woman. This is like sawing. This hurts. I keep dabbing at myself with egg whites. My mind drifts to Bix, to that scruff at the jawline, to the steel eyes, the scent. I picture lifting that expensive sweater over his head.

Gary grunts and we're done. We did it. He collapses on top of me. For a while I like being crushed, pinned down; the man-weight is comforting, like those gravity blankets that increase serotonin and decrease cortisol for stress-free sleep. But the buzz between my legs is insistent, my hair is in my eyes and mouth, he is heavy and sticky and sleepy. I wriggle politely. We adjust ourselves to face each other. Our faces are inches apart. I focus on his eyes, blur his black hair which gleams in the soft dark. His eyes are the light-wash denim color I have always loved. The lids, upper and lower, pull down now, droop in a way that makes him seem introspective and kind. His salon helps him out with the sprouting nose and ear hairs, but he's got old man eyebrows, shaggy and multidirectional. There are impressive bags under the eyes, which I don't find unattractive. I love his changing face. I'm pretty sure that's not mutual. Gary sees his own decline in mine.

My Gary was the first person—and to date, the only person—I've told the whole Marx story to. The words rushed out of me at Joe Jr.'s, the diner on 16th Street, near his grimy studio in 1973. There was no internet then, but our family had been in the newspapers a few years before, with pictures of our mother and a couple of the more scandalous photographs, with black bars redacting our genitals and our eyes to protect our identities, even though our names were right there. Gary, the Goldbaum's beloved only child, listened intently. He told me in Joe Jr.'s that it sounded to him like we kids had been exploited, and maybe abused. That I was traumatized. This was new terminology at that time: trauma, abuse. He was concerned for me. He was.

He really was. Our age difference, seventeen-year-old girl, twenty-seven-year-old man—it's more suspect now than it used to be. A relationship with this age gap today, of course I'd question the guy's motives. But it wasn't like that then.

Or was it? I have to stop and think.

I mean, I *was* a kid, and according to Gary himself, I'd been, at the very least, exploited for my mother's work. It was the atmosphere in which I grew up. Gary was older and more experienced, with drugs and money. I can see how if I wrote out our story in a memoir, it could appear that Gary took advantage of me. But. We were so consumed with each other, in such hot lust, desperate, tearing at clothes and pulling hair and merging our bodies and minds and souls. After days in bed together, I didn't know where he left off and I began. It was like that for him, too—that I know. Under the stoned, sexy circumstances, neither of us considered the age difference. Nobody was worrying about power imbalances. We couldn't stop. We were in love. My body and brain were soaked in it. The romance of that!

And yet.

It flares in my memory now, as it has many times over the years. A moment. There was a lawyer meeting about the songs. I—the cowriter—was in the background keeping the coffeepot going, emptying ashtrays, eavesdropping. Gary kept saying *I* this and *I* that, expounding on his ideas, expressing his creative needs and setting forth his contractual demands, things he wanted from a record deal. I was too intimidated to say a word, but when we were alone, entwined, I prodded him. "How come you kept saying *I, I, I* when you were talking about the songwriting? It's *we*, isn't it? On some of those songs, it's just me."

Gary laughed and said, "Beanie, when I say *I*, I mean *we*. You know that. I mean *we*." I accepted it—there was nothing malicious about it—but it stung then and it stings now. The offhand way he disappeared me and my work, the way I gave my tacit consent to being erased. He was a young baby rock god and in the unnatural natural order of the times, everything belonged to him. I do believe he had my best interests at heart, and still does, as long as those interests don't overshadow or conflict with his. My own best interests for myself, because I was so young, were unformed. I'd had no guidance, and he stepped in and claimed what should have been shared. A power imbalance.

On the other hand.

We left Joe Jr.'s and walked a few blocks south and west to the registrar's office at NYU. I stood at his side, saying nothing, while he took forms from the clerk. We sat on a low windowsill. He went back to the counter to borrow a pen. He wore a suede jacket with fringe, despite the heat, and his hair was cut in a long, dark shag. He had a Camel tucked behind his ear. His jeans dragged a ragged hem at the heel of his Frye harness boots. I was wearing a striped poor boy sweater and bell-bottom jeans and water buffalo sandals, the kind you sloshed around with in water and then let dry to form fit to your feet. He pulled a crumpled check out of a battered wallet, and within twenty minutes I was registered in the College of Arts and Sciences at New York University—non-degree, not yet, I still had to formally apply, but it was a start—in Greenwich Village. I was surrounded by other young freaks who'd escaped to New York like I had.

I loved school, but I was too young to manage it along with the distractions of our rock-and-roll life. I left classes unattended, papers unwritten, warning letters unopened. After a while, I stopped going to class altogether. I never graduated. All that seventies-era fun was weirdly demanding, the nonstop partying, the intensity of Gary's schedule, the here-and-gone lifestyle, the delusion that it was my lifestyle too, that I might actually be a songwriter in my own right. Then the falling out over "*I, Alive.*" And just like that, he was done with our marriage and I had no choice but to be done too.

After Gary, I lost decades. Lost. I had lovers and a couple of live-in boyfriends. I faked my way into temp jobs that became real jobs but I always got bored and drifted away and on to the next. I had colleagues and acquaintances I thought of as friends whose names I can't remember anymore. I spoke to Albert once a month, I thought about Henry, I avoided anything to do with Miriam Marx. I think back to those years and it's like a long, indistinct smear on the timeline of me. Things happened, nothing happened. The one thing that stayed sharp was Gary. Me with Gary. We went for drinks or dinner and had sex again. We exchanged emails and chatted almost daily. Our sensibilities matched, because our thoughts were joined, and then he found someone else and then another someone else, and etcetera, and we simply stopped fussing about it, or I did, and we fell into friendship. Good friendship.

Until we married the second time. He had just moved to the loft on lower Broadway, and I was still hanging out two sexy days after a boozy Saturday-night booty call, although I don't think that's what the term was then. On Tuesday morning, I had a ten a.m. meeting for work at a financial services firm. I remember searching Gary's closet for something of his I could adapt to look corporate and competent, a dress shirt I could belt, a vest, since I had no time to go home—I still lived on Third Avenue. I heard a boom. Gary called my name. I walked across the loft to him, buttoning up one of his white shirts, to where he stood looking out with his hands flat against the tall windows. I remember saying, "What's going on?" Smoke and ash clouded lower Broadway.

We walked to City Hall a couple of weeks later, just the two of us. We recruited strangers as witnesses. Looking back on the days after the towers fell, what else could we do? I thought we would finally be our best selves. But we were still who we were.

I surprised myself by being good with clients and a better free-lancer than an employee. I was a million miles from rock and roll, and my resentment of that world and Gary's place in it increased every time I had to say no to partying or staying out late, every time I heard "*I, Alive*" or noticed a just-his-type new backup singer. Gary was in his fifties by then, and terrified of getting old. He was ready for a girl who wouldn't eye-roll stories of the glory days, someone who didn't know him so well. He succumbed to all the usual temptations again, and I felt betrayed, again.

Our second ending seems inevitable now. My cancer scare came a few short months later. We had a friendly glass of wine to tiptoe through divorce number two issues, and I told him about my diagnosis. He pulled back, visibly repelled. He went pale. Pale! I patted his arm and asked, "Are you okay?" His reaction was partly generational, from a time when the C word was whispered; but also it was selfish and irrational, and my theory is it's some stupid man thing to do with boobs. For all these years, I've actively hidden the topic from Gary, I've never mentioned Dr. Keswani or my mammograms, let alone my free-floating terror. He has never once asked about my health. It all reminds me that there are things about him I don't like, and I guess that's something I hide from myself, too.

And yet.

We still stayed friends. Close. I do give Gary credit for that. Gary never stopped picking up the phone or shooting me an email to check in, to get my take on something. I held—hold—that space in his life, wife, and after a while I forgot to worry about not having the full package. He was the only family I had.

Now, here we are, same loft, same bed, same Gary, same Bea. He reaches across me to the night table and grabs a hair elastic, mine I hope. He pushes at me to turn over. He braids my wild hair for me, as he has always done. He is good at it. He knows exactly how tight I like it. His fingers rake and tug and tuck.

"Gary."

"Bean."

"Bix. I don't know."

"Leave it for tonight, Bean."

"Do I really need this? For money?"

"Well, Beanie baby, you're sixty years old. Why not use those damned photographs to your advantage for once? Get some closure."

"I hate that word. And I'm not sixty. Not yet." We are quiet for a while. "Are you sleeping?"

"Yes. But my dick hurts. I need something. Some lotion."

"Aloe. Like I said."

"Don't you run out of smart remarks at midnight? Do I remember that correctly?"

"I wrote you a hit. '*I, Alive.*'"

"Bean, you were paid for the song. And I subsidize you. Must we do this?"

"I was paid a fee. I never received royalties. Like you still do. If you'd set it up right, I wouldn't need to be subsidized!"

"Get a lawyer."

"I can't afford a lawyer. Get me a lawyer."

"Okay, it's time to stop talking. You're hysterical."

"This is not hysterical. I'm practically whispering."

"You're pre-hysterical. I know the signs. What makes you think I can afford to give you more money? Pay for lawyers? Maybe Bix is our answer."

"You're always working. You have money! I've been your wife for four decades, almost. I don't want to pawn my mother's fucked-up legacy to be able to live out my golden years."

"You're not my wife."

"Then stop telling me what to do."

"Then stop spending my money."

This is our pillow talk, our sweet nothings. He curves around me. He pulls me close. He presses his groin, sticky with egg white, into my ass. I move back into him, tighter, closer, for comfort, but I can feel him stirring against me with Viagra aftershocks. I say, "Move off," which of course he does. He's not into it either.

I don't sleep well entwined with Gary, or anybody. I try to breathe his way, to sync my breath to his, and I lose my breath and fret and toss and turn. I hear the clock, I watch the numbers change. I worry about disturbing him by moving out from under a heavy arm or leg so I do it in millimeters and it becomes like a slo-mo tai chi exercise. I'm not sleepy enough. I'm throbbing, honestly, with Bix in mind. His magnetism. I picture myself leaning into him, inhaling him, pulling him to me, on top of me. I wait Gary out. His breathing steadies and he sinks down deeper into his pillow and then into his body and then into his sleep. I move slow. It's like a game, how slow I can go. Just one finger between my legs, a little tap and a little swirl. I know the spot, and it only takes a minute.

Chapter Five

"I'M HOME!"

It's midmorning and I'm back from Gary's with a hangover. I hold out hope every time I return that Dory will greet me like she loves me, but no. It hurts because she wags herself silly for Echo.

Echoe's not home. I can tell she's been out all night too because the door is as I left it, unlocked, which she would never do. I don't use the deadbolt or the lock on the doorknob. They both stick and I can work myself into a panic thinking I might not get the door open from either side. I don't want a lock guy. That costs hundreds. Echo is appalled by this. New York City! Unlocked door! She grew up during an era of exaggerated emphasis on stranger-danger but this is Riverside Drive. It seems unlikely that rapists would make the effort to get past the Armenians in the lobby—the doormen and the porters, who are brothers and cousins—and ride the elevator or climb the ancient fire escape twelve flights to target me, the lady in #12D.

Out all night. I didn't think Echo knew anyone in the city. It's none of my business and why shouldn't she stay out all night? After the first divorce I was Echo's age. I left bars with men I'd met two hours prior. I say men but they were boys, younger back then, earnest long-haired fellows in flowered shirts, with their belts buckled low on nonexistent hips, wearing corduroys and gum-soled desert boots, grateful, really, for sweet, dirty fun. Echo's entitled, but I'm curious.

Dory snores and drools on my pillow. "Come on, girly, you need a walk." She doesn't open an eye. She's uninterested in me. I'm not imagining it. She snores through me dropping my bag, rolling my leather pants off and sweatpants on and pulling on socks and winter boots. I tug a ratty old cashmere turtleneck over my Balthazar shirt and wrap the old silver Kamali sleeping bag coat around me. My hair has half escaped from Gary's braid and my mascara has slid and smudged beneath my eyes. My ears are ringing with exhaustion and the effects of all the good wine, courtesy of Bix. I see myself in the mirror and do a double take. "Dear god," I say.

When I catch my reflection lately, I never see what I think I am going to see. I don't look like I think I look. My first thought is always, *Who is that?* It's jarring. I wish people would stop saying, "Age is just a number." Hello, the outside no longer matches the inside! My changing looks is a situation I have to manage from here on out. It's work. I'm working on it. I don't want a nasty shock every time I unexpectedly see my reflection.

I rattle the leash next to Dory's ear. "Get up, Dore. We need to get out there before it snows."

Before Dory, before Echo, during a Gary-less phase, I worried about being lonely. Not because I *was* lonely, I wasn't, not yet. I did miss intimacy, touch, so I got brave, ate dinner alone at bars, got picked up, dallied a bit, slipped out before dawn without leaving my number. That got expensive and a little bit sad. I'm not good at online dating. I'm a fool for frisson and chemistry, sniffing and sensing and waiting to be circled and circling, like with Gary, like with Bix. Anyway, I came to love living alone. Talk to most women who live alone and they'll tell you, don't knock it until you've tried it.

I was fifty when AARP found me and let me know I was officially old. AARP was relentless. I fell for the offer of a free insulated lunch bag which I didn't even need since I work from home. Next thing I knew my inbox was filled with dire AARP articles. "Aging alone is bad for your health." "Your vagina atrophies no matter how many Kegels you squeeze." "Your money disappears, get ready to live on the street with all your belongings in a trash bag." "You'll die alone." The articles were dolled up by images of faded beauties in pastel cardigans sitting in a too-clean kitchen with hand to brow, the universal representation of female despair.

I decided to get a pet. I established my online search criteria—*Senior Dogs*—and immediately fell in love with a collie-shepherd based on photos featuring her long nose and amber eyes. She was around ten so I kept the name, Lady, out of respect even though I hated it. Lady didn't last long. It cost me a couple thousand dollars to keep her going for a few months after the adoption, and then a thousand more to give her some peace at the end. Next I tried a cat, pulled from a crate—I had to undo her grip on the steel grid to embrace her—on Adoption Day at Petco. I named her Mittens because she was, in fact, gray with white forepaws. Mittens left me by squeezing through my window into a blizzard. The window was open three measly inches, Manhattan apartments being notoriously overheated in winter, and the opening was blocked by the snow, but I can still see her flattened ears, her skull and body going boneless as she cat-paddled out, and her high steps and the delicate paw prints down the fire escape, into the storm. I threw on boots and a bathrobe and went down a few treacherous steps, calling, *Mittens, Mittens*. She never looked back. For days, I walked the neighborhood waving an open can of tuna fish and taping flyers to lampposts. What commitment she had to leaving me, despite a well-stocked pantry and the organic kitty litter. I still don't know what I did to make her go.

I went back to the screens and revised the search criteria: *Men, 40-60*. I was skeptical about finding love online, nevertheless I invested thirty-nine bucks a month. I wanted to see how I stacked up so I pretended to be a man and did a search in my zip code. I recognized women, my neighbors from the shops or the park or the subway platform, all with clever usernames, snappy headlines, game responses to intrusive questions. Just like me. For a while, I was addicted to browsing the men in the privacy of my own device, thrilled to judge and dismiss their images. I would yell at the screen: *Move the laundry basket! Toss the pizza box! Get out of the bathroom!* It got compulsive, flicking men away with a fingertip. Now, even the possibility of true love bores me if it requires hours of forensics-level profile reading.

Last autumn, just in time, along came Dory. She belongs to the fellows next door, Patrick and Ronaldo. I could hear her yapping in there over the summer, but I hadn't seen her until one day the guys, both in popped-collar polo shirts and festive Bermuda shorts, knocked on my door, holding a white toy poodle wearing a barrette on her forelock. They said they were traveling for work, the hospitality business, for an extended period; would I be interested in dog sitting for a monthly stipend? I reached for her and Dory side-eyed me and curled her lip in a snarl. "Don't worry, she's friendly," said Ronaldo, and handed her over. The minute I held her, I was hooked on her. I loved her. I see

Patrick and Ronaldo on Instagram, so happy in the sun with their perfect resort clothes and their tropical drinks, and I've started to hope they might not come back. They check in by text and they Venmo the money, which I could use.

Haughty little Dory shakes herself awake. I say, "Let's go, let's go." I urge her along to the elevator, which she hates. We get close. She backs up. It's the same thing every time, three times a day. "Come on, Dory, please. I'm sorry, we have to go, let's go."

The elevator sets off the shivers in Dory. The door opens with heaving effort. It's an old building, and the mahogany-paneled lift needs frequent servicing. As I tug her over the threshold and into the elevator, the door closes too soon and hits me in the shoulder and I step on Dory who has pressed herself against my ankle in desperation. She yelps, disproportionately to the infraction, and lies flat out. My hangover head throbs. "Dory, please, come on."

Inside the elevator is a smiling family. I don't recognize them; they must be visiting. The little girl says, "Oh, she's so cute! She has a little clip in her hair! Why is she shivering? Is she cold?"

I make a tight smile that I hope the parents will understand to mean, *She bites.*

The mom says, "Aww! Precious! What's her name?"

"Dory. She doesn't like the elevator." Dory is splayed out in a final attempt at resistance, so I pull her sliding across the floor on her belly and position her behind me. "She's not very friendly. Sorry."

The mother says, "Dory! Like the movie, Arabella! Like the fish!"

Dory is making a guttural noise that I know is pre-growl. I block her from Arabella's view. The elevator car doesn't move. The dad looks at me and shrugs. I say, "It sometimes takes a minute. They'll reset the button in the lobby."

Arabella has knelt to Dory's level. Dory is crouching behind my ankles, baring her teeth. The mom is smiling away, the dad is looking at his phone. Signals are missed. The mom and I speak to Arabella simultaneously. I say, "Please don't do that." The mom says, "Be gentle, darling," as the little girl reaches. Dory shoots out and snaps at the kid like an alligator, catching her on the side of her gloved hand. The elevator lurches and we inch down.

Arabella is stunned. The dad says, "Jesus Christ!" and Arabella starts to cry. I say I'm sorry, so sorry, I'm sorry. He examines his daughter's hand and holds up a ripped glove for me to see. "That dog shouldn't be allowed near children!" Dory is now as calm as a monk. She is in the perfect sit position, waiting patiently as the elevator descends to the lobby. The family marches to the front desk to complain. I call, "I'm really sorry!"

We head out into a dim late morning. The sky is heavy with what's coming. It's like the underside of a dark gray bowl. It feels like the end of the day with the weight of the weather, but it's the beginning of the middle. We have our routes, our routine. Dory walks tall for a small dog, and fast, and I keep pace and my heart races in a way that makes me feel refreshed, good, less hungover. She marches on, never glancing back to me at the end of the leash. The walk gives me talking-to-myself cover, and I give her the lowdown: *Gary dyed his hair! I met this Hollywood guy, Bix! I got laid, finally!* We walk to Broadway for my American Spirits. Back at home we warm up with a little fresh water and some freeze-dried liver tidbits for Dory, wine and a cigarette for me.

After the usual ten-minute search for my glasses, at the computer, I open the memoir file. I'm protective of my idea and competitive because of Bix and the film title conversation. *Exposed* or *Exposure*.

I have to navigate around MoMA and Bix and Gary, who have entire teams that could bring my story to lurid, lucrative life. All I have is my problematic memory, sketches and scenes I've written, dwindling time with Albert, and the black hole waiting for me behind the door of the storage unit in Congers, New York. Why not let them take over? For a long time I stare at the blinking cursor on a blank Word document. Now and then I sip Sancerre from a mug. I jump and nearly spill when a hand rests on my shoulder.

"Echo, you scared me!"

"Lunch?" Echo has Dory in her arms. Dory looks down at me. Looks down *on* me, I swear.

I am happy to be interrupted, grateful that I get to stop not writing. I make tuna melt sandwiches. I pour myself another mug. Echo is twenty-two, old enough to drink, although she never does at home. When I was twenty-two, eek. We sit across from each other. "Where have you been?" I ask.

Dory is draped across Echo's lap, relaxing, not begging for food, which I find astonishing. Echo says, "How about you! Did *you* come home last night, Bea?"

It's satisfying to flaunt sex at my advanced age to a young person. "I stayed at Gary's."

"The famous Gary. When do I meet him? Does he ever stay here?"

Echo is interested in Gary. He's part of rock-and-roll history for her. She's too hip to be interested in the Stones or other oldies acts. She mines the past for more obscure stuff, like Chalk Outline, from a time when cool stuff, by definition, could not be mainstream. You couldn't just tap to it, scroll for it, you had to know people, read the right papers, hang out in the right bars.

"You'll meet him. He'll love you." I give her an approving nod. "I like your look. Where'd you dig all that up?"

She is wearing my old New York Dolls T-shirt, an XL, tucked into skinny jeans, with a studded belt and flowered Doc Martens. She looks down at herself. "Is it okay? There was a box at the top of the closet in the little bedroom. The boots fit."

"That belt is from Trash and Vaudeville on St. Mark's. And the shirt. I got that shirt at the Dolls show in 1973. The night I met Gary."

"Seriously?"

"Seriously. It was prom night."

"You went to prom with Gary Going?"

"No, no. With my high school boyfriend, Danny Auerbach. From Grand View. His dad was a liquor salesman who sold booze to a bar in Queens called The Coventry, and he got a bunch of free tickets to a New York Dolls show. So we went to the prom and then took a limo to the show."

"How did you meet Gary?"

"You would not believe what I wore. A cornflower blue, high-necked, long-sleeved Victorian-ish gown with black Chuck Taylors, high-tops. I was covered from neck to ankles. But there we were, six of us from upstate, sitting at a table eight feet from the stage, in our prom clothes. Chalk Outline was the opening act. And there was Gary."

"And what? He spotted you?"

"We looked so completely dorky, in tuxes and long dresses. Sitting right in front of him. He screamed at us from the stage. 'What are you? What are you?' Over and over, it became part of whatever song he was singing. It was punk. The whole place went nuts. We went nuts too. And he was at the bar after the set. Just standing there, drinking a beer with the boys. Now, he's the only one still alive." I hate tacking on the morbid comment, the death toll, but once you hit a certain age it creeps in.

"What happened to Danny?"

I laugh. "That was it for Danny. Gary brought me backstage to watch the Dolls. He was hoarse and sweaty but so sexy. He unzipped my prom dress and I stepped out of it and he put that shirt you're wearing on me. It came to my knees. I was in a T-shirt and the Chucks. I never even picked the blue dress up off the floor. The limo left without me. Danny never spoke to me again. Although he friended me last year on Facebook. Anyway, the next day, Gary drove me home. He waited outside the house in his car. A Karmann Ghia. I packed some stuff and took off. The house was sold anyway."

"Oh my god. What did Daddy do?"

Echo calls my father Daddy, like I once did. Hearing it from her now stops me and I lose track of the story. Any memory of Albert as "Daddy" is rare. Albert was there but not there. He was fun and silly when he wanted to be; he boomed at us and teased us when Miri wasn't around. He liked to cook and sing along to standards and pop songs. He was loud from a loud crowd, he'd say. These memories, though, don't stand up to the truth: the frequent absences for work and my mother's complaints about it because she had to parent us, or his vague presence when my mother was around. He was devoted to Miriam Marx, the artist, and indulged her sensitivities and catered to her needs. My theory is he was in awe of Miri. If he had any qualms about his wife using her children as subjects in her work, the questionable nature of that, he never broke ranks. He's still there but not there because of the dementia and lung cancer and pain and fear, which I know is not his fault. But it feels like my same old idea of Daddy.

The prom night story stops being fun to tell. "Eh, Albert was in his own world by then. It's ancient history. You can keep the boots and the belt. But the shirt, I'm not ready to part with it. What have you been up to?"

"Dropping résumés at every restaurant on the Lower East Side. I can't believe you need a résumé to be a server. That's so New York."

She's been out overnight, not dropping résumés, but I don't push it. I study her face across the table, over the tuna melts. A good face counts for a lot. I don't mean pretty or attractive. Those are easy to mimic. You can shade and highlight the hell out of yourself to turn into a runway model. My barista has his own YouTube channel. He pulls out a palette and transforms his skinny, blond bland self into Rihanna right before my eyes.

Echo's face is vulpine, angular, just shy of sharp with a long jaw and strong chin. The eyes are hooded. They are set so deep you almost can't see what color they are: wolf blue. They are deepened beneath by lavender curves like opposing commas from the inside corners, along the tear troughs to the top of her cheekbone. She thinks the curves are ugly dark circles but they intensify her. They make her face. The eyebrows are neat and thick and run nearly straight. The vertical cleft between her nose and her upper lip looks carved. The lips are pink, unglossed. Her bare face shines with everything makeup can't deliver: youth, with the sheen of out-all-night.

She makes a hair statement. It's blue-black, overdyed and stiff with product. The sides are short and close to show off her biggish ears, and she's got this hank of long hair from widow's peak to crown that is constructed into a pretty impressive pompadour. The finishing touches are a ring through her septum, a barbell through her eyebrow, and who knows what else under her clothes.

I see my family in her face. It stands to reason. My father saw something familiar in Miri's face, and later in Jeanne's face, and there it is in Echo's face. I have studied the Wedding Announcements section of the Sunday *Times*. It doesn't matter—any race, two men, two women, older or younger, mixed up—there's something similar in the couples' faces. Check out the jawlines and chins. So what I'm trying to say is, Echo is familiar to me. Deep down I recognize her.

I mull her over. She might be my person. I've never really had one. The internet says a person is *your person* if they would be your first call when you needed help burying a body. I am not planning to kill anyone, but if I were, I would not call Gary. The kvetching alone would get us caught. But Echo might possibly be able to set aside her ideals and help me dig.

Echo says, "More wine?" and I think, *Just enough to tamp everything down, just enough so I can nap, just enough to give me an excuse not to work on Exposed/Exposure.* I promise myself that when I wake up, I will deal with at least one of the 212 numbers chasing me down. I'll call Violet Yeun, set up a meeting. Maybe I'll bring Echo to MoMA for moral support. Dr. Keswani and the test results—I'm still dancing in denial. I'm not ready to know.

Chapter Six

WE WAIT ON a black biomorphic bench in the vast entrance to the museum.

Sound is muffled, lost in the heights. It's crowded yet quiet, with an expectant atmosphere. Visitors move to the ticket counters, to the stairs, to the wintry sculpture garden behind us. They consult their phones or maps with their heads tipped together. People are excited to be here, to see art.

Echo says, "Here she comes." Violet Yeun is a woman of imposing size and style. All this time, seeing her name in my inbox, hearing her voice messages, I assumed she was Korean, but now I see she is Black, too. I forgot I can google what people look like. The crowd parts for her. She strides through. She wears a black column dress with a long zipper spiraling and encircling her, from high neck to mid-calf, and short, sharp black boots. Her eyes are rimmed in dark plum shadow. Plum lipstick defines her mouth. Her hair is shorn, gray stubble. She wears gold tassel earrings that graze her broad shoulders.

She has kept up the pressure on me in her minimalist, elegant, art-world way and now here I am. There is a touch of victory in her approach and the way she extends her hand. "Finally, Ms. Marx, we meet. Violet Yeun."

"Seger."

"Ms. Marx-Seger. Of course."

"Just Seger, no Marx. Anyway, it's Bea. Call me Bea. And this is . . ." I stumble every time I introduce Echo. I want to say "my sister," but that's too much, too soon. I want to use "Hannah," because Echo sounds a little flaky. "This is Echo."

We follow Violet Yeun through the galleries and into the elevator to the Photography Department office. A big bright room with windows overlooking 53rd Street is lined floor to ceiling with flat drawers that slide into the walls, like in a morgue, but for art. There are four long white enamel tables under articulated boom lights with scopes that hang down from the ceiling, used for examining images.

Echo says, "Wow."

Violet Yeun nods. "I get a little thrill in here, every time." She fits her hands with white cotton gloves. She opens a drawer and takes out a print and carries it by its edges as if it might disintegrate. She sets it on one of the tables, then pulls and positions a boom and turns on a bright light. "Here, have a look."

Echo looks for a long minute. "It's freaky. At first I thought it was a movie still. From olden times. I thought she was posing. Like a movie star."

"What else?"

"It's not one face. I mean, it is one side of a face, split in half and then, like, pasted back together. The eyes are off. Kind of like Picasso. Except it's a photograph."

"They were working at the same time. She's distorted."

"She looks like an alien. She kind of glows."

"She does glow. It's a silver gelatin print. Miriam loved it too. She saw it at MoMA, in the early sixties. She referred to this image in an interview from around that time."

"Who took the picture?"

I don't have to look at the photograph. "Berenice Abbott. She was the photographer and the subject." I look at Violet. "*Portrait of the Artist as a Young Woman.*"

"So it's a selfie," Echo says. "Two selfies, really, like in a funhouse mirror."

Violet says, "Exactly. Abbott took a picture of herself in 1930, and twenty years later went back and distorted it to make this. Cool, yes? And of course, Ms. Seger—Bea—is Berenice Abbott's namesake." She flips off the light and pushes the viewing boom up and away. She lifts the photograph by its edges again and slides it back between the thin protective paper and places it in the drawer. She takes off the white gloves. "Come. Sit down. Thank you for coming, Bea."

"Here I am. Here we are."

We move to an impossibly deep-cushioned sectional sofa, very low to the ground, upholstered in tufted fuchsia velvet. I worry I won't be able to get up now that I've sunk in. Violet looks at me. "May I speak freely?"

"Absolutely. Echo is my sister, sort of. My father's daughter."

"Adopted," Echo says. "Sort-of sisters." My heart hears her and my head tilts to her and I give her a little smile.

"Your father—Albert—is still alive?"

"He's in and out. Down in Florida."

"This is complicated for you." Violet pours water from a sleek carafe into amazing water glasses. I've seen them in the gift catalog. They are handblown, colored from the base to look like an ocean up to a pink horizon and then to a pale blue sky at the rim. Sea to sky, forty bucks each in the gift shop. I calculate how much I can hide from Gary's guy on my Amex card and make a note to stop on the way out as a reward for coming.

Dr. Yeun is not unlike Bix, except she's East Coast elite and swathed in creative clothes and pouring water with cucumbers floating in it into iconic water glasses, instead of wine at Balthazar. "I've studied your mother for a long time, Bea. I've read every word of every interview. I've read monographs, the exhibition catalogs, reviews, the newspaper articles, even dissertations by art history and photography students. I'm not the only person in the field who believes Miriam Marx's work was before its time. The notoriety was a terrible distraction from her achievements."

She pauses, providing a well-timed moment of silence for me to fill. She's too polished to speak directly about child pornography. She's leaving the messy parts for me. I believe what Dr. Yeun says, but what she doesn't say says a lot, too. She is well aware that notoriety brings crowds. She is counting on it. Echo shifts in her seat, unconsciously signaling me to relieve the tension of silence and say something, which I don't.

Violet continues, "I'm not Miriam's only champion, but I am in a good place." She waves at the surroundings. "I think the time is very right for a survey of your mother's work. The museum is one hundred percent behind it. The entire sixth floor would be devoted to Miriam. That rarely happens. In fact, it's never happened for a woman. Cindy

Sherman got two-thirds of the space in 2012. It would take a year to organize. At least eighteen months, two years. The timing remains to be seen."

"Why do you need me? You can go to collectors. Other museums. Right?" Just like with Bix, I want to know, Why can't she do this without me?

Violet smiles. "I believe there are more images. Perhaps many more. Maybe imagery that was too controversial for the times. If that is true—and there is no question in my mind that it is true—a MoMA exhibit would be definitive. If we discover new work, her reputation would be restored. She'd take her place alongside the women she admired: Arbus. Imogen Cunningham. Dorothea Lange." She gestures to the wall of drawers. "Berenice Abbott. Your mother belongs on that list. With new work, the value would increase dramatically. From a cultural perspective." She looks me dead in the eye and holds it. "The work would be a gift to the museum. There's no compensation, per se, except obviously all her work would increase in value. Tremendously. So whatever else you have, what doesn't make it into the show, there will be collectors and galleries around the world interested. You could certainly sell other works."

Echo watches our exchange back and forth as if Violet and I were playing Ping-Pong. The stakes feel higher in this setting than with Bix at Balthazar. I try to look aloof but my stomach is flipping and my throat feels tight. I drink the cucumber water from the amazing water glass. Dr. Yeun believes my mother belongs to the history of photography, and feminism, and art. With Bix, it's Hollywood. If a Miriam Marx biopic bombs, I can distance myself. Everyone loves to hate Hollywood. Hollywood never gets it right.

With MoMA, Miri becomes Art with a capital A, what she always wanted, what Albert wanted for her. Plenty of people don't relate to art, especially the contemporary stuff. A lot of it is hard to get, but if you look, if you stay with it, you see that there are infinite ways to be human. And that's a relief. MoMA will give new context to my mother, her era, her influences. MoMA will hang us Marx kids high, with excellent lighting and little plaques. MoMA will reframe my childhood in a way I've dreaded but that might, in the long run, benefit me.

I am gripping the water glass. I smooth my breathing and bland out any expression on my face and I shrug. "New work would be good for you, too, Dr. Yeun?"

Violet lets out a big, unguarded laugh. "Yes. Definitely. The chief curator is talking about retiring in a couple of years. I'd love his job. A show like this would help."

That disarms me. "There's a storage unit upstate. But it's a lot to take on. For me. I'm a freelance writer."

Echo can hardly take her eyes off Violet. She's impressed. "I could help you, Bea. Like an assistant."

Violet leans in. She grimaces as if we must eat our vegetables before we get to dessert. The tassel earrings shimmy, her plum mouth shimmers, her black eyes bore in. "As I said, I know it's complicated. The museum would do the heavy lifting. Every step of the way. Starting with the lawyers, of course. I assume you've had legal counsel about your mother's work over the years? An estate lawyer, at the very least?"

Everybody thinks I need a lawyer. I've been diligent about avoiding legal advice on everything—my work, my divorces, my mother's work. Lawyers dig in, it's expensive in more ways than one. I don't want to pay for the misery.

"We'd start by inventorying the archives. Cataloging everything, digitizing everything. Getting it out of the storage unit. Which is not a safe environment, not at all." She widens her eyes at me for emphasis.

I'm out of my depth. I sit quietly. Inside, I have a wild moment of wanting to confess my money problems and health concerns and relationship woes to Violet Yeun. I want to turn everything over to her. Let her sort me out, because Dr. Yeun knows me. She has lowered that boom down and swept its icy light across every millimeter of the Marx children. My body. Ansel and Henry, their bodies, with me between them. She has examined my eyes in the photographs. She can see we were coerced. Can't she?

In any case, Dr. Yeun could not care less. Her interest, from her Columbia undergraduate days through her Yale doctoral dissertation to the fancy job she has today, is Miriam Marx and the Marx Nudes. She believes, as Miri did, that the work—The Work—transcends my childhood trauma or late middle-age powers of denial. She is bringing the full force of her education, her coveted job at the museum, her ambition, and her wardrobe to bear on me. I am only a subject in the photographs.

At least it is a role I know well. I say, "I guess I have some thinking to do."

We stand and gather our things. Dr. Yeun hands Echo her card and invites her to come back any time. I hitch my bag onto my shoulder and drape my winter coat over my arm and I turn to go and my coat sweeps all three forty-dollar sea-and-skyscape water glasses on the low table to the marble floor. I step carefully, apologizing and picking my way through the shards and I know it's safer to skip the gift shop.

Chapter Seven

I'M HAVING MY picture taken.

"Don't move. Stay as still as you can for about twenty minutes. Or we'll have to start again." The technician speaks through a microphone from behind a glass wall and tall monitors. I have been fitted into the curve of the scan bed, a hotdog in a bun. A wedge has been placed under my knees for my comfort. A warmed blanket has been tucked around me. My arms ache, stretched up over my head, already tired. I concentrate on relaxing them, and at the same time, I try to forget about them.

The diagnosis in my late forties was a tiny thing, prognosis excellent. I was very alone at the time, broken by the second divorce, still dragging Marx baggage, still unwilling to open it up. My thinking was chaotic. I made decisions using a frantic calculus. I said no to radiation—my skin!—no to chemotherapy—my hair!—and no to the standard five years' of tamoxifen—weight gain!

More than a decade later, I'm revisiting those decisions from inside this tube. The mammogram showed clouds where it should be clear. This time Dr. Keswani said, "Let's get a closer look."

With a situation like this, once you get the news, you probably call your mother or a sister or a best friend. I haven't been good with women friends. It's a trust thing, meaning, I don't trust them with my past. Certainly I can't burden Echo yet. I don't want to scare her away or make her feel she has to tell Albert. I can't discuss any of it with Gary, he's so easily freaked out. I did unfold Dory's ear and whisper, "I might be sick," and she pressed a paw against me, to push me away or make contact, I don't know.

Every form I filled out in the waiting room asked about family history of this or that, but I don't have relatives to ask. I mean, I do, maybe Miri's brother is still alive, but I don't know him. There were so many in Albert's family, there must be some left in New York, but I've never tried to get in touch with them, even when he moved to Sandy Edge. A chill fell over Albert and his family when he married Miri, and I guess they froze him out completely when the photographs became notorious. Surely they were appalled and disgraced by my mother's work and probably grateful that Albert had Americanized his last name to Seger and no longer shared theirs. I think the Segrettis had a very concrete concept of evil, and Miri's images must have made them believe my mother had invited the devil himself into the home. Ansel's death and Miri's suicide proved it.

Suicide. I rarely let myself release that word into my thoughts.

Staring at all the blank spaces on the forms, I yearned for Henry with an intensity I haven't let myself feel in years. All the cloudy images. All the unanswerable questions. Henry. Henry?

On the forms, I wrote, "Not available."

I am tucked in and moving. The tube takes me in and glides back and forth, in and out of range of the lens. Tears of relief run through wrinkles at the corners of my eyes and into my ears, my hair. There's something comforting about being seen on a cellular level. The camera lingers at my groin, my belly, my chest, my throat, my brain. At each pause, there is a soft, clicking sound, pictures, taken. I envision bad memories floating alongside renegade cells on a current of radio-active tracers with which I've been injected, debris in a stream. There is a gentle breathing sound that fills the tube and engulfs me, and I match mine to the machine's. By the way, you don't have to take your clothes off for a PET scan. The camera sees through them.

I drift. I doze. *Don't move, stay still.*

I was three and the boys were six, the first time. She posed us, entwined us, and retreated under the canvas hood. Her camera found us. I followed her directions, I did what the boys did, and yet I looked to Henry because I was confused. It felt wrong. Henry knew. He felt my eyes asking his, and he replied with his eyes, quick glances or blinks, a squint or widening, our secret conversation that lasted for years. Until he left.

The scanner searches me. Maybe I sleep.

I was eight, my brothers were eleven. By then we were hostages to our mother's art. On a primal level, even though we were kids, we understood viscerally that the photo shoots were strange. We were naturally embarrassed by them. We were bonded together by shame and in a kind of love with each other, but also, we hated each other. After the shoots we put our shorts and T-shirts back on. I wore the boys' old clothes even though Albert would try to interest me in shopping trips to the mall for candy-colored outfits. I preferred the muted stripes and worn denim, each garment's pockets sandy from the treasures they'd hunted and stowed after expeditions along the Hudson riverfront, or the Old Erie Path behind our house.

My memories of the lavender hour at dusk after the photo shoots made me think for a time I'd had a happy childhood. The tension and adrenaline had flushed away and we were languid and loose. The boys horsed around for a while, but then Ansel would wander off, needing to be alone. Henry and I went to the kitchen, ravenous. He would pour me a glass of milk with ice and a scoop of chocolate powder from a box, the only way I could tolerate it. He put dusty vanilla wafers on a plate. I took an apple or a peach. We went to the porch, to the swing. When we were a little older, he would produce a paperback from his pocket and read Agatha Christie to me. He did a British accent for the dialogue. He made his voice shrill for the lady characters. He rocked our swing forward and back, pushing off from the porch planks with his toes. I leaned against a pillow, listening, and kneaded his thigh with my toes. We handed the fruit back and forth, taking bites, getting sticky.

I am dying to lower my arms. My knees hurt, despite the wedge. Maybe I dream.

I swing on the porch swing while a fire rages and roars and races in the woods behind our house. I hear branches crack and the crash of a tree falling to earth. I smell an acrid scorch, I see the early evening sky eclipsed by black smoke and red blaze. I feel heat. Still I swing. They say if you want to interpret a dream, think of it as a newspaper article and give it a headline that consolidates its meaning.

Local Teen Succumbs after Old Erie Path Fire

AUGUST 19, 1969, GRAND VIEW-ON-HUDSON, NY—A backyard fire leapt out of control on Sunday, August 17, and claimed the life of Ansel Marx-Seger, 16, of River Road in Grand View-on-Hudson. State police report that the young man may have used an accelerant to burn debris on family property that runs along the Old Erie Path. Firefighters responded to the call at about 5:00 p.m. to battle a fully involved fire and found the teenager engulfed in flames. He was rushed to Grasslands Hospital in Valhalla, New York. Assistant Chief Roy Quigley reports that firefighters fought for two hours to keep the fire from spreading through dry foliage. Ansel Marx-Seger died as a result of his injuries. He is survived by his parents, Miriam and Albert, his fraternal twin brother Henry, and a sister, Berenice. Funeral and burial arrangements are not known at this time.

The headline appeared in the *Rockland Journal News*. The accelerant was grain alcohol, which a reckless teenager might drink, of course, and I knew the boys had tried it already, and I had been sworn to secrecy about it. I've always thought that's why it was up in the woods that day, but its intended purpose, along with collodion and ether and silver nitrate, was for my mother to make her pictures in the darkroom. Henry was somewhere outside, out back, I'm not sure where, relative to the fire. Albert was "occupied elsewhere," as he so often was at that time. Miri was on assignment for *Outtasight* magazine, ninety minutes away in Bethel, New York, at Woodstock.

I drift and I doze in the tube. The lens examines me, watches me, sees inside me, its breath alters mine, its choosy clicks here and there along and within me seek and stop, seek and stop. I notice where it loiters, at the sternum. My arms ache. I am between a dream and a memory.

Henry left for Columbia University two weeks later, as planned, except without his twin. I don't remember Henry packing or saying goodbye. Four months after Ansel's death, on December 30, by her own hand, in our attic.

I think I'm asleep.

Albert must have organized Miri's funeral and her burial, after Ansel. During this time, my father went off to work every morning, came home and retreated to his basement office to haunt the house, as lost in spirit as Ansel and Miri and Henry were physically gone. For a year, two, Albert got an occasional phone call and conversed with Henry in monosyllables for five minutes and then passed the phone to me. There was so much to say that there was nothing to say. Henry wrote me three or four obligatory letters. Our bond dissolved in the time before email and texting. It was just Albert and me for three years. My grief-shocked father was there but absent, and his plan was that as soon as I started college, he would make a new life for himself in Florida.

I was already a freak in high school because of my mother's photographs, and after the deaths my freak status grew. I was too young to be on my own, too old to stay out of trouble, stoic about my father's utter lack of interest in me. I ate dinner standing at the kitchen counter. I sneaked out most nights. I chased boys. I smoked cigarettes and pot, I drank apple wine in the woods. I had no girlfriends, not one. I took up with Danny, who had hair to the middle of his back, jeans dragging in the dirt, an oversized vintage Harris Tweed coat that never came off, no matter the season, and perpetually glassy eyes. We went to prom. I met Gary and left for the city.

The whole time period is a black hole in my memory. That was the idea behind the memoir, to chart the events, fix them on a timeline so I can have a look, so I can make them make sense, so I can write my way out of the dark. I start and start and start, but I lose track. How can I write a memoir? If I were under oath, I would swear that Ansel and Henry and Miri simply vanished, and Albert was a ghost I lived with in Grand View for a minute, a day, three years.

I come to. I'm stiff. I shiver. I need to move. I wonder how much longer. I find my own breath. I squirm. My arms are numb but I am still not supposed to move. I need to get out of the scanner. I have to get to storage finally, obviously. The archives lurk like a dangerous mass in need of treatment.

I'm startled when the tech's disembodied voice says, "All done, Berenice."

She has seen inside me. She knows what's there but can't comment. That's the doctor's job. She says, "Have yourself a beautiful day," and as I put my boots on I say, "I'm going to have a cheeseburger as a reward," and she says, through her speaker, "Go ahead, indulge!" and that makes me worry that the scans will confirm what I think I know.

Chapter Eight

SOMETHING IS GOING on above me, I can't tell what.

The air is still and then it shifts, it's still, and then it shifts. I hear a mechanized sound, a whir, and distant metallic squeaks, like resistant gears. I stop and listen. The whirring is wings flapping and creating currents in the air. The squeaks are caws. There are a lot of them, flapping and cawing way up above, overhead, some perched on girders like on the telephone wires in the Hitchcock movie. I don't like birds. They are unpredictable and quick, primordial but clever, incoming from the past. The skin behind my ears tingles and my scalp draws tight.

I fumble and swipe and aim my phone's flashlight to light my way. I follow the beam, past everything locked away. Long row after long row of steel storage units housing everyone's overflow of mistakes and memories. My boot heels *rap rap rap* on the cement floor, my breath is in my ears and is puffing out in front of me, it's so cold, and above me are the busy birds.

I find my unit, #201. There's no light switch. I worry that I'm going to have to walk all the way back to the front desk to ask the guy to turn on the lights but then my beam finds a master switch on a far wall. Finally, *whoosh*, house lights flood all of StoreSpace. The birds on the girders go silent, wary and watching, like in the movie.

The Birds came out in 1963. Miri took me to an afternoon show to spend time together, just the two of us. She said, *Let's get away from the boys*. The movie theater was a few miles from home. My mother looked small and tense driving Albert's Chrysler Town and Country, the New Yorker model—the long station wagon swaying on the road, Miri's eyes fixed ahead, her grip tight on the steering wheel, with a lit cigarette between the fingers. The tension I felt watching the cigarette ash grow and shiver, watching the paper burn closer and closer to her fingers, was nearly unbearable. I couldn't say anything because she demanded total silence while she drove. She had been a city child, got her driver's license as an adult and found driving stressful.

The movie theater smelled like old wool and butter. The floor was sticky. The walls and curtains and seats were rusty blood red. Everything looked already ancient. Motes of dust hovered in the projector's beam aimed at the screen. Before *The Birds*, I'd only been to Saturday matinees with my brothers and other kids, where we'd filed in and sat in an orderly way until the parents left. Then the popcorn and candy flew, the shouts and banging seats echoed, Technicolor flickered across the faces, the older boys and their girls melted together in the back rows, and it was hard to pay attention to what was onscreen.

Until *The Birds*. I remember a long scene, the blond woman in the green suit smoking a cigarette outside a school on a bluff above the sea. I was transfixed by this actress, despite her manipulations and mean mouth. There was something selfish and reckless about her. Something that reminded me of my mother. Behind the actress, unbeknownst to her, black crows amass on a playground jungle gym, one by one, and wait for the schoolchildren who sing a jangly nursery rhyme off camera. The movie birds blink, cape-shaped, and shift from bony bird claw to bony bird claw on the rails of the jungle gym, like impatient foot-tapping, wanting to get at those kids and peck them to death. I couldn't take my eyes from the screen. I gripped the armrest between me and my mother. I had assumed birds, which I'd not given much thought to, were benign, decorating the sky and the branches of our trees. But in the movie, they conspired and attacked.

The movie's musical score accelerated my already thudding heart. When I could no longer take it, I buried my head in Miri's side. She pulled me close. She put her arm around me. She stroked my hair. "Shh, silly. It's not real. It's only a film." She wore a sweater that was fuzzy and tickled my nose. She wore musk oil, heavy, that I can call up. She smelled like cigarette smoke, too, a scent that comforts me still. It's the only time I remember being embraced by my mother.

With StoreSpace lit now I see the rows have street signs: River Place, Woods Road, Boundary Avenue. #201 is on Hilltop. The door has a keypad. I realize I don't have my bag, which has the code. Gary has it but I made him promise to just sit still for a change and wait until I summon him. I call him for the number, but he doesn't answer his phone.

Gary hired an Uber and picked me up and came along to support me today, which is sweet of him, which is nice. Bix wanted a crew to film me at the storage unit for the first time, footage they could re-create later. I said no, much to Gary's disapproval. In the car, he reminded me again that Bix is ready to hire a screenwriter, with his own money. That phrase is tagged on to the end of every conversation

Gary and I have about Bix—*with his own money*—in the reverential tone men reserve for richer men.

I was quiet on the drive, managing my anxiety about what I was about to find after all these years of next-level compartmentalizing and denial. Here's what's funny. For anxiety relief I shifted my thinking to worrying about cancer. I'm not worried about dying, not yet, because I feel fine. I am worried about losing my hair.

Gary kept talking, thank god. I leaned my head against the car window and let it bounce a bit with the ride, and closed my eyes and let the light of that white sun strobe against my eyelids from between the trees along the highway. The tires rocked a regular rhythm and Gary's voice fell in with it and it all soothed me until he said, "Really, who knows what we're gonna find!"

"What *I'm* going to find, not what 'we're' going to find."

Gary said, "Fine, *you*. You. I'm only trying to help," and then ran through, again, every possible scenario about what "we" might find.

I waved him off. "You're repeating yourself."

"So? You know, my father repeated himself . . ." And he was off to the musing-about-repeating-himself races. I've heard it all before. I revert, he reverts. We bicker like we're still married, like I'm the volatile little woman and he, the exasperated television hubby. He complains that I yell help and then I dismiss him when he tries to help. It's true, I do that. What can I say? I'm irritated by the quality of his assistance. The Uber driver's ears twitched. Finally we got to StoreSpace, a massive gray garage, the same color as February.

I left Gary up front with Jeff, the StoreSpace guy, holding my tote bag and my coat. He loves to bullshit with a guy with some odd-ball job. They are always Chalk Outline fans, in this case Jeff, who manages a cavernous, remote location with rows and gates and secret codes and who knows what hidden away. Gary was a hippie before he was a punk and then new wave, and now that he's an old guy he's going hippie again with libertarian leanings, and a touch of conspiracy theorist. He watches a trashy reality show and is convinced there are storage outposts and secret locations all over the world loaded with piles of money, Russian mainframes, dead bodies, priceless stolen artifacts. Who knows. After all, there's a trove of Miriam Marx's work sitting on the other side of the door to unit #201.

The birds watch me, blinking robotically. I try to visualize the door code numbers from the email I got from Jeanne, Albert's wife. I'm blank. I try some combination of numbers that feel vaguely familiar. I try the code again. Finally the readout says, LIFT NOW. Because of the touch-pad technology, I expect the door to glide up easily, electronically, but it's just an old-fashioned thing on a track and it resists. I do something stupid, which is I get my left shoulder under to prop it so it doesn't drop down. Now I'm in a bad spot since my shoulder is supporting the door while I'm trying to push it up with my right hand but it won't budge.

The door gets stuck halfway, with me crouched under it. I can't push it up and I can't jimmy it down. I am now not only barred from unit #201, it is trying to kill me. The birds caw with glee, psyched by my predicament. I pointlessly call out to Gary—*Gary, I need you!*—but he's too far away, staying put like I told him to. I scoot out and let the door hang halfway up, halfway down.

I track back and there he is, leaning on a counter, expounding to balding, ponytailed Jeff about the storage place reality show. He looks relaxed. He looks happy. I love Gary. I promise myself I'm going to be nicer to him. I'm not going to bicker with him. I know he's here to help me and he's my guy, he's Gary Going, who, at seventy, still has muscles; who, at seventy, still has some great guns.

Chapter Nine

"Okay. Wow."

"Wow is right."

"Shh. You promised. Let me get my bearings."

"All I said was what you said. Wow."

"Gary! I'm asking you! I can't hear myself think!"

Gary takes four steps back from #201 and bangs up against the across-the-aisle neighbor's unit. The corrugated metal door wavers and reverberates for long seconds. Gary says, "Like cymbals," and puts his hand against it to stop the sound. He slides down and sits cross-legged and keeps back, as he has promised to do.

I say, "You'll never get back up without my help."

He says, "True," which, in our love language, means he gets how hard this is for me, and more important, he doesn't want to be exiled back to Jeff. He busies himself with his phone, pretending he's not interested.

I have spent years envisioning what I now see. I expected a TV-hoarder horror-show of the contents of my mother's darkroom, her library, and the rest of it that extended past her workspace and into our home. I imagined precarious stacks of files and photographs and grimy jars and piles of rags and tripods tangled with extension cords and cables, broken cameras, and even mice, chewing nonchalantly on naked photos of me and the twins. I pictured piles of old newspapers and magazines with headlines about us. I pictured yellow crime scene tape—which never actually happened, which is only something I've seen on television—from when the cops visited us, first because of the photographs, and then when Ansel died, and then again when Miri died.

In fact, unit #201 is a marvel of careful, thoughtful organization. Everything in place, all the tools and accessories of Miri's work—her "gear," as she called it—the things I'd grown up navigating around or fetching or hunting for, because Miri couldn't remember where she'd dropped the whatever-it-was in her quest to rush to the light or hole up in the dark and make the pictures. Someone has done the work that I'd been dreading for a long time.

I'm in shock. I can't reconcile my memory of the chaos into which our household descended with this well-kept room. I'm the one with my shit together, kind of, but this level of intimate organization would have to come from someone who knows, for example, that a stained stiff old scrap of canvas is not a discarded drop cloth, but the photographer Miriam Marx's famous hood, from under which she waited for the clouds to diffuse the sun or the sun to drop so that she could click the shutter at us and turn us into the Marx Nudes.

I look back at Gary. "Let's see." He extends his hand for help and I give him mine. He nearly pulls me down and we spend a few minutes squabbling, trying to figure out how to compensate for my lack of muscles and his new hip until at last we sync our moves and get him up off the floor without me getting pulled down. We step inside holding hands like children in a fairy tale on the threshold of the witch's cottage. Gary lets out a whistle. Two hundred and fifty square feet have been divided into aisles custom fitted with tall wire shelving units that run floor to ceiling along each side, along the back and down the middle, with just enough room to walk between the rows. Every shelf is labeled with a little snap-on plastic thingy. There's no dust, nothing is yellowed, the bins are contemporary—what you could buy today at Lowe's.

I didn't help pack the Grand View house. I was with Gary by then, at NYU by day, clubbing and drugging and drinking and dancing across the city all night every night. There was a message blinking for days on our answering machine, and I hit Play one afternoon, and Albert was telling me to come and take what I wanted. It was too late by the time I played my father's message, but I didn't care. I didn't want any of it except *Carry the Dog*, which Albert sent. I had a life in front of me: Greenwich Village and Gary. My songs. It's hard to admit, but I didn't think about Henry. I missed him but I was so young and thoughtless, I assumed the distance between us would take care of itself.

When I speak to Albert on our monthly call, sometimes I drop Henry's name into the conversation, to test his reaction. He is unresponsive and yet his silence makes a racket. Both sons, lost to him; the mother of his children, too. I avoided Albert because I don't like hearing the massive silence he holds inside himself. I hear it, because it's inside me too.

I say to Gary, "I guess Violet can worry a little bit less."

Gary says, "Who's Violet?"

Damn. "Oh. I forgot to tell you. A photography person. From MoMA."

"MoMA? What do you mean, MoMA?"

"MoMA. You know MoMA, right? The place with all the art." I shrug like it's no big deal.

Gary looks at me. "I know MoMA." But he lets it go.

The shelves on the left hold the bulky equipment, everything labeled: TRIPODS, UMBRELLA HEADS, LIGHT STANDS, BACKGROUNDS, BACKGROUND STANDS, STOOLS, STEPLADDERS, FOLDING CHAIRS, BLANKETS, DROP CLOTHS, CANVAS, MUSLIN, CUSHIONS, DAY BAGS, CRATES, WEIGHTS, on down the aisle. On the right, the shelves have been sectioned into smaller units, and each of these is labeled too, and each holds a clear plastic bin with a camera and bins alongside to hold that camera's lenses, batteries, flashes, flashguns, flash diffusers, reflectors, cleaning kits and cloths. Gels and filters are categorized by color and size. There are electrical cords, small cables, power strips, clamps, and clips. Many rolls of gaffers tape and electrical tape and duct tape and Velcro, fishing line and twine. All the things Miri used to create her tableaux.

I stop at a bin and lift the lid and see a dozen boxes of Dritz T-pins. I pull out a little box and empty the T-pins into my palm, and with the tangled pins, memories tumble, crossed and caught on each other, too. They all have a point. I want to untangle them, set them straight. I touch and am pierced. "Ow."

It was midsummer. At breakfast my mother said, "I want to take some pictures today."

The boys groaned and protested, knowing it would make no difference, knowing she would not change her mind. I was beginning kindergarten that autumn, a small girl with a small voice. Miri said, "We'll start at a quarter to four."

At the appointed hour we trooped out of our kitchen across the yard to the woods, each of us lugging a bulging tote or a piece of equipment. Miri was in her work uniform: hair held back by a thick rubber band; a discarded white dress shirt of Albert's, the length of it nearly to her knees, sleeves rolled up above her elbows; black Capri pants and black Keds. She climbed the packed-earth steps cut into the steep slope behind the house, the metal valise that encased her camera bumping against her legs. I brought up the rear, and I can still picture the little parade of my mother and my brothers, marching ahead of me.

It is hot and dry and buggy. We crush leaves and twigs underfoot and swat away mosquitoes. The tree stands get denser and denser. The air cools, the light changes, the shadows darken. Miri stops at the border of our property. Along the edge of our world where the slope crests, a crowd of bamboo grows dense and tall, impenetrable silver leaves like coins flattened into oblongs on a train track. To get to the flat path, a long-abandoned railroad bed, the Old Erie Path, we push through the bamboo. This is as far as we usually go, but Miri has an idea. It's in the set of her shoulders, in the sweat above her upper lip. She indicates a direction with her chin. "A little farther. Right, boys?"

Ansel and Henry, who've been arguing as usual, quiet down. We come to a thicket hundreds of years old, the trees' ancient trunks, fat or narrow, all tall with distinctive patterns engraving their bark: diamonds and rectangles and long grooves. It feels like a different day here, black and green, a chilly, deeper world, just a five-minute climb from home.

She's discovered a hideout. The twins' secret, ruined. Ansel engineered it and Henry built it, with logs for borders and branches for a bower and a purloined canvas for the ground cover. It is sited well off the path, out of range of parents and a nosy little sister, camouflaged by two-hundred-year-old white ash and white oak trees, and situated snug up against a tulip poplar with branches at the perfect height for a lookout and a wide view of the Hudson River.

She says, "You picked a good spot."

Ansel mutters, "Shit," and Henry shakes his head and I say, "I knew it was here!" Ansel says, "Shut up."

Miri sets up her equipment, checks the sky, moves the gear, resets the tripod, over and over. When she is satisfied, she says, "Okay, let's go." We undress and drop our things on top of each other's. We don't look at each other's bodies.

Miri motions Ansel into the hideout's recess. He finds a place and lies on his side on the tarp. She positions Henry just outside the hideout, with his hands crossed in front of his genitals. She pulls muslin from a bag and drapes it around my waist, and with a mouthful of Dritz T-pins, she folds and fastens the fabric around me.

She gives me a little push. "Berenice, sit in front of Ansel, but close, okay? Cross-legged. Stay very, very still, and look over at Henri. Can you do that?"

I can do that. I feel heat behind me from Ansel's groin. I squirm to scoot away and am stung by the prick of a pin on my bottom. "Ow!" Tears fill my eyes. I cry, "Ow! Ow!" and I twist around to see the blood I am sure is there and as I twist, the muslin pulls away.

Miri says, "Berenice."

I turn to look at her, still twisted, my eyes brimming and spilling over. Ansel looks at me—I'm the baby, always slowing things down—in big-brother disgust. Henry turns away from Miri and angles his head to see what is going on behind him with Ansel and me, forgetting to hold his hands in front of his genitals. I look to my mother for comfort, but she is under the hood, her voice muffled, encouraging, "Okay, don't move," and "Stay like that," as she shoots us.

The first time I saw *Hideout* was a couple of years later at a group show in a gallery in some little bohemian town in the Hudson Valley, when Miri was almost famous. It was the same show where *Nap* was hung. Adults milled around with glasses of warm Chablis. Miri had printed the photograph big. Really big. It was mounted all by itself on one wall. The little girl is silver-skinned with shiny black eyes. Her eyes brim and tears track through grime on her face. The reclining boy behind her smirks in the shadows. His twin is in the sun, unprotected, vulnerable, with a halo of yellow white around him. The angel boy looks at the other two with great concern. They are under a bower in a copse, a silver-and-gray-and-black anti-Eden.

Do I remember the afternoon or the image? Standing here now in #201, Dritz pins in hand, I am only an outline in my own memory, a sketch of a girl, like Eloise at the Plaza, with hands on hips and eyes intent, trying to reconcile what I see on the gallery wall—the image the wine-buzzed grown-ups murmur about—and the afternoon in the woods. Our naked bodies, the boys' bird chests and mauve genitals and their arms as long as legs; my shiny round belly and translucent skin of not-yet breasts, the muslin dropped away, my mass of curly dark hair, and the gray curves under my eyes.

I made the note in my middle-of-the-night ruminations: *Albert?*

He might not have been in the vicinity when she took the photographs, but he was at her side when they—we—were mounted on the Hudson Valley gallery wall. Albert was there with a wineglass in his hand. Of that I am sure. My father was in awe of my mother's work. Maybe confused by it, maybe intimidated by it, maybe even repelled, but he had no will to challenge it. She was Manhattan to his Brooklyn, Art to his GI Bill mentality. She was everything the women in Albert's family were not.

He had grown up around women who protected their children, first and foremost, but he turned a blind eye to our "chores." When he was out of the house, Miri would say that Albert was "occupied elsewhere," insinuating that he was with other women. She seemed not to care. Maybe it was part of the deal of their marriage. She got to do her work, he got to escape it.

My knees wobble and my hands shake. I put the pins back in their box. I feel the same old low-grade, relentless rhythm of anger and guilt. Everything that happened that summer afternoon—Ansel's smirk, my pain, Henry's curiosity—was a moment about to move into the past, that should have become the past. Instead, our mother the photographer chose to click the shutter and freeze the moment and print it and hang it on a gallery wall, and the moment was never dissolved by the mercy of memory.

Hideout and all the other prints from all the other shoots are filed and labeled on the shelves in the middle of #201, stacked high in archival boxes of every depth and dimension, in folio cases, binders for negatives, and slide boxes. Gary's curiosity gets the better of him. He pulls down a black buckram box with a tight-fitted lid whose label says, *Porch Swing*. He struggles to loosen the lid. I pull it from him and we tug the box between us.

I say, "Let go."

"Just one box. Just this one. Let's look."

"I'm not digging in to everything today. I'm seeing what's what. That's all!"

"But, Bean. All these boxes. Who knows? Maybe pictures no one has ever seen. The negatives alone. Maybe hundreds never printed. You've got to look."

I should say, "MoMA will take care of it," but I don't. I shake my head and return the buckram box to the shelf.

I go deeper in. The stretch of shelving along the back wall holds office supplies and a half dozen thick photo albums with warped black pages, black-and-white photographs stuck at their corners by paper triangles. Are these from Miri's childhood? Albert's? I don't know. I can't look. Two shelves are crammed with photography books, all first editions: I see Robert Frank's *Les Américains*; *Paris de Nuit*, Brassaï; *The Decisive Moment*, Cartier-Bresson; *An American Exodus*, Dorothea Lange and Paul Taylor; *Changing New York*, Berenice Abbott; *Sierra Nevada,* Ansel Adams; André Kertész's *From My Window*. I tip up the lid of an archival box. It holds original *Aperture* and *Life* magazines. There's also a dark red box among the magazines, duct-taped, with Albert's handwriting. It's seems out of place, so I want it. With my back blocking Gary's view, I drop it into my tote.

On the very bottom shelf near the floor is an oversized Ziploc bag. I recognize the gray canvas compressed within. The hoods. Certainly the hoods—so anachronistic, so retro, so creepy—are items any self-respecting archivist or movie producer would snatch up immediately. "Give me a hand."

Gary says, "I thought no touching," and he braces for me to hang on to him as I bend for one of the Ziplocs. I unzip and split apart the plastic and without thinking, pre-thinking, primal, I put the bag over my nose and mouth and inhale. The canvas releases ghost odors trapped in the folds for all this time, her cigarette breath, her coffee breath, her wine breath, the breath of her murmured directions. I inhale my mother holding her breath to wait for the light to be right, her tiny sips of breath so she can keep the camera still, stopping her breath to make herself an extension of the camera so that my brothers and I would forget she was watching, so that none of us would lose focus, so that none of us would blur the image.

I gag. I am dizzy and my knees give way. I try to say, *Let's go.* Gary grabs my elbow and his voice recedes and the birds scream. I need air. I make myself breathe through the dizziness, the hot eyes, the racing heart. I don't let myself look up at the birds in their skyless sky. I count my inhales and my exhales, four in, seven held, eight out, to put distance between my lungs and the reek of my mother. "Please! Let's go!"

I stumble along the Hilltop aisle, queasy. Her smell is lodged in my nostrils and caught at the back of my throat. I am on a verge, fainting or vomiting, it could go either way. My vision tunnels. Everything is a blur. I blink and blink and think I see, I do see birds. I don't know bird types, but it is a pair flying in tandem, screeching, aiming down the aisle at me like arrows. This can't be real, I remember this scene from the Hitchcock movie, or I am making it up, but I crouch and put my hands up to protect my eyes, and this might not be real but I am not taking any chances. I say "Gary," but maybe I don't, maybe it's just gagging and retching and then the bile rises and the next thing I know, I am on my knees to purge the odors, the taste, the memories.

Chapter Ten

A CHUGGED DIET Coke from the gas station store did not flush her.

The Uber driver had to pull over twice on the way home to Manhattan. Gary rubbed my back while I leaned and heaved out the car door, but he was glued to his phone the whole time so I did not feel soothed.

I'm home by dusk. No Echo, no Dory, just me. I leave my coat on, stop in the kitchen for my supplies and in the bathroom to brush my teeth, and on through the bedroom, and I climb out the window to the fire escape. I arrange an old cushion on a rusty step. The icy air freezes my nausea and my anxiety. I have my American Spirits and my mug of Sancerre. I don't have PET results yet. I shouldn't be smoking and drinking, I'm not stupid, I'm well-informed, I don't think I have a death wish. What am I supposed to do? Yoga? Meditate, after the day

I've had? That kind of self-care doesn't make sense to me right now. Of course I want to loosen my tight throat, shut down the banging and clamoring thoughts, silence the caw of the birds and the rackety roll of the steel door on unit #201.

But the door to #201 has been opened. This is where I am.

A cushion, a cigarette, a mug full of wine, a higher altitude. I prop my pillow, light up, take a sip, have a look. From my step, I survey my domain twelve floors up, my city view, the backs of buildings, the courtyards and rooftops of 103rd Street. Lights flick on above, below, around me. Neighbors work in their kitchens, move through their rooms, set plates on tables, settle into chairs. Televisions blink. I watch strangers reach and chop and stir. I pull from my cigarette, I follow with a good swallow of wine. My whole body eases. My stomach unclenches.

I haven't forgotten the deep red Ferragamo scarf box, taped with such care. It's mine but I feel like I've stolen it. Under the designer logo, my father's Catholic school cursive curls in black marker: *Outtasight* Interview 1969. Still wrapped in my coat, back at my desk, I scissor through the tape. Inside, flat aluminum canisters of 16mm film are labeled with white masking tape, also in Albert's handwriting: MM/IAN MCNALLY. There are four compact discs in jewel cases tucked in there too, numbered, so I have in my possession the original film and its digital copies. Albert must have had help having copies made at some point in the last decade. I adjust my noise-canceling headphones; I don't know why, I'm the only one home, there's no one to disturb. I slide the first disc into my computer. My heart thumps. I tell myself I can mute, I can pause, I can eject the disc.

I make it start.

A camera looks at a chair, as familiar and human-seeming to me as any other member of our household. I hit Pause to examine the chair. A wing chair. It has a high back that curves around the sitter, like protection; even my mother's chair had boundaries. The chair has claw feet and armrests discolored from her grip. It's upholstered in a Scalamandré fabric of striped zebras and black arrows scattered across a mustard yellow field. It sat squat and wide in our living room in front of the bookshelves, deceptively cheerful looking, although it was so thoroughly shaped to Miri's body it might as well have had a KEEP OFF sign. That chair lives in my senses. It smelled of smoky menthol Newports and something cottony, and I know the feel of that fabric under my fingertips and against the backs of my thighs, and the sight of the chair on film calls up an entire household buried in the past, my childhood home, still alive inside me. I am only now noticing that the zebras are not frolicking happily, as I always thought, but dodging the arrows. Where is that chair now? Why haven't I thought about it before?

At this rate, I'll be here for days. I tap Play. There she is, and here she comes.

Miri fills the stationary camera's line of vision. At first all I see of her is a headless torso swallowed by a worn man's chambray work shirt with mother-of-pearl snaps instead of buttons and a Wrangler label on the pocket. I want to pause again and examine her, compare our bodies, but I can't see her shape because of the big shirt. She folds into her chair.

Miri sets herself to face Ian McNally, publisher of *Outtasight*. I can only see one quarter of the back of McNally and his dark shaggy hair, but he is an icon of the counterculture, instantly recognizable. He is also in a chambray shirt, the back yoke of which is embroidered in rainbow colors and happy shapes. It's the kind of shirt reproduced and hanging in the window of Urban Outfitters over on Broadway, and makes me cringe when I walk by.

I tap the Back arrow to start again. My mother walks into the shot and takes a seat in the wing chair. Another young man approaches and adjusts the arm of a microphone set on a small table next to her.

Ian says, "Ready?"

Miri murmurs, "No." She shakes her hair out and brings her hands up and runs long fingers under her black tangled hair to mess it up more. She has my hair. I mean, I have her hair.

When she's good and ready, she looks not at Ian but directly at the camera. At me. She nods. A chill runs through me. I feel caught out. In trouble. I hit Pause. I go to the kitchen and fill a bucket with ice and stow the wine in the bucket, and set it up on my desk. I tap Play.

Ian says, "Don't look at the camera, Mimi. Look at me."

Mimi? I've never heard my mother called Mimi. The way he says *Look at me* makes me think, *Jesus Christ, were they sleeping together?* My mother bends one leg beneath her and crosses the other bare leg, shaved smooth, on top. A bare foot, toes unpolished, dangles. She looks at McNally, her eyebrows slightly raised, like a coconspirator.

I say it out loud. "They were sleeping together."

"Okay, we're already rolling. Don't worry. Keep going if you mess up. This is just for us. You'll get the transcript. We can edit that together. When we're done, I'll take pictures for the piece. For the cover maybe, if it goes well. Sound good?"

Miri keeps her eyes locked on Ian.

"Thank you for doing this with *Outtasight*, Miriam Marx. We're the new kids. You're our fourth interview. We did two last year, we'll do two this year, and next year, fingers crossed, a full slate. One a month."

"Lucky me."

Ian says, "Well, we talked to Mr. Dylan a few months back, so maybe that makes up a little bit for our inexperience. He was a tough interview, too." The way he prefaces *Dylan* with *Mister* makes me hate him.

Miri turns her head and looks at Ian, from an angle. Her eyes slide and assess from the side. Her eyes sweep up from under her skeptical brow. Her eyes are black and white; they round out when she speaks but narrow when she listens. Her eyebrows are ungroomed. She wears no eyeliner or shadow or mascara, she highlights nothing, emphasizes nothing, but her eyes burn.

Ian is solicitous. "How are you?"

"Exhausted." My mother loved talking about how tired she was.

"Because of *Car 1967*?"

"That, and everything else."

"You mean the FBI? The confiscation of the work?"

"Is this all part of the interview?"

"Well, we'll see. I want to keep it loose. I have notes. Nothing formal, you know? When we're finished we'll see what we have and make it great."

"When you say *we*, I have final approval?"

"Well, at some point one of us might have to compromise. I want readers. You want . . ."

"A serious discussion about my work. So it's better understood."

"Good. We're on the same page. Let's pick it up. You were saying you were exhausted because of the events of last year. Your big show going up, the press attention, and then the FBI's attention. Which all brought about a grand jury?"

"Yes. All that. Which ended up being just a lot of ringing telephones. Paperwork. Guys in suits."

"What about the children?"

My mother laughs. "What about them?" I feel cold in my coat.

Ian reads from notes in his lap. "This is from the *New York Times*, May 27, 1968: *Controversial photographer Miriam Marx has been threatened with removal of her children from the home in the wake of her most recent exhibit, which features disturbing images of twin sons Ansel and Henri, 14, and daughter Berenice, 11, in the family's station wagon.*"

He looks up. "That must be pretty upsetting."

"It is. They turned that show into a tabloid scandal."

"I meant that your children were taken away. That's the upsetting part, I would think. You almost lost them."

"They were close to 15 and 12 when I shot *Car*. And none of them were lost, they spent time with relatives in Westchester until it all blew over. Trust me, they're all still accounted for." I feel struck, physically, by how flippant she is. How dismissive. Where were we during this interview? Albert was probably at work. The boys, up in the woods or down at the river. If so, I was lurking, spying on them, or maybe Henry and I were on the porch swing and Ansel was in his bedroom, as far away as he could get.

"Let's hold that for a minute. We'll go back to that. Let's talk about the exhibition first. Tell me about it."

"There were ten images hung at Stoffel Gallery in Soho. They all sold."

"Before or after the FBI got interested in them?"

My mother stonewalls McNally but he is undaunted. "Okay, then. Can you tell me about the image that got you into trouble? How did *Car* come about?"

Miri smiles and her eyes crease at the corners, almost sweet, and she covers her mouth to hide her teeth which are big and bright white. Her smile makes her seem less formidable. I'd forgotten that.

"It wasn't . . . I wasn't trying to do anything special. I used the car like any other subject. Like the kids. It was sitting there, in a good spot. With good light. I used it."

"How about the kids? Your subjects. They didn't object to being used?"

Miri's eyes narrow. She pulls her bare legs up, crosses her arms and hugs her knees. Her ten toes grip the edge of the chair. "They've been helping out with the pictures for a long time. Our little family business."

Ian says, "Well, right, but I guess the perception is—"

"I don't really care what the perception is. You were asking about the photographs."

"Okay, then tell me about the photographs."

"I shot them the same way I always do. Large format. It was Indian summer. After an hour or so it got hot. Really hot."

"You were under the hood?"

"Yes, a canvas hood. Not the hood of the car."

I snort, something between a scoff and a laugh. She's trying to be charming in her way. Ian seems surprised that Miri makes this little joke. He turns to the cameraman and gestures at Miri with his thumb as if to say, *Check her out.* I still see only McNally's back, but when he turns there is the side of his face, his fuzzy sideburns. I hit Pause. I make the screen smaller, open the browser and google Ian McNally. I filter by image.

Dozens of pictures assemble. I don't have to enlarge or focus on any particular one. They're all from the sixties—macramé and spider plants, a bushy-headed man-boy in oxford shirts and narrow ties and scruffy Levi's, half clean-cut, half hippie; half revolutionary, half corporate. There are pictures of the early days of *Outtasight*, McNally with his wife, Nora, a Celtic beauty with flaming hair and a flinty stare. I'm retrofitting, I'm overidentifying, I'm sure, but the look on her face says, *I do all the work and he gets all the credit.*

I scroll past image after image of Ian in the olden days of magazine publishing, drafting tables at a tilt, rubber glue cans and X-Acto knives, pen-and-pencil caddies; rock posters taped to the walls; Ian with his feet up on a battered desk next to an Olivetti Lettera; Ian on a flowered sofa, arms long along the back, legs crossed at the ankle, commanding as much space as possible, a big bay window behind him, everything faded now but so San Francisco then. There are more images of Ian McNally later, emeritus, honored, smiling wide in front of his magazine's famous covers: Mick, Jimi, Dylan, and Miriam Marx. My mother the cover girl, to jarring effect, is sitting on a stool holding her Leica, naked except for her black Keds. There is a black outline around the image, and underneath it: *Miriam Marx 1932–1969.* I've seen it before, of course, but not lined up next to the iconic men of music at that time, all fully clothed. I click and the cover photo credit goes to Ian McNally.

I resume the movie.

"Okay, you're under the hood and the kids are in the car. And?"

"We were an hour into the shoot. It was hot. They were bickering. I didn't know how it would go, with the kids in the car. They do usually fight, that much I expected. I was losing them. I was about to call it a day. Then I saw the shot."

"You put the kids in the car without their clothes. You figured they'd start fighting about something?"

Miri laughs with unrestrained delight. "Yes! I hoped!" My heart tightens at this but I can't stop watching. She shakes her head with the memory of the moment. "It was perfect. The big American station wagon. The fogged windows. Naked teenagers. Lover's lane in suburbia. But twisted."

"That's what people object to. That it seems twisted. Since they're your kids. And siblings. Berenice was eleven."

"Almost twelve." Miri roughs up her hair again, it's like a tic, it's how she flirts. She raises one arm and bends it behind her head like an actress. Her long fingers grasp the curved-in wing of her chair. "It's just a photograph."

"Louis Lefkowitz, the Attorney General of the State of New York, disagreed with you on that. The state of New York called it pornography."

My mother shrugs it off. I gulp for breath. I haven't thought about *Car* in a long time.

Okay, that's not true.

I think about *Car* 1967 all the time. *Car* gives me insomnia. The insomnia View-Master clicks and lingers on that image, showing me what I should see, but I can't see. Now here is Miri, turning the story of that photo shoot into an amusing anecdote, with her girly hair-toss thrown in for good measure. Miri's retelling of the shoot that day feels upside down to me, just like the glass plate images she used to take her photographs. Every inch of me curves in and contracts. My shoulders rise, my neck strains, my jaw is so tight. I haven't noticed that my glasses have slid so low on my nose that I'm squinting. I lean in too close. She's lying about the way the photograph happened.

Ian says, "Let's keep going. I'm interested in the process. Tell me about it. Tell me about Berenice in the image."

"Berenice." My mother smiles. "She must have been kneeling on the front seat. She opened the window a few inches. She held the edge of it. She was angry. Hollering for me to stop shooting. White knuckles. The boys were fighting behind her. They're big boys. Berenice pressed up against the window to get away from her brothers. She flattened herself against the window. Screaming at me to discipline them. To stop shooting."

"Without clothes."

Miri dips her head for a defiant nod.

Ian says, "Did you think about the implications of that while you were shooting? Two teenaged boys and a girl, brothers with their sister, no clothes, fogging up the windows of a Chrysler? Pretty suggestive."

"Did I think about it? Of course I thought about it. But I didn't necessarily plan it. I do wait and watch for an opening that I can shoot through. And of course, Berenice, complaining, one thing I could always count on. That made it dramatic."

"Didn't it feel wrong, as a mother? Seeing how upset she was?"

"It wasn't about right or wrong. It was about the light. That's my goal. My job."

"What about your husband? Albert? Al?"

"What about him?"

"Does he ever object to the images? Of how you . . . work with the children to get the images?"

"Al's opinion of my work doesn't matter. I'm doing my thing. He gets that." Miri shakes her head. "So, no."

"Does it matter to the kids?"

"Does what matter to the kids?"

"Being with each other, that way. For your work."

"We've been doing the pictures since they were little. It's not a big deal to them."

"Isn't it possible that they do it because it's what they've always had to do? Chores? They've never really had a normal childhood, right?"

She narrows her bird-black eyes. "Normal? I'm not trying for normal. That's not what we're doing."

Ian pushes it. "We? Isn't it just you, Miriam Marx?"

I'm almost convinced that Miri truly believed Ansel and Henry and I—like Albert—were willing, even enthusiastic, collaborators for her art.

But here, I hear it, she says it herself. I was a complainer. A resistor. I realize I am holding my breath. My heart is racing. I am close to the screen. Sharp seams of pain have stitched up either side of my spine. The muscle that hunches between my shoulder and neck pulsates. I am about to hit the square to stop the movie at the precise moment Miri says to Ian, "A break."

She does not wait for his answer. She gets up and moves out of the room. I can now see that she is wearing very short Levi 501 cutoffs with frayed hems, which the work shirt nearly covers. She is thirty-seven at the time of this interview, in the summer of 1969, and is as far as she can get from the typical appliance-worshiping, stay-at-home mom of that era.

The running camera is fixed on Miri's empty chair. Ian sits and waits, back of work shirt, shaggy hair. He is looking down, flipping through notes. He says, "What time is it?" to Eddie. Off camera, Eddie says, "I don't know, man. I think we lost her."

Ansel enters and passes across the frame. It's so shocking to see him alive that I gasp and cover my mouth. I hit the Back arrow and watch again. His scuffed belt is threaded through the loops of his sagging jeans. I feel a catch in my throat: he's missed a loop. His torso is tense and slender. I can see his brown hair curled at the top of his white T-shirt. He wears a braided brown leather cord around his neck. I can't see his face. Ansel, who would soon be dead.

McNally asks, "Ansel, where's Mimi?"

My brother says, "She says she's finished for today."

Ansel knows the nickname, Mimi. Ian says something I can't quite make out but the tone of his voice pokes at me. Ansel responds with a laugh and it feels like it's at my mother's expense. Ansel and Ian seem familiar with each other. I tap Back to hear it again, try to make out what Ian says to Ansel. I lean in and close my eyes and hold the headphones tight against my ears to hear better, to make it make sense.

Echo knocks lightly on the top of my head, breaking the spell. Her cheeks are bright red with the cold after a long dog walk. She holds Dory, who is panting and smiling. I take off the headphones.

"Wow, you look crazy." Echo leans over me. "What are you watching?"

"And you two look beautiful." I fumble the mouse, the cursor, the tiny ✖ to escape. "Nothing. Just old family movies."

"With Daddy? I want to see."

"No, it's . . . it's mostly my mother. Photography stuff. And my brothers. Brother. So far. I've just started." My hands are shaking, my voice quavers.

"Are you okay? How was the storage place? Is that where you got the video? Why are you still wearing your coat? I was going to make tea. Want some? You look like you need it."

"Yeah, good, I'm fine. I guess I'm cold. We left after a quick look. But, it's all in good shape. I mean, whoever organized it did a good job. Yes, tea, please."

"Who did? Organize it."

"I don't know. I have to figure that out."

"Have you spoken to Violet? Maybe she can figure it out. Maybe just hand it over."

"No, god no. It's too soon. I have to see more." I do. A window that might be a mirror has opened onto the past. Like Mittens, I might have to squeeze through and into the blizzard. An idea comes to me. "Actually, I was thinking I'd talk to Albert about it. In person."

"At Sandy Edge?"

"Yeah. Maybe get away for a few days. Some sunshine. Interested?"

"Oh, me?" Echo pauses. "Well, I don't know. My mom would love a visit, obviously. Daddy too. I can't really afford . . ."

"Oh, no, I know that, I know. You'd be doing me a favor."

Chapter Eleven

ECHO TRAVELS SMARTLY.

She starts out in fleece and layers and zones out under head-phones through the flight and ends up in shorts and flip-flops when we land in Palm Beach. I'm frazzled and sweating in my down coat and my black pants and my black boots. I look ridiculous, over-dressed, but then I remember that at my age, no one looks at me anymore anyway.

Sandy Edge Delray lies between the Intracoastal and the Atlantic. A cab takes us past daytime neon bars opened onto sun-bleached sidewalks, past boatyards and yacht clubs and Lego-like condos, one after the next. It's February. The streets swarm with half-dressed locals and snowbirds dodging pool-toy flamingos and sharks hanging outside shops. Cars are parked packed tight. The cab noses around beachgoers heading to the water; they walk without a glance at our vehicle. Everyone seems slightly drunk or stoned.

Eventually the cab finds and follows a winding driveway with bright green lawn on either side. It could be a country club. The grounds are anchored by white stone benches in shady spots under glorious old trees, but no one sits outside at this hour, high noon. We enter a cool lobby where the staff in polo shirts and khakis greets us cheerfully, and the residents loll or kibitz quietly in their bright clothes on designer sofas and chairs. I think, *This is so nice,* and, *I can smell the ocean,* and, *I will never be able to afford a place like this for myself.*

We are directed to a walkway that crosses the boulevard to a boardwalk that leads through dune grass to the beach. There's a ramp down to a stretch of sand reserved for Sandy Edge residents only, no teens or tourists to disrupt the tranquility. The beach is unpopulated except for my father and his minder. He sits in his wheelchair at the shoreline in full sun facing the ocean. A woman in a Sandy Edge uniform sits in a chair next to him holding her shoes, shaded by a Sandy Edge umbrella. He is dressed in loose white pants and a pale yellow guayabera, and he is barefoot. The tide rushes to his ankles, his feet sink into the sand, his chair tilts a little, he laughs, and his feet emerge as the tide recedes, again and again. I choke up at the sight of my father laughing with his feet in the sea.

Echo throws her arms around Albert from behind and he doesn't look up at her, he just pats her forearm and says, "Who's that. Hannah."

The woman stands and hugs Echo. "Hannah!" She is stout, with a tight swirl of beaded black braids wound on top of her head.

I enter my father's field of vision. I stand between him and the ocean. I am in full sun. He squints up at me. "Miriam."

"Dad, no, it's me. It's Bea."

"Bea, Bea. The hair. It threw me." He squints harder. "You're not in New York."

"No, I came down for a visit. I'm here."

Echo sits in the sand. "Daddy, where's your sunscreen?"

Albert's companion ekes out a smile in my direction. She doesn't extend her hand. With the tight smile and the withheld handshake, she chastises me. My father has been here for five years. This is my first visit. I call monthly, but now that I'm here, I can see how it seems like I've neglected him.

"I'm Clara," she says. "I look after your father. When he allows it." She reaches into her pocket and hands Echo the sunscreen. Echo squeezes cream onto Albert's bald head.

I say, "Dad, you're okay out here? Why don't you sit under an umbrella?" He's got a tan but the sun is brutal. "Where's your hat?"

Echo and Clara both answer. Echo says, "He hates the umbrella," and Clara says, "He won't wear a hat." I am the only one who doesn't know his ways.

Albert says, "I dreamed about this. Retire. Sit in the sun and watch the ocean. I'd like to be smoking, too, but this one." He indicates Clara. He looks at me. "You're still smoking. I can smell it on you."

I laugh and say, "No way. I quit a long time ago."

"So. All of a sudden you're here. What's up." Nothing is a question with him.

"Nothing. Nothing's up. I came to visit, that's all."

"Since when," he says, not expecting an answer.

"Can we go inside?" I look at my watch. "Maybe have some lunch?"

Clara says, "Lunch is over. It's at eleven."

Lunch at eleven? So what, dinner at four? I stop myself from interrogating Clara about the infantile meal schedule. Albert's chair is fitted with special tires for the beach terrain, and Echo steers him across the sand, up the boardwalk. She says, "Say goodbye to the ocean. You'll come back later." Albert waves at the Atlantic like a monarch.

Out of the blinding sun, in shadow on the terrace, my father looks small and bowed and age-spotted and milky-eyed. He's got hearing devices. He's got a medical ID bracelet on his narrow wrist. A male aide takes over. He aims a scan gun at my father's ID tag. They keep track of the old people, it's a good idea, but it's hard to watch the aide raise Albert's bony arm and scan him like a box of cereal at the grocery store. "Shower time, Al."

My father flips his thumb in the guy's direction. "That's Sergio. Don't let the name fool you. He's Cuban."

Sergio says, "I told you a million times, Al, I'm half and half. You need to read your history. My pop was a good Marxist from Naples. He went to Havana in '59 for Castro. But he stayed for my mother." They wheel away, arguing.

Clara takes us on a tour. Sandy Edge is lilac and sea green, institutional beachy. The space is divided according to levels of care, one wing for the high-functioning, where Albert resides for now, and another wing for those needing constant attention. There's a garden, a library, and a gallery hung with framed photographs of the residents and their families. There's a game room and a music room and a fitness room. Clara says, "We love our little theater," and behind a door is the little theater, with about twenty seats, all taken. On stage there is a placard on an easel: FALL LIKE A CHILD WITH SENSEI JOHN.

Clara whispers, "It's a safety demonstration," and Echo and I nod our approval. After a minute, I am totally absorbed. Sensei John is an older Japanese man, a once-upon-a-time martial arts master and a bit of a star. He wears the outfit. He pretends to trip and fall onto a mattress. He throws out his hands to break his fall. Wrong! He mimes not being able to get up, hip pain, wrist pain and boo-hooing. He hams it up. The audience laughs.

He pretends to trip and fall again. This time he doesn't try to stop himself, doesn't throw his hands out or stiffen his legs, he relaxes and curls and rolls beautifully. He flops on to the mattress and kicks his legs and waves his arms to show he is unhurt. He stands, straightens his martial arts outfit, and concludes in all earnestness, "Resist all instincts. Accept that you are falling. Find the momentum. Spread the force of impact. Pliability is your friend. Remember how to tumble and then tumble. No fear, no embarrassment. Fall like a child."

What gets me is some of the residents are taking notes.

Clara ushers us through a state-of-the-art memory care section, called, with the least amount of nuance possible, Memory Lane, for residents who are losing the past to dementia and Alzheimer's. There is a dining room outfitted like a mall food court. There's a nursery with a baby-friendly mural and a crib and a rocking chair. A sixties kitchen, avocado green appliances, speckled Formica countertops. An old-fashioned reading room with a card catalog, a crafts room. The residents stroll or sit with aides or relatives. It's disorienting to see everything retro. It feels like vintage virtual reality, the past with all the bad memories designed away.

We go to the elevators. Clara puts a casual arm around Echo's shoulders and Echo leans into Clara. They chat and laugh. I trail behind trying not to feel left out. I am itchy in leggings, with my giant coat over my arm, my hair in full frizz, my feet sweaty in city boots. As we ride up, I say, "So how's he doing?"

Clara says, "He's having a good day. There are bad ones, too."

"You mean mental? Or physical?"

"You'll speak with the medical staff. They can update you. They check in on him every few hours."

"But you're with him all the time. What do you think?"

"He's ninety-one. He has lung cancer and dementia. On his good days, like today, he's still got a spark."

Echo says, "He can go for a long time like this, right?"

Clara gives a little lift to her shoulders but says nothing.

I change the subject. "By the way, Hannah has a new name. She's Echo now!" I am flaunting my insider knowledge of Echo to Clara, whom I feel threatened by, who is obviously a better human than I am. I regret it immediately.

Clara seems confused. She looks at Echo. "You've changed your name? Echo?"

Echo blushes. "No, not really. Not officially. That's just for New York. Like a stage name. If I decide to do music."

"You should be proud! You're reinventing yourself! You go, girl!" I exhort Echo, like the kind of women I avoid, overly supportive types rah-rahing the rest of us. Clara side-eyes me, just as I would side-eye her if our roles were reversed.

Clara says, "Well, maybe don't try to explain all that to your father. That might be hard to process."

Albert's room is gray and white and the windows are wide sliding doors that can open onto a little balcony, with the ocean and the big sky close by. The bed is the only thing that looks institutional, with rails you can raise, a high mattress, and wheels. Everything else is boutique hotel-like, compact and fitted and functional. There's a closet and a dresser and stocked bookshelves and a big television screen and a round table with a flower in a vase and a couple of chairs, and a little sofa. My father sits in fresh clothes in a motorized scooter chair that he can drive himself, his Jazzy. Sergio fits him with nasal cannulas attached to tubing and tucks a portable machine into a compartment in the chair.

"What's that? Oxygen?"

"Yep, a tank." Sergio says. "It helps."

Albert says, "Hannah, watch this! Watch! I got Alexa! Watch!" He gives a command. "Alexa, *Judge Judy*!" The television blinks on and loads for a few seconds and then there she is, the judge. My father is agog at the screen.

Clara winks at Echo. "He loves Alexa."

"He has a crush on the judge, too." Sergio says, "Al, come on, shut that off. You've got company."

Albert says, "I know I've got company. My daughters. I'm just showing them. I knew Murray, Judy's father. That's why." He commands, "Alexa! *Judge Judy*! Off! Off!"

I sit on the sofa near my father, not too close. "Can we talk, Dad? A few minutes?" He shrugs. I say to Clara, "Can I speak with him alone? Is that allowed?"

She points to a bedside button. "Of course it's allowed. Hit the buzzer if you need me."

Echo says, "I'll be here. Don't worry."

I make my voice neutral and say, "Maybe me and Albert, for a few minutes? I'll text you?"

When we are alone, I take Albert's old-man hands. They are thin and loose of skin and gnarled and knobby and his nails are too long. For all this hyper-attention, why haven't they cut his nails? They are definitely my father's hands, wide and coarse. He is an educated man, a white-collar man, but he has always had the hands of a man from an old country. I look into his eyes, milk brown, ever watchful.

"Dad," I say. I don't say, *I'm worried about a PET scan.* I don't say, *What was wrong with us?* I don't say, *Why didn't you stop her?* I make my lips a tight line. Holding everything back requires physical effort. I default to, "You look good, Dad!" He nods. I say, "How do I look?"

He says, "A little bit older. You're still in New York."

Nothing is a question. "Yep, yep. I'm still in New York. And I'm definitely older. Almost sixty."

"The rents! You don't have to tell me. But there are plenty of cheap flights."

"I'm sorry. I know."

"Don't worry about it. Phone calls are okay. I can get you up on the screen. With FaceTime."

"FaceTime makes me nervous. I feel like I need hair and makeup. Better lighting."

He shrugs. "You still look good to me. Don't worry about it."

It's like a beam from the firmament. I don't say, *I do, Daddy? I look good?* I'm fifty-nine years old but needy as a child. I lean toward him. I want more praise from him. I want him to know me and approve of me anyway. I want him to think I am smart and good and pretty. I want him to tell me he left, but he didn't leave me. A cloud moves across the sun and shadow falls over us and we fall quiet. He's here now, and this is my chance to dig into the bedrock of fossilized fear and anger and abandonment I'm built on. I should ask him, *Where were you?* I should but I don't.

Taking stock is tough. I appreciate what I did get: the laugh, the compliment. I breathe, he breathes, the oxygen concentrator marks the beats. I find lotion on the table. I massage his hands. It occurs to me that "closure" also means being okay with no closure. The sun comes back. We sit together inside the bright afternoon. I rub lotion into his palms.

He pulls away from me. "Enough with the hands. Let's go." He Jazzies himself around and heads for the balcony.

"Wait, are you allowed out there?"

"Open it up, hurry up!" He winks at me. "Come on! Help me over!"

We get the Jazzy over the threshold. We have an expansive view of the beach and the sea, the sea and the sky. I lean and look. "This is pretty good."

"I'm using up all the money. And my pension. And the government kicks in. Jeanne writes the checks."

"That's great. We're seeing her tonight. Echo—Hannah made a dinner plan."

"Hannah. She's good. Drives her mother crazy."

"You know she's in New York? At my place?"

"Do I know. I know! Where else is she gonna go. She's got a ring through her nose. She's into music. Tell your famous husband. Let me have a cigarette."

"A cigarette! I don't smoke! You're crazy!"

"Demented, that's the word. What's the difference. Cancer, too. What's the difference." He takes out the tubes.

"You have dementia, Dad. It's an illness. You are not demented." I don't say *I might have cancer too.* What's the difference is right. I salivate and my fingers twitch. I feel breathless too, in that way of smokers who need it to catch a breath. "They'll freak out."

"By that time we'll be halfway through."

"I'll get thrown out!"

"Nah, not at these prices. They don't want to lose a paying customer too soon."

I fit a cigarette between his dry lips. I say, "Don't you dare die on my watch."

It's another bad joke I shouldn't be making, but Albert gives me a that's-a-good-one nudge with his elbow. I flick the lighter and touch the flame to the tip of his cigarette and then light my own. I inhale all the way.

My father draws at the American Spirit and looks at it with disdain. "What is this crap?" He closes his eyes. His blows the smoke up into a tight curl. He looks like a blissed-out baby. "I guess I gotta take what I can get."

This is maybe the worst thing I've ever done but it is also the best, sharing a smoke with my father as we watch the big Florida sun play on the water.

"Daddy, I went to Congers. To StoreSpace."

He shrugs and sips at his cigarette. "So."

"I don't know. I was surprised. Impressed."

"What about Zillow. Brooklyn! I looked up my old building. Hart Street."

"Daddy, I'm asking you about storage. With all the . . . with Miri's work."

"You look like her. She was a good-looking woman, your mother."

"It's so organized. Who did that?"

"Zillow. What everybody paid, right there. And then Google. The maps. You can zoom in. You can practically see in the windows. Take a walk around the block. I was born there. I lived on Hart Street. Railroad rooms. A tenement building in Bushwick. Now, that same street. I can't believe my eyes. Showplaces. Millions!" He shakes his head. "I couldn't wait to get out. I met your mother."

"Dad, I wanted to ask you about storage. About what happened. At the end. After, you know, that summer, the fire. And later. Can you tell me about that?" I can't bring myself to say their names. Ansel. Miri.

He seems far away. He takes a long power drag. I realize, too late, that is not good. That's bad. My father gasps and then gurgles.

He clears his throat but it doesn't help. He chokes and coughs. He is racked with coughing. He puts a hand to his chest. His eyes bulge and brim and he bends over. His cigarette drops and I drop mine. I stupidly slap his back. "Daddy? Dad?" He shakes his head vigorously, *No, no*, so I stop slapping and pet him gently as I can and offer the water bottle from the Jazzy. He shakes his head again, *No, no*, but he's still hacking and nearly retching and clutching his chest. I maneuver the chair back into the room.

"Clara!" I call. "Clara!"

My father shakes his head again, *No, no*. He is consumed with the struggle to breathe but he points at the buzzer attached to his bed and I run and within thirty seconds Clara arrives. We reek and two cigarettes burn out on the balcony floor. She doesn't look at me as she inserts the tubes back into my father's nose and adjusts everything on the concentrator. She knows.

Chapter Twelve

HE'S OKAY, AS okay as he was before the crappy cigarette.

The Sandy Edge people reprimand me but Albert is right, they don't want to alienate a family member who might have money. They pretend I didn't understand the rules. My punishment is that next time I have to let them examine my bag.

We drop our things at an Airbnb and Uber to town to meet Echo's mother for dinner. It's a red-sauce Italian place on the beach, Caffe Luna Rosa, and crowded with sunburned, overdressed tourists. Echo has toned down her look, nose ring removed, her hair less aggressive. She is unhappy with me. We wait in silence and people watch.

I can't take it. "Echo, I'm sorry about the smoking," I say.

She fiddles with her phone. "It's just. You know. Thoughtless. I mean, he is like literally dying of lung cancer because of smoking. And you gave him a cigarette. You enabled him!"

"No, I know. I just wanted to make him happy. It was stupid. Don't be mad. I'm sorry. He's okay."

Sorry, not sorry. But as Albert pointed out, what's the difference. He's ninety-one years old, he lives in a weird world of then and now, here and gone, *Judge Judy* and the Jazzy. Strangers know his most intimate moments, they record them on charts. The cigarette gave him back five minutes of himself. He got to say, *Fuck it*. I feel that way when *I* light up. Fuck it.

I signal for a waiter. I really need a cocktail. Echo decides to forgive me by relaying a Dory update from the city. Dory is with a neighbor who dealt with her successfully before I took her on. "Lauren texted. Dory is grumpy. But fine."

Jeanne Seger, Echo's mother, my father's wife, sails in on a surge of fragrance and dangling accessories. She's got the Palm Beach look: a bright green tunic, white pants, Chanel ballet flats, the bag, long necklaces, bracelets, diamond earrings, a frosty blond bob. The maître d' presents her to us as if she's a celebrity. Mother and daughter kiss the air near each other's ears. They make rapid, sharp small talk as if they are picking up in the middle, in a way that telegraphs that even though they don't get along, they are close. They skim over the details of Albert's afternoon choking episode. I try to look humble.

Jeanne says to Echo, "Still in the rebellious hair phase, I see." She turns to me. "My god, Bea. After all these years." She moves to hug me, which I make myself accept. I am not used to having family. Her strong scent surrounds and attaches itself to me. She pulls away. "You look fantastic. You look like your mother. Exactly." Jeanne and I have spoken on the phone, and it was Jeanne who sent the code for StoreSpace, but we've never met in person.

"You too," I say. "I mean, you look fantastic, too, not that you look like my mother. Although, I have a theory about familiar faces. I think Echo—"

Jeanne cuts me off. She turns to her daughter. "Oh, are we doing Echo tonight? Feel free to correct me if I call you Hannah. The name I gave you at birth. Your actual name."

Echo fixes a hard look on her face, one I haven't seen, and scans her phone. "Bea's apartment is really cool. It's great, actually. Right near the park. And we have a dog." She waves a selfie in which she's cuddling with Dory.

Dory and I are pawns in a mother-daughter war game, but that's okay. "Jeanne, I love having her. You don't have to worry."

"I'm not worried. I just don't want to be the ATM machine anymore." She turns to Echo. "Do you have a job yet? A boyfriend? What are you doing all day?"

"Drugs," Echo says. "Watching porn. Figuring out a career in identity theft so I can steal all your money."

"There's no more money. Okay? The money faucet is turned off." She glares at me. "You have no idea how expensive Sandy Edge is."

She and I both put on our glasses for the menu. I say, "Actually, it's just ATM. No *machine* on the end. The *M* already stands for *machine*." I think I am serving up a little mood-lightener, but neither of them acknowledges it. I wave for a waiter. "Should we order?"

Echo sips iced tea. Jeanne and I drink the same thing, dirty martinis, and make an effort not to gawk at each other. We are the same age. She met my father twenty-two years ago at her own mother's wake. Her mother was Albert's secretary at Pan American Airlines back when there was such a thing as secretaries, and such a thing as Pan Am, in what was once the Pan Am Building on Park Avenue. Albert was in his late sixties when he re-met Jeanne. Jeanne was nine months pregnant with Hannah/Echo. I don't know who Echo's biological father is. My father has been her father since she was born.

The three of us split a salad, rigatoni alla vodka, and a linguine con vongole. We have red wine with dinner, Jeanne's choice. The drinks and the wine and the pasta do their job. We relax.

"Jeanne," I say. "Can I ask you? About Albert?"

"He's your father, ask away."

"When we were out on the balcony, I was trying to find out a few things. About the storage place? In Congers?"

She nods. "Yeah, StoreSpace. It's all yours. Whatever's there."

"Well, I know. But I was wondering about before that. When Albert was still paying the bills."

"Did you come down to see your dad about money? After five years? Is that what this visit is about? Because there's no money. Whatever there is—was—goes to Sandy Edge. And it's not going to last forever. I'm up at night wondering which goes first, the money or your father."

Echo says, "Mom, that is a fucked-up thing to say!"

Jeanne gives a quick shake of her head. "Reality, babe."

I say, "I don't want his money. I want to know who set up the archives. I'm curious."

"After all these years, you're curious about the 'archives.'" Jeanne makes air quotes. "Please. You mean all that crazy trash of your mother's. You're telling me this isn't about money? Pardon me if I'm skeptical."

She's not wrong. We drink our wine and eat our pasta. I let her simmer down but I've gone this far which has taken me more than half a lifetime so I keep pushing. "When I was talking to him this afternoon he spaced out. He was fine and then I asked him a question about StoreSpace, about my mother's work, and he just started talking about Brooklyn."

"Bea, he's demented. Okay? He shuts down. Do you blame him? It ruined his life, the marriage to your mother. Everything that happened. A dead son. Her suicide." She drains her glass and tips it my direction. "You."

"Me? What did I do?"

"I don't want to get into it with you. You ran off to be a groupie. You went wild."

I hoot in surprise. I say, "Wait a minute," in protest, but it shuts me up. A groupie? My knight in a shining Karmann Ghia whisked me off to Manhattan. A groupie? For the first time in my life, I consider Albert's point of view. His seventeen-year-old daughter went to the senior prom in a proper dress with a local kid and came home at six in the morning wearing only a T-shirt and smeared eye makeup, and then packed up and jumped in the foreign car of some punk rock freak, ten years older, and never came back. A groupie.

This is the problem with memory. It's mostly made up. My synopsis of my life from fourteen to seventeen? I was abandoned by my father and Henry, and Gary saved me. What came right before—the fire, the suicide—in my made-up story? They are blackened and flat events, there's nothing to see, like the burnt ground behind the house. I have spent my adulthood, such as it is, drafting my version of what happened, which I then wrote across my brain: thoughts, feelings, assumptions, my View-Master memories.

I try to defend myself to Jeanne. "*Albert* sold the house and moved away to Florida. I was a teenager. I fell in love. I chased my dream. And not to correct you, but I don't think having dementia is the same thing as *being* demented."

"He put up with your crazy mother all those years. On top of it all, he lost the Segrettis. He deserved some happiness. He's been happy here." Jeanne looks at Echo, who nods solemnly. "Don't you agree, Hannah?"

"I do think of him as a happy person." Echo says. "Everyone deserves to be happy."

That stops me. She says it like it's fact. I've had pleasure, I've been satisfied, I've been content. I've been buoyant for a few hours, I've been relaxed, mostly through artificial means. But happy, as in a baseline state of being? I've never considered it. It occurs to me that Gary is happy, and Echo is finding her way to happiness.

Jeanne is still going. "And those disgusting photographs. I hope you're not snooping around that storage unit with any ideas. Don't drag all this back up. Let him live out his life in peace."

"Who's been there?"

"What do you mean?"

"The unit is completely organized. It seems recent, like somebody's been there."

"Well, it's not me and it's obviously not your father. That's all I can tell you." Jeanne widens her eyes and shakes her head and shrugs defiantly. Echo is fixated on her phone, not taking sides.

We drink dessert wine. We share a tiramisu and find new footing. She tells me proudly, in a way I admire, that she has new love in her life, she has met "her person." My father will never know and I don't judge. In fact, I'm a little jealous. I say, "Did you meet online?"

Jeanne scoffs. "Are you kidding? I don't have the patience to weed through losers. I was introduced. Properly."

We commiserate about online dating. I tell my funny stories. I make them laugh. I compare her look and my look, all her color and aroma and shiny jangle compared to my own somber urban aura. Maybe there's something to this Florida thing. Maybe this *is* the place to get old. I like tunics. I could cut my hair, accessorize. Maybe I've been swept into premature invisibility by the tsunami of young, beautiful, rich, smart, ambitious women of Manhattan. Maybe it's time to escape inclement weather, black clothing, the noise, the attitude. Leave behind the many failed selves I've been. Get distance from Gary, once and for all.

Outside Luna Rosa, the valet pulls Jeanne's car around. It's a little Fiat with the top down. Now I *am* jealous. I have always kept a driver's license. I've driven over the years, but only when Gary lets me have the wheel, to joyride out to the beach or the mountains, with him kibitzing from the passenger seat. I've never owned a car.

Jeanne kisses the air in farewell. She hops in the Fiat and adjusts her mirror and puts a gold headband in place to control her hair for top-down driving. I can't help being distracted by the Chanel handbag, blinding white with the gold latch and the braided chain handle. It occupies the Fiat's passenger seat like an indulged little dog, like Dory would. She says, "Next time, Hannah, I expect you to stay with us, not some bed-and-breakfast. You too, Bea." She waves and zooms away and just like that, she feels like family.

Echo and I take a long walk back to the Airbnb. We are mostly silent. I say, "Would you hate me if I smoke?"

"Only if I can, too."

"You don't smoke! You're like, the opposite of a smoker!"

"Only when I drink. Or after I've seen my mother. Tonight was the double whammy."

I laugh. *Double whammy* is an Albert expression. We stop and smoke and watch drunk kids go by. All the young women are Instagram-ready, jewelry and heels and full makeup, and all the young men look like they are dressed to get wasted, big baggy cargo shorts, slogan T-shirts and flip-flops.

Echo says, "Let's be weirdos." She puts on her sunglasses, even though it's ten p.m. I put mine on too. We do selfies in sunnies with cigarettes. I hate selfies, I hate the way I look, I don't want to see myself, I hate having my picture taken at all, ever—but I love our selfies. We lean over her phone and zoom in and select our favorites. She posts us to her social media and I am secretly thrilled.

Echo says, "I'm sorry about my mother."

"Don't be. I like her. She's got a lot of opinions. That's a good thing."

"She's cheating on Daddy."

We stub out our cigarettes and walk. I put my arm through hers. "I don't think it's cheating. Not really. She's still taking care of Albert. But she's taking care of herself too. You said it, everyone deserves to be happy. I wish I were more like your mom."

She says, "I like the way you are." My heart skips. It hops. Since she's come to live with me I have been trying to think of her as a sister, but we're so far apart in age; and me with no children, just my incomplete pregnancies, and even though Echo has a mother—a perfectly fine mother—I feel like a mother to her, too. I wish I'd had an extra mother in my life, a spare.

We walk. We stay linked. We keep the sunglasses on.

In the morning we stop at Sandy Edge on the way to the airport. The concierge inspects my bag. Albert is in his room, watching *Judge Judy*. He glances at us, and calls out, "Ahoy!" He pats the sofa and Echo sits next to him. She shows him pictures on her phone of the night before. He tries to finagle a cigarette. He is having another good day. Even I, The Great Neglector, can tell that.

I wait for Judy to take a commercial break between cases and command, "Alexa, mute *Judge Judy*."

Albert throws his hands up in irritation. "My show!"

"Just for a few minutes. We're on our way home."

"Here's your hat, what's your hurry."

"Daddy, I want to ask you about the storage place. StoreSpace."

"Just ask already. Stop telling me you want to ask. Just ask."

"You rented it, right? Years ago? You moved everything from Grand View."

"Right, right. Everything was my problem. Now it's your problem."

"Who helped you? Who moved all the stuff in?"

"Good morning, ladies." Clara comes in to the room. "Albert, lunchtime soon. Can we get you into your chair?"

I try again. "Who helped you, Dad? Who organized the archives? Who got all those bins and made the labels? That was a big job. I've been out there. It looks great. Who did it?"

Clara wheels the Jazzy close to the sofa. She and Albert work together, her hand goes under his arm, she guides him to the seat, helps him sit, helps him place his slippered feet on the Jazzy platform, helps his old hands hold the handles. He motors toward the door. Echo makes the backing-up noise, *beep beep beep,* as if he's a truck. He snorts.

I try again. "Dad, who else has access to StoreSpace?"

He rolls away, making the backing-up noise himself. *Beep beep beep.*

On our flight home, I wrap myself in a cocoon of sleep mask, wool beanie, down coat, and cashmere wrap, even though it's a short flight, even though it's midday. I'm disturbed. The organization of #201, it must have been Henry. Who else could it be?

Echo wants to disappear down into whatever distraction she's tapped into on her phone but she can't help fussing around me. "Are you okay, Bea? Do you want something? Water? A snack?"

I slide my eye mask up. "I'm sorry. I need to think about this. I thought he could help. He seemed fine this morning and then he just flaked out. I don't know. I'm just trying to figure out what to do. It's so complicated. It's always been so fucking complicated." I catch myself by surprise. My tears spill. "God, I'm sorry. It's okay. I'm fine. Ignore me."

Echo says, "No. Tell me."

I buy two small wine cooler cans and a can of Pringles and I turn to her in our close cocoon of side-by-side airplane seats and tell her what I think I know.

Chapter Thirteen

MY PARENTS MET in a black-and-white time.

It's a story Albert loved to tell. It was like a poem he memorized or lyrics to a favorite song. He knew it by heart. I should have asked him to tell it when I was at Sandy Edge. For Echo. Next time, I'll record him. I'll go back in a couple of weeks, get him talking, tape him. I promise myself.

When I was a kid he'd sit with a cigar and a whiskey on the porch swing. The boys were an unreliable audience, diverted by jumps off walls and races to the road, bickering and besting each other, but I sat and listened. Albert didn't need prompting, and he told the story the same way every time. I made him start over if he deviated or left something out. I wanted it to be like a book at bedtime, words on the page, unchanging. We weren't praying people, so bedtime stories carried me safely to sleep. Albert's porch stories had the same power. In his stories, my mother and my father fell in love. We were safe.

He was a bookkeeper for Emery Roth, the architectural firm in Manhattan, known as Al Seger to neutralize his Neapolitan surname, tone it down for the colleagues. He left at five o'clock five nights a week and took the train to Queens College to finish an accounting degree paid for by the GI Bill. He went home to Bushwick to study, three rooms in a brownstone on Hart Street, with his parents and two older brothers and two sisters.

He skipped school one night and went out with colleagues for drinks, and to see a half-naked woman writhe with a reptile— Cleopatra and Her Snake—at a club on Broadway called the Top Hat. When he told us the story, Albert said "Cleopatra and Her Snake" in a salacious voice, with a tilt to his head and a twinkle in his eye.

Echo is in the middle seat. She's got an airline blanket around her legs. She says, "I can just picture him!"

Miri worked at the Top Hat as the souvenir photo girl. She wore a skimpy dress meant to hug a woman's curves but in her case it fell without interruption from bodice to calf. She circulated with her thick hair twisted up, a heavy camera hanging from her neck, straps biting skin, watching, snapping—*Look here, look here, look here*—Barbaras and Bernards, Harolds and Ruths. The Top Hat let her print the film in a pantry in the basement outfitted as a makeshift darkroom. Miri slipped the fresh photos into the cardboard holder that promoted the club, a dollar each, and pointed out the note on the back: *Extra copies available by mail, Constellation Photo, 341 West 47th Street, BRyant 9-7740.* On Monday mornings, the Constellation Photo guy noticed that despite his squad of girl-photographers in Manhattan nightclubs, copies of Miri's photographs were in greatest demand. Everyone's eyes were open, smiles were not grimaces, candles flickered flatteringly.

Was there a box on a shelf in StoreSpace labeled CONSTELLATION PHOTO? Violet would swoon. Bix would, too.

Miri was twenty years old, with only a high school diploma—but not just any high school, as Albert liked to say. Miri had gone to the Ethical Culture School in the Fieldston section of the Bronx. Fieldston was a haven for wealthy, creative city kids. Miri's father was footing the bill with the small fortune he made from the skins of Eastern European sables. It was right up Miri's bohemian alley. The school offered photography as a course of study, and Miri signed up immediately.

I tell Echo, "It's all on Wikipedia."

"Bea! I know! I've seen it a dozen times." She gets exasperated when I steer her to the internet. I forget that she's grown up with it. She pulls it up and reads, *"Marx became a student, like Ethical Culture alumnae Paul Strand and Diane Arbus, of Lewis Hine. Hine took pictures of children toiling in factories and fields and the disturbing photographs woke people up to the terrible conditions and exploitation. Child labor laws were reformed because of Hine, and his work instilled in young Miriam a passion for photography. Marx absorbed Hine's teachings, and then realized a more personal vision by turning the camera to the intimate conditions within her own family."*

Echo looks up. "This whole entry sounds like Violet Yeun to me. I bet she wrote it."

It's true, there is certainly one Miriam Marx expert who'd want to make sure it's right.

Echo says, in earnest, "What's the big deal anyway about the photographs? I mean, naked bodies. It seems like the whole thing got blown out of proportion."

I'm surprised by how much Echo knows about us. Of course she's looked it all up, seen the images, drawn her own conclusions,

probably long before we met. She has never shown any extra interest
or discomfort. Echo, Echo's generation, they're more generous in their
judgments about things, the Marx Nudes included. She's probably
seen way weirder things on the internet for her whole life. Maybe time
has caught up with Miri's work. Maybe social media has made the
Marx Nudes kind of ho-hum.

Miri refused college after Fieldston, no Sarah Lawrence, no Vassar.
She needed to begin. Albert always said, *Your mother had a calling.
You should appreciate how unusual that is.* She left her parents' East
Side townhouse for a junior four on the west side of Central Park to
begin the artistic life, albeit subsidized by my grandfather the furrier.
Whom I never met.

She freelanced for Constellation at night, and built her own little business by day, Manhattan Moments. She was shooting school
photos, bar mitzvah photos, wedding photos, family photos and the
club souvenir photos. Manhattan Moments helped Miri develop
her eye and her confidence with the equipment—no small feat for a
slight, anemic-looking girl—and build her own darkroom in the second bedroom. She sold her pictures to travel magazines, newspapers,
gazettes, pictorials, wherever she could. *Carry the Dog* has Manhattan
Moments rubber-stamped across the back with the telephone number,
MOnument 2-0761.

That night at the Top Hat, Albert spent the first hour tracking
Miri with his eyes, the second hour planning his overture, and the
third walking her home. He loved Jewish women. The Jewish women
he worked with at Emery Roth, despite lesser titles and smaller pay-
checks than the men, seemed to Al to be running the show, with their
snappy comebacks and frank eye contact, their style, their infallible
bullshit detectors. They were different than the women in his neighborhood, who didn't go out to offices, didn't mix with non-Italians.

Miri effortlessly batted back Albert's banter. She didn't prattle to him about movie stars or clothes or petty slights or family obligations. She had no clique, no sisters or girlfriends. Her parents had parented her from a distance, had hired help for the practical aspects, and had traveled a lot. Her brother, Stanley Marx, whom she revered, was a painter of growing renown.

Albert was in love. *What can I say. I met my match and she lit me up.* He'd crow and puff at his cigar like a victor. Of course, it was all told in euphemism and innuendo, but we got the message: after the exchange of one burning look outside Miri's Central Park West door that first Top Hat night, they went upstairs but barely made it inside the apartment, so overcome were they with lust. Within weeks, Miri presented Alberto Segretti, not Al Seger, to the sophisticated Upper East Side Marx family in order to infuriate them. In turn, she was presented to the Segrettis of Brooklyn. Extreme consternation was mutual. "Greaseballs," Miri's mother concluded. "Ebrei," Al's mother whispered in Italian. Stanley, Miri's brother, refused to even meet Albert, and in fact, for the years of my parents' marriage, there was an estrangement that was never resolved.

Echo goes back to her phone. "Stanley Marx. Is he still alive?"

"I don't know. I haven't come across an obituary. He'd be in his nineties, too. Albert's age."

"Yep, here he is, Stanley Marx, still alive. Sagaponack, New York."

"They didn't speak. He wasn't at the funerals."

The families could feel the heat between Albert and Miri; there was nothing to be done. As both mothers suspected, Miri was already pregnant with the boys. My parents were married less than sixty days after they met, on Valentine's Day in 1953. Ansel and Henry were born in October of that same year.

I stop storytelling. I'm slightly drunk—alcohol works quicker on a flight, something to do with cabin pressure and high altitude. I reach into the Pringles can for "food" to ameliorate the situation. My hand gets stuck. I wave it at Echo. "Am I boring you to death?"

She frees my hand from the can, shakes her head. "No. I like it. I love it."

Who knows why Miri chose Albert? He was handsome and lively. He made her laugh. He had a great head of hair and a steady paycheck and he was ambitious too. He could dance. He wasn't Jewish, and her family was appalled. Even more irresistible, Albert looked at Miri—I can hear this in his voice and see it in the few snapshots that remain—with reverence. He saw her the way she wanted to see herself: artistic, existing on a higher plane than other people, with special gifts that needed nurturing and protection. Also, she was sexually liberated. Albert used to say, "Your mother was free. Never uptight about things. She was like a man that way."

Echo casually says, "So she was slutty?"

I laugh. "Judging from his stories, they got together the first night. Women didn't do that back then. They were worried about their reputations and getting a man to marry them. So, yeah. I guess that made her slutty. At the time."

"That is so cool. She was so cool!"

Despite myself, pride fizzes along my jaw. I can't help it. I like that Echo admires Miri. It lets me admit to myself that I do too, from a safe distance. Telling the story of Albert telling our story helps. I don't know it all, I don't know enough, but it's comforting to retreat to Albert's version, as long as I don't dwell on what went so wrong once we were born.

By the late 1950s, my father was managing Emery Roth's big project, the Pan American World Airways headquarters in the middle of

Manhattan. Al fell in love with Pan Am, the company that began by flying sacks of mail from Key West to Cuba. He had a hobbyist's knowledge of aviation, air routes, globalization, and, I came to learn years later, stewardesses, although by the time my father's interest in them became known to me, they were called flight attendants.

The stories he told of those years—I heard them on the porch, or when he chatted with neighbors, or during the few times we'd get together with the Segretti clan. Now and then Albert would take us, without Miri, to his sister's place in Westchester. She was also named Jean, like Jeanne, Echo's mother. Cousins I barely knew ran wild and ignored me and my brothers. We were too strange. My father was adored and indulged by his sister, with whom he could drink and be a version of himself he didn't show my mother: Al of Brooklyn.

"We stayed with them for a few weeks," I tell Echo. "But that was later."

"What do you mean?"

"Child welfare sent us to the Segrettis while they investigated my mother. To see if she was . . . you know. Abusing us."

Echo with great kindness just nods.

Pan Am hired Albert away from Emery Roth for an accounting job at HQ. He was a sterling employee until his retirement and loyal long after. It was boom time. The Pan Am job, the mood of the country, the bright future, it all seemed secure. The next step for the family was to get out of the city. My parents' contemporaries were going east to Long Island or north to Westchester, but Miri was repelled by houses of worship, supermarkets, public schools, drive-thrus, neighbors, and, especially, other suburban mothers. She wanted riverfront. She wanted undimmed starry nights and the light off the water. She wanted dark woods and privacy. There was an artsy enclave farther north on the other side of the Hudson, so our family crossed the river and headed for Nyack, but on the way Miri spotted a For Sale sign at the bottom of a sloped lawn in Grand View-on-Hudson. I don't know if this really happened or if I've made it up to fit my memory, but my mother put her hand on Albert's arm and made him stop the car. I was in the back seat of the Chrysler with my brothers and we all, all five of us, looked up the hill to the house. Our house. I see it, but that might be from Albert's telling it so many times.

The Grand View house was built in the Arts and Crafts style with a low profile, a foursquare footprint and a wide white porch with worn decking and a faded aqua blue ceiling. It sat on a ridge with a dense black wood behind it. Town was a ten-minute walk away, but town consisted of a gas station, a post office, a grocery store, a bar with no name, and a bench to wait for the bus to the city. The house itself was old and in disrepair, nothing like the model-home settings my parents had previously toured. Albert resisted. He wanted to give his family a cookie-cutter home, new and shiny and push-button easy. He wanted to impress his own family and Miriam's. *But no,* he said. *She had to have the house north of nowhere.*

Again, it's either a memory, or there exists a blurry snapshot of Al mock-throwing away the For Sale sign, maybe taken by a new neighbor or the realtor. Miri is standing up the hill on the porch steps, arms folded, hair in a high ponytail, serious. I sit on a step at my mother's feet. I am leaning against her legs. I wear black Mary Janes, white anklets, and a dress with little flowers, smocked at the bodice. I have a high ponytail too. Ansel is at the bottom of the hill, cheering my father on, making a muscle-man pose. Henry lies in the grass. Just a normal moment stopped and framed with scalloped edges and faded by time, a moment you can find in shoeboxes and albums, attics and flea markets, stuck in frames or the corners of mirrors, all over the world. This one is probably sitting in one of those old photo albums in StoreSpace. I see my shoes, a tilted mailbox, cracked concrete, the mound of my brother's biceps, the gleam in our father's eye, right before we disappeared into the house in the woods.

My parents were fine in Grand View, at first. I think. My father gave an aggressive shake to his starched white shirt each morning before he put it on. He fastened buttons, pushed links through cuffs and knotted a silk tie tight. He donned his Brooks Brothers suit jacket like armor. He wore a watch but no wedding ring. He got in his big car and commuted from our bohemia to his fancy office in Manhattan. His secretary held a steno pad, awaiting every dictated word.

Miri rose late, retreated to the darkroom or her chair, printing or reading and smoking for long hours, barely remembering to feed us, always dieting herself. My brothers and I inhabited the separate land of "the children," in a way you don't see much anymore. We were completely unsupervised. The twins were minding me, which consisted of me trailing after them, trying to keep up. I watched them catch fish from the Hudson with twine and worms, and poke them to death on the shore. I watched them take blue-tipped matches from their pockets and flick them against their teeth or the zippers of their pants and light small fires. One time, they hauled a rotted canoe up from the river and into the house to "repair" it, but lost interest and moved along to some other adventure. The canoe sat across the threshold, propping the front door open, allowing a raccoon to find its way inside the house. I remember screaming and shouting and the three of us swatting the critter with brooms and mops. In that memory, my mother is nowhere to be found. The canoe sat that way until my father came home from work. Every now and then a school friend or a neighbor kid would make it inside to use the bathroom. They'd trip over camera bags and tripods. They wrinkled their noses at the chemical smells from Miri's darkroom—the developer, the stop bath, the fixer—odors we kids didn't even notice. Visitors surely saw that every table and counter and mantel, every dresser top and stair step, the window seats and ledges, the piano top and its bench, even the top of the refrigerator, was stacked with art books, newspapers, technical magazines, torn-out articles on every topic under the sun, steno pads and notebooks, her contact sheets marked with grease-pencil slashes. Miri would gather those up quick and hover, cigarette between her fingers, cigarette brought to her mouth, cigarette burning like a signal, until she could usher the interloper back outside.

I unbuckle my seat belt and stand and walk the narrow airplane aisle to stretch my legs. It's a full flight. I hold on to headrests to stay steady. Each traveler's space glows with a screen or rests in shadow. People are asleep or distracted by work or entertainment as we cross the sky. We are a planeful of vulnerable bodies, trusting souls in adjacent seats. We've all decided to believe mechanics have tightened every bolt, the plane will lift and stay aloft, the pilots are unimpaired and focused on the controls, the flight attendants will provide creature comforts but also save us if there's trouble.

My internal color commentary sounds familiar. I realize I'm reciting an old Albert monologue to myself.

Fine, I was in some creepy photographs in the olden days. Fine, I was nude. With my nude brothers. Fine, our mother sexualized us, exploited us. It was not normal. Fine, fine, fine. The world we're in today? Is it even such a big deal? I go back to my seat. I buckle up.

I say, "Until Gary told me otherwise, I kind of thought I had a normal childhood. Can you believe that? Nothing about it was normal." This is the most I've said to anyone in a long time about my childhood, about my parents as a couple, as parents, that isn't a smart remark, flippant or dismissive or cynical. This trip, our father, the selfies, the motherly-sisterly feelings I have for Echo, her interest in the family, our family—it's good. This is good.

"Can you believe your mother thought I was a groupie?" I look over. Echo's asleep. I stop talking into the dead airplane air and slide my sleep mask back down over my eyes. We both doze through the landing. We're here, it's New York, time to deplane. We stumble out, sleepy and disoriented, into a busy afternoon at JFK. I'm bleary and headachy from the wine and salty snacks, but invigorated too by the airport's energy. Passengers and greeters rush to and from the gates. Kids run. The shops and cafés are filled with people killing time.

I say to Echo, "Albert brought me to JFK for a company event when it was all brand new. There was a special Pan Am terminal, the Worldport. It looked like a building from outer space. With a flying-saucer roof. I was a little girl. We were all dressed up. Just Albert and me."

I realize I am talking to myself. Echo has stopped behind me. She is staring down at her phone. I go to her. "What?" She looks up and shakes her head. A busy terminal at JFK seems as good a place as any to get the news.

Chapter Fourteen

WE GO BACK.

Ticket counter, boarding passes, security, separate seats, we take what's left. I try with Echo, a word, a touch, but she's unavailable. I leave it alone. Albert had a heart attack during his after-lunch nap. I rationalize. His death couldn't possibly have anything to do with smoking on the balcony. I rationalize, but I don't dare say it. I also don't say it doesn't seem like such a terrible way to go at ninety-one. Sad, yes; bad, no.

Clara is reserved. Sergio is stoic. Jeanne introduces me to Deborah and I am chastened to see that her new love is a woman. I've drawn wrong conclusions from colorful tunics and logo bags and blond bobbed hair. I'm mad at myself for my assumptions. I need to embrace everything. Nothing is how it used to be and that's the way it should be. I ignore Deborah's outstretched hand and awkwardly clasp her to me in a hug, in penance.

I realize something. "Jeanne, what about Henry? Have you called him?"

Jeanne says, "Henry? No, Bea, I haven't. Maybe someone from Sandy Edge did. He checks in with them. Occasionally," and she shrugs, and that one word, *occasionally*, indicts Henry and me. Jeanne and Echo were Albert's real family. His kids were not around. Even Deborah knows more about my father's day-to-day life than I do.

We spend a couple of days wrapping up. We nod and agree on everything. There's not much to do, Jeanne will review, Deborah's a lawyer, she'll help, there's no money, keepsakes will be mailed. It's orderly and efficient. Sandy Edge arranges the end-of-life business, including sending Albert off for cremation and organizing a generic Albertless gathering under a canopy on the back terrace where my black city wardrobe finally feels right. I realize this is part of why Sandy Edge is so expensive, the smooth way they manage death. *Here's your hat, what's your hurry.*

"Can you give me a minute? Can I go back to his room?" I am assured that it's completely empty. There's nothing left. It will be freshly painted and prepared for the next to arrive at the sandy edge of the Atlantic. "No, I know. I just want to get one last look at the view he had. At the end." I wave my phone. "Just a picture of my father's view of the sea." Everyone understands.

I enter Albert's room alone. I close the door behind me. The device still sits on the nightstand. The On light glows. First, I step out on to the balcony and I snap a quick picture of the view but that's not what I'm after. The two half-smoked cigarettes are still there. I pick them up and tuck them into a pocket of my tote bag. Everyone has a different idea of a keepsake. I go back inside. One more thing. I have a hunch.

"Alexa," I command. "Henry's phone number!"

Alexa replies, "Call Henry?" and I panic.

"No, no! Don't call Henry! Give me Henry's telephone number," I enunciate, and just like that, I have it. I jot it down on the yellow Post-it pad I keep in my bag.

Echo decides to stay with her mother for a few more days, to grieve and to avoid the last of February in New York City. I go home alone. Lauren the dog watcher has dropped Dory off, and Dory is happy to see me. She ducks her head behind my leg, a quick nuzzle to sniff out where I've been. She does a slight wag of tail. I say, "Dory," and she lifts one tufted eyebrow at me. "My dad died." Her ears flicker. She gives me an intense look, which probably means *Where's Echo?* or *Feed me* but at least someone is here, someone hears.

I am home. The Armenians, my neighbors, the wheezy elevator, the crown moldings and Art Deco vibe, all of it tended to by Marcus, the super. I've probably lived here too long. Gary says I should have moved downtown years ago, in the eighties, to Tribeca, when it was scruffy and cheap. I'd be sitting on millions by now, the square footage alone. But I'm home. With Dory. I don't even take off my coat or shrug the tote off my shoulder. I go for the mug and the wine and my lighter and cigarettes and the fire escape. I sit on a step with Dory in my lap and the snow starts again, lazy bug-fat flakes that melt as soon as they hit the steel steps or me or my dog.

"My dad died." I say it out loud again to test how it feels for this to be true. I review the day. I feel okay about things with Jeanne and I'm proud of myself for getting Henry's number without asking Scary Clara, who would undoubtedly have cited some Sandy Edge privacy policy and declined.

I've forgotten something. What have I forgotten? It takes me a while to step through my short-term memory.

I didn't record Albert's Brooklyn voice.

In the middle of my nights, during my endless review of the past, I can sort of see my family with a sense-memory of gestures and expressions and motion inside the blur of the household. But their voices, I can't hear them. I forget how anybody sounded. When I heard Ansel and Miri on the *Outtasight* disc, I was electrified. They were alive in another dimension. I could have captured Albert's voice with my phone, listened later, shared with Echo, and now it's too late. I could have added it to the tangible mix of video and images and the storage unit full of gear, and Henry's phone number—everything that is not memory—and maybe understand how it all happened. How our father let it happen.

Where was Albert?

He was there. He knew everything. He saw the pictures. He squired Miriam Marx to exhibits and cocktail parties and galleries where pictures of his children hung on the walls. He saw the hate mail that crammed the mailbox. The *Journal News* ran an op-ed by a local pastor who condemned our family to hell. Still, Albert stood by Miri. He signed for the certified letter letting Miriam Marx know that she was the subject of a federal grand jury investigation into possible criminal violations of child pornography statutes. Child protective services pounded on our front door with warrants authorizing the removal of "the children"—even though we were teenagers by then, or at least the boys were; I was on the cusp—pending the grand jury decision, and Albert let them in. Miri retreated. My father examined the paperwork and nodded politely. Ansel, Henry, and I were hustled out and sent to the other Jean, Aunt Jean in Westchester, where there was a regular father, a stay-at-home mother, unruly cousins, and the only art on the walls was family photos and pictures of the pope and JFK. It was like vacationing on another planet. Flat lawn, tended flowers, bright sun. There was a pool. No woods. I was shocked when my cousins back-talked or broke the rules or complained about *their* chores: walking the dog, mowing the lawn, cleaning the basement.

The grand jury decided not to go after my mother. The judgment was that Miri was not a pornographer or a criminal. According to the newspapers, she was, however, a really bad mother. Albert came off as kind of a hapless dummy, a workaholic bookkeeper trying to provide for his family, who trusted his wife. A couple of months after the raid, a truck trundled up our long driveway and brought all Miri's gear back home. Albert signed for it.

Here's what's worse. Albert got the *Outtasight* film transferred onto discs somehow. He labeled each disc and the Ferragamo box. There is no way he didn't view them. I know what I saw, and so I know what *he* saw. The painstaking way that box was taped says a lot to me. He watched her flirt with her lover, Ian McNally. He heard the pet name, Mimi, and he saw the dynamic between Ian and Ansel. Which makes the porch love story Albert was so enthralled with, that he was so good at telling, a black-and-white lie based on his own manipulated memories and needy nostalgia and massive denial.

That's probably how I got so good at all of that myself. I learned it from my father.

I hear the faux old-school ringtone of my cell phone in my tote bag. It's Bix. I tap Ignore. I also see a missed call notification and a little red circle telling me I have one voicemail, from Dr. Keswani. This is how it goes, right? When it snows, it blizzards. What a life.

I don't procrastinate. I can't delay. I need to know. Dr. Keswani's recorded voice says, "You're fine."

I'm fine. Dr. Keswani said so. I'm fine.

I search the depths of my bag. I come across the two half-smoked keepsake cigarettes I retrieved from Albert's balcony. There's the Post-it with Henry's number. I still have wine in my mug, so I light up a fresh American Spirit. Snow falls in earnest. The flakes stick to my hair, which is a nest of knots from traveling. Snow falls into the mug. Snow dampens the thin paper of my cigarette. It's time to go inside. I brush off Dory's fur. She burrows into me, so close. Alive against me. My father died. I'm fine. I have to rest. I stand. The slatted fire escape is slippery. I lose my balance and the mug slips away and clatters to the edge and down. I lean over to watch it go and thank goodness there's an empty courtyard down there and not the sidewalk, no one's in danger. It's going all the way, and the snow continues to fall and becomes dense, and I get a little bit hypnotized. I realize that the keepsake cigarettes and the yellow Post-it have slipped from my grasp and gone over the edge, too.

Jesus fucking Christ. I push Dory back through the window into the apartment and lean over the railing. I can't see anything except swirling flakes. I assess the twelve flights of steps, more like a rusty ladder now covered in slick snow, and even though I'm drunk, I applaud myself for deciding not to climb down. Inside, I add a hat and gloves and snow boots to the coat I'm already wearing and I take the elevator. I weave past Artur, the night guy, and he looks distressed and asks, "Ms. Seger? Bea?" but I wave him off. I need the Post-it.

The building's back gate is unlocked and I drag it open. It carves a semicircle through the snow. In the courtyard the snow has already massed and drifted. Black garbage bags stacked along the fence look like miniature snowy hills on the landscape. I take a couple of big steps and lean way back to peer up and find my apartment window, to gauge where the Post-it might have fallen. I lose my balance and fall, of course, but I'm caught by a drift and I'm drunk, and now I am sad. I am an idiot, I have lost Henry's number, Ansel and Miri and now Albert are all dead and I'm old, and grief for all of it, which I thought was black, burnt ground inside me, is alive, and it makes me stop and see that it's been there all along. I realize: the absence of grief is grief too.

Here I am. I've fallen and been caught by a drift. I'm fine, Dr. Keswani said so. I'm flat on my back, it's snowing on me. The night is navy blue. It's New York so the stars are far but I see them. Sensei John said, *Pliability is your friend.* I sink into the snow and I fan my arms to make a snow angel, and my tears are released. Daddy died.

In the lobby I stamp off the snow. Artur says, "Anything you need?" which is so discreet and respectful that tears threaten again and I say, "No, I'm fine. It's okay. Thank you, Artur."

I'm still me facing another night with the same old worries and fears. There's a newly broken slat on a blind so the security light across the way glares and the room is too bright, and there are screamers on Broadway and sirens slicing the night, and Dory is wheezing and the old refrigerator is buzzing. But I sleep like a worn-out child.

Dory and I step out into a dark blue morning. I check the courtyard again, but the snow has really accumulated. There's no point digging; the cigarettes and Henry's number will be sodden by now. If I wait out the snow, I might get lucky. At least I know he's here, in the 212, in the city.

The lampposts, the crouching gargoyles, the awnings and steps, the run of the promenade and the long bare branches of trees, and the long white quilts of snow that blanket the park. The benches are iced with a fondant layer of snow, pristine before the sledders and the snowman builders come, before the plows, before the hour rushes in with cars and trucks and foot traffic, before it all turns to slush and sludge. Dory and I find our park path by making it as we walk. My favorite thing is stamping my boots in the snow, and another favorite thing is watching Dory high-step and burrow with her snout and snort and toss the snow and look back at me so I can admire her and exclaim over her. One more dark night is behind me, and Dory and I make the first visible footprints of the day, and that's all I need to know.

Chapter Fifteen

NEXT UP, BIX.

He lures me with an invitation to an afternoon movie, no Gary. I've got the time. My work obligations are nonexistent. It's early in the year, before projects gain traction, when my usual clients' resources and budgets and my consulting services are being juggled and wedged into a calendar. I hope. My checking account balance is a couple of thousand dollars away from extinction, and my New Year's resolution, I keep forgetting, is to need Gary less. I tell myself it's okay, it's been worse, and one day falls into the next, and I magically make the money last. So I'm going to the movies with Bix.

I'm sleeping well and this me in the mirror is as good as I get. I do my face. I braid my hair to the side and admire the streak of white at the front. I wonder for the hundredth time how to afford subtle surgical intervention. I pull a big gray turtleneck over my go-to black leggings. I step into mukluks from the eighties, and although I am no longer a fan of fur, I own these boots and it seems a shame not to wear them. I am so fond of my belongings these days, I keep digging in my closet and pulling things out. I twist a big scarf around my neck, grab my gloves and go.

Bix is standing outside the theater in a gray shearling coat and narrow jeans and a black V-neck sweater with a heather gray T-shirt showing underneath. He's rocking a fur trapper's hat and puffy mittens. It's like we planned our matching outfits. It's like we're a couple. I say, "You don't look very L.A. today."

"I'm trying to live up to your New York standards." He touches my arm. "I heard about your father. I'm sorry."

I nod. "Yeah. It's strange. We weren't close, but we were."

"It's good you were there, yes?" He puts a hand on my back. "Maybe the movie will take your mind off it." He chose a fancy cartoon, not my thing. He corrects me when I tease him. "Not a cartoon, Bea, not at these prices. This film cost 175 million bucks to make. It's Pixar Animation. You'll see."

"If you say so, Bix."

"Will you ever call me Malcolm?"

I flirt back. "No."

He kisses my hand. We line up for refreshments. It's endearing, this movie mogul waiting for peanut M&M's, a supersized Coke, a giant popcorn. I say, "Wow, that's a lot of junk. That helps me know you better."

He smiles. "Well, the Balthazar menu didn't work on you so I thought I'd go in another direction." He winks. I might actually be on a date. I have a flutter of guilt about Gary which is absurd, but I can't lie, I'm a heterosexual woman with a pulse. It's energetic and insistent, and I'm a bit desperate for male attention and Bix smells so good. The skin on my hand where he kissed it is still damp. I hate myself for it, my undiminished desires, but I love myself for it too.

Bix leads us to seats dead center, four rows back. I like close. I hate having a lot of heads cluttering up my line of vision. The theater is nearly empty anyway.

Bix says, "So, did it work? My pitch? At Balthazar? I notice you're not rushing to sign."

"I went to storage, I'm sure Gary told you. I just needed to get past that first trip. I'm going to try again. Make some decisions. I promise."

"Let the production take over. That's what we do. Don't overthink it."

I laugh. "I've spent years overthinking everything. I can barely get dressed in the morning, I've got so much overthinking to do. And this topic, it's a doozy." I look at him. I even like the way he munches on popcorn. I sink down into my seat and put my knees on the empty seat in front of me like I'm young, and I have to remind myself not to make achy-bones noises when I change position.

He says, "We'll save these for later," and wags the M&M's package and tucks it in a cup holder, which perfectly complements my own rigid movie-crap eating agenda. He elbows me and says, "*You're a doozy.*"

I tip my head toward his soft, sweatered shoulder. "And you're fun."

The trailers start and I say, "Shh, I love the trailers." Bix makes an of-course-what-idiot-doesn't-love-trailers face, and we watch together. The cartoon movie is lovely and sweet, but the minute we stand and make our way up the aisle, it evaporates for me.

Bix says, "Let's get a drink."

I love movies in the daytime, I love emerging into the afternoon light, and I love a cocktail in the afternoon. He leads. In addition to "the bungalow" in West Hollywood, he "keeps" an apartment on Central Park West, a couple of blocks away. The building's lobby is magnificent: murals and gold leaf, delicate settees I'd be afraid to sit on. A lone ancient doorman presides over the grand space and gives a little bow as we pass. We wait at etched bronze elevator doors. I'm about to have a drink with a man I want, we're going to ride up in this fancy elevator in this swanky building on the park. It's so adult. I'm titillated until I catch sight of myself in the enormous mirrors that line the elevator.

This is how it goes now. I leave home, I've done my best, I think I look good, I feel good and then I catch my reflection in a window or a mirror. There is a split second before I recognize myself. My neck has sunken into my shoulders, my scarf is swallowing my head. My jawline has softened and squared off; I question braiding my hair the way I've always done. The eyes are the giveaway. I am not tired but I look tired. I'm surrounded by mirrors. There are too many of me. I have to resist putting on my sunglasses and pointing out how bad I look to Bix. He's chatting, telling me about the building, the apartment, without even a glance at the mirrors or any awareness at all of how *he* looks. *Imagine that,* I marvel to myself.

The apartment is, of course, perfection, completely contemporary with classic Manhattan accents everyone covets, moldings and high tray ceilings and herringbone floors. Bix goes to a white enamel paneled wall and pushes lightly and a well-outfitted bar is revealed. He makes Negronis, what I think of as a summer drink, but I forgive him because he's from L.A. where the sun always shines. He hands me my cocktail and says, "Come see." A gracious terrace wraps around the apartment and sits above the winter trees. The snowy landscape is like a scene from a Woody Allen movie, except this is the inspiration.

"I'm sorry, Bix, but . . ." I take out my American Spirits. "I know it's horrible. Do you mind?" To my great delight, Bix joins me. We take delicious drags in easy silence, and in my mind I start to plan how we will overcome the challenges of bicoastal coupledom. How we will quit smoking together.

"Does Gary smoke?"

"Oh, no. Not ever. He's radically antismoking. Except weed. But now not even that. He uses the CBD oils."

"He must nag you about it. Your smoking. Didn't you have breast cancer, years ago? I think he mentioned that."

"It was a long time ago. I'm fine." *Why has Gary discussed my breast cancer with Bix?*

Bix reads me. "Well, Gary's a good guy. I've known him a long time. He seems to have your best interests at heart."

"Mostly, he does. How about you? Do you?"

"Has anyone ever told you you are a tough customer? I have to watch every word."

"I'm the opposite of a tough customer. I'm a squishy ball of confusion. I always feel like I don't exactly know what's going on. That's why I ask a lot of questions. Anyway, why are we talking about Gary?"

The sun is setting and boundaries and edges are fading in the late afternoon. I like the dusk, when everything is blurry. The park is behind me, lights all around the city are switching on, I'm switched on from sitting next to Bix in the dark movie theater, from the cocktail. I'm loose from all the deep breathing smoking brings, the cloudy calm. Bix reaches. I close my eyes and think, *Yes, please*, but he only flicks lightly at my hairline. "An ash," he says.

"I thought you were going to kiss me." I look at him in what I think is a frank, confident, worldly older-woman manner. I try to act French and sexually sophisticated. It's a persona I'm cultivating because a blog

I follow for menopausal ladies says this is the upside of aging. I am entitled to have no fucks left to give. I must seize the moment. I feel a little actressy, but I use my eyes on him. I tilt my head, asking for it. I take the elastic from my hair to loosen the braid and also to hide.

He looks back into my eyes, hard, and says, "That hair. Your mother's."

That's unusual but I don't let it stop me. I reach to touch his, Streisand to Redford.

He intercepts my hand. He kisses the back of it, same spot as at the movie theater. Now it seems like shtick. He says, "Believe me, I'm tempted."

It takes me a beat. My body understands before I do. My face gets hot, and, I'm sure, blotchy red. I snatch my hand away like it's burned. "Oh, shit, I'm sorry. I am so sorry." I make a messy ponytail. I back away and rattle at the doors, trying to get back into the living room. Is there anything more humiliating than assuming desire is mutual and getting it wrong? "I am ridiculous. I thought . . . I don't know what I thought."

"No, Bea, please. Don't run out. Wait."

"Oh, wow. I am so sorry. Thank you for the movie!"

I'm mortified. He's ten years younger than me and rich and gorgeous and a famous Hollywood guy. Of course he's not interested in me. He is only interested in making a movie about my mother. I struggle into my coat. I try to be funny. "I don't want to keep you. You must have hordes of twenty-two-year-olds after you."

Bix laughs. "Maybe not hordes, and maybe not the twenty-two-year-olds you're picturing."

Oh. Wait. Oh.

I've done it again, made my stupid old-lady assumptions. The alpha-ing of Gary, the manly stubble, the take-charge gait, his smooth dealmaking conversation. It occurs to me that the online dating stock photo lumberjack guy is probably gay too. I don't know if I feel better or worse.

"I thought because Gary wasn't invited it wasn't a business meeting. I'm an idiot."

"You're not an idiot. I wanted to get to know you." He takes my hand. "Come meet Danilo. He's back in the office."

This is why I am here. Handled, outnumbered, overmatched, outflanked, and as I always forget, the subject is money. An entire other wing of the apartment lies behind French doors. We turn a corner to a long hallway hung with Mapplethorpes, one after the other. Gorgeous black and white, printed with such intensity of vision that they glow, nearly electric, and make me blush. Here are the BDSM images, the ones I can't look at without wincing and can't *not* look at because they are majestic. Those are hung next to the equally luminous photographs of the babies and the flowers. "Wow, that's a lot of Mapplethorpes."

Bix nods. "Yep."

Danilo is sitting in front of a big monitor in an office deep in the apartment. Bix says, "Danilo, this is Bea Marx, Miriam Marx's daughter. And our producer, I hope. Bea, this is my husband, Danilo Gomis. Our screenwriter."

I am racking my brain, the name is so familiar. Danilo Gomis unfolds from an Aeron chair and he must be six-foot-three, topped off by another three inches of Afro. He is wearing a T-shirt under a cardigan sweater and a pareo tied loosely at his waist. He is unsmiling with coal black eyes and very white whites of the eyes. He could have stepped out of a Mapplethorpe himself, and that thought makes me blush again. He looks me up and down. He stares into my face. He assesses me, and then he extends his hand. "Bea. You look the same. A few years older, of course."

I keep my eyes on his face. I say, "Thank you, I think." I don't know if I'm intimidated by Danilo, A Real Screenwriter, or dazzled by his physical superiority as a human specimen, but I don't correct Bix's introduction of me as a Marx.

"Danilo is working on *Exposure*. Among other projects."

"A script? Already? *Exposure*? Is the title decided?"

Bix says, "We want to be ready. When you're ready. Danilo is building the package. Pitch, treatment, scene ideas, character sketches, drafting the bible. With *Exposure* as the working title."

"Wow. You're far along."

Danilo says, "We're as far along as we can be without the source materials from the archives." He does something with his mouth that aims a smile like a dart in my direction. It's clear he thinks I'm the weak link in the process.

Bix intervenes. "Dani, I've promised Bea we're on her timing. As soon as she's ready, we'll budget her in, cut her a check." He looks at me. "I can work all this out with Gary. Yes? Bea? Does that sound good?"

I can feel the magnificent Mapplethorpes lining the hallway and the hair on the back of my neck stands up. The choke collars, the tumescence, the bound limbs hung next to the babies and flowers—it's disturbed me. I know we contain multitudes but maybe don't hang them all next to each other. It occurs to me that Bix and Gomis might have a private context to their interest in my mother. In me. I ask Bix, "Are you collectors? Photography?" I wave in the direction of the hallway.

Bix ignores me. "I think we need some champagne. To toast the collaboration."

The notion that they want to make the movie because of the porny implications and not in spite of them hits me hard. When I wrestled with whether Bix was creepy or artsy in Balthazar, I let his smooth moves and good clothes and expensive scent bust my gaydar and set me off course. I want to get the hell out of here, so I back myself further into a corner and say, "Yes, that sounds good!"

Bix claps his hands together, then squeezes Danilo's shoulder, folds me into a hug and says, "That's terrific. That's what I wanted to hear," and I realize that maybe I've just agreed to something I didn't mean to agree to and Gary knows more about it than I do.

I try to reclaim my dignity. I chat and chug a glass of excellent champagne. Bix comes at me with the bottle for a refill but I demur and thank and apologize. I rewind my scarf and adjust my hair and button my coat, with more apologizing and thanking. I pass back through the gilt and the velvet and the mirrors that show my disappointing reflection, my unspent desire. I step alone into another Saturday night, unfulfilled, buzzed, jittery.

I'm not dexterous with my phone when walking, but heading uptown in pedestrian traffic on Broadway, I do what the young people do. I stay fixed on my screen and let everyone navigate around me while I search. Danilo Gomis is Senegalese. He has written three indie-film screenplays within the last few years, each centered around a dysfunctional art genius, all men. Gomis is also the author of one book, a biography, *Marx Xs the Spot: Stanley Marx and the Broken Color Field*.

Surely I have come across this title over the years. A biography of Miri's brother exists, and I have done an excellent job of ignoring it. I marvel at my own powers of willed obliviousness. I step away and into the brightly lit doorway of the Price-Wise. I google images for Stanley Marx's work, which, even after Echo and I talked about it on the flight, I have never done. Perfect squares of color fill my little screen, including black, including white. In some part of the field of color two **X**s are placed in relation to each other, every variation you can imagine, overlapping or side-by-side or at a distance or as far from each other as the canvas will allow. Canvas after canvas of the same theme, the field of color, the ✖s in some kind of formation. Variations on this is all he paints. They look like diagrams of football plays to me. I don't get it.

Once again, I'm trying to understand my actual life by deciphering images that hang on museum walls.

I need Gary. I press my phone to my ear. He answers. "What?"

"Don't what me."

"Now what?"

"I've been to the movies. With Bix."

"Nice. What did you see?"

"An expensive cartoon. It was pretty good."

"Good. So?"

"I tried to seduce him."

Gary laughs and that hurts. "I guess I'm not too worried."

"You know Danilo?"

"I know him. Of course."

"You know him! What else do you know? Did you know that he was Stanley Marx's biographer?"

"I knew he had an interest. That's why Bix likes him for the project. That's how it works."

"An interest? They're collectors! They have Mapplethorpes! Do they also collect Miri?"

"That I couldn't tell you. That I don't know. What are you so upset about? It's all money in your pocket."

"They are far along on this screenplay. They think I'm on board. You haven't committed me to anything, have you?"

"Don't be silly."

"They hung the dirty Mapplethorpes alongside the babies and the flowers."

"Why am I in trouble here? Because of the Mapplethorpes?"

"I'm feeling pressured. Very pressured. Like a lot is going on behind my back. What else is going on?"

"Bea, the trip to storage was weeks ago already. Bix has his own money in this. You could be pulling a paycheck starting tomorrow."

"Gary! My father died! Right? I'm allowed to take it easy. Not to mention everything else that's been going on."

"What everything else? What else?"

I disconnect from Gary, with whom I can't share my health news: I'm fine. I can't tell him. Protecting Gary from my cancer fears has left a hole in our relationship which I blame him for, that he doesn't even know about. I have a reason to be happy, but I have no one to share it with. It hits me then. Happiness is, by definition, shared. No wonder Gary never shuts up about everything good that happens to him.

I'm on Broadway. I'm lost. How can I be lost? I'm on Broadway. I need to get my bearings. I look for the street sign. I'm in the 80s, trying to go north, trying to go home. I'm agitated. The flood of relief at being healthy, the delicious anticipation with Bix, the desire, plus the streams of Negroni and champagne have loosed my wobbly moorings. All the mirrors, the rejection, Danilo. Money, no money. Gary! What he knows, what he doesn't know! Stanley Marx and Miri, estranged. Why?

There I am again, my reflection in an empty storefront window, between the peeling stickers and posters and a forlorn broker's sign, Berenice, distorted and fragmented, still unrecognizable to myself. Baseline shame, intense embarrassment, and effervescent anxiety make me break a sweat.

Where is Henry?

I do the 4-7-8 breathing technique Dr. Weil taught me on YouTube. I put one foot in front of the other and I walk. I repeat, *I'm on Broadway, I'm walking myself home. I'm on Broadway, I'm walking myself home.* Maybe a mantra will help me make my way. Who knows.

Chapter Sixteen

I CAN'T GET in.

The Medeco is jammed. I try the key, all directions, and then I try every key on the keychain. I knock and then pound. I say Echo's name low near the jamb—I don't want to disturb my neighbors—but then I call out. Dory is on the other side of the door, pacing, her nails ticking along the hardwood. Her anxiety ratchets mine, or vice versa. I text Echo, no answer. I call her phone, no answer. Dory whines in intermittent bursts and then nonstop. I am picturing a crime scene inside the apartment, with bloody paw prints. I'm cold and I need to pee. My next-door neighbor, Arnold, opens his door a crack.

"What're you, locked out?"

"Yes."

"You need to use the phone?"

I wave mine. "No. I've got one, thanks."

"So call Marcus!" Arnold shuts the door.

I slide down and sit against a hall wall to wait. Marcus, who lives on the first floor with a wife and two small daughters, comes with one badass multi-tool in hand. He wears a tight navy blue pocket T and navy blue chinos, no belt. He has a heavy orange Stanley tape measure clipped to his back pocket that drags the pants down a little bit. As he works, his T-shirt lifts and the dimples of Venus on his lower back are on display. He twists the tool so that his shoulder pumps and his scapula extends and retracts. His arms are striated with veins. His fingers splay against my door. I redirect heat for Bix and flashes of the gleaming skin of the Mapplethorpes to a Marcus fantasy, for private time later: he backs me up against my kitchen counter and lifts me up and sits me there and spreads my knees. He kneels. I scoot close and pull his head against me.

I will not have a young man's arms around me ever again. My fingertips will never tap along the indentations, this side, that side, at the base of a young man's spine. A taut torso, the tender spots, his hair, the muscle and bulk and height and width of him. Gary had the dimples of Venus once. They don't hold up. Aging, it's an accumulation of small losses and tiny glitches that you don't notice and then you do and you ignore them at first and then you can't. I can't buckle a strap on a shoe anymore without getting a stomach cramp. I can't reach a top shelf without spasms in my shoulder and neck. The pills on the counter. The magnifying mirror. A special pillow. Miriam used to say she hated old people because all they talked about was their ailments. I do think about my ailments more frequently, it's crept in, and Gary never stops talking about his, but maybe we're not just complainers, maybe we're saying it out loud over and over until we accept it. Age is not just a number.

Marcus pops the brass plate, unscrews the screws, ratchets the through bolts, and the old lock works clatter to the floor. I try to get up gracefully. He offers me his big hand and hauls me to my feet. I'm embarrassed about the fantasy porno I made in my head starring Marcus and me, but he is a professional superintendent, and by the way, I am interchangeable as one of maybe a dozen older ladies in this building locked out of their apartments regularly. He hands me a locksmith's card and says, "It'll cost you five hundred bucks to have the whole thing replaced."

I've asked Echo not to lock the Medeco a million times. I can't help it. I mutter, "You're costing me money," to her room. I think about texting her again, but I don't want to appear too needy. The Florida trip brought us closer together, despite the enabling cigarette and Albert's death. I can't mess that up.

So I walk the dog, keep my coat on, pour the wine, smoke and drink on the fire escape, come back inside. I think about writing, prepare to write, avoid writing. I stare for a long time at the little blue folder on the screen labeled *Exposed/Exposure*. I position the cursor. I let it hover. I've added Word documents titled by year. My idea has been to just write about anything I know . . . feel . . . about a particular time. Just to start. Albert's birth in 1924 and his Lower East Side life; 1932, Miri's birth up to *Carry the Dog* in *Life* magazine; 1953 when my parents marry and the boys come right along; me in '56. The apocalypse years, '68 and '69, and then 1973, when I meet Gary. And on from there. So far, every document has a name, some have a page or two of writing, some are blank, and that's all I've got.

I add a new document for this year, the year of my father's death. I close my eyes. I wiggle my fingers to tell my brain: time to write. About Albert. My new grief, which prompts my old grief. Just start with Albert. What I feel. Just notes, that's all I have to do. I make my mind a steady lens trained inside to find outlines and shapes as they emerge. Instead of my father, I see storage bins labeled *Hideout; Nap; Porch Swing; Picnic; Car 1967*. It's dark but I can't stop searching. My eyes adjust—or do they? The light shifts—or does it? I can almost see the little girl I might have been before my mother's camera stopped me in time. I can almost see the woman I could have become. I'm peering into the dark so hard that everything behind the open lens of my closed eyes dissolves. The harder I try, the less I see. I've always said I have a terrible memory. Maybe that's because I don't want to look.

I want to look. The disc is still in my computer. I scroll over the desktop to the icon. I hit the Play arrow. She's ensconced in her chair.

The light is late afternoon. The zebras and arrows are fuzzy behind her, the mustard yellow fabric reads gray, her face is shadowed. Her legs are folded beneath her. Her feet are bare. She leans her chin on her hand. Her dark eyes show that she is waiting. She wears a gauzy white peasant dress embroidered with flowers across its bodice and down the billowing sleeves. She's a hippie married to an accountant. Ian McNally, a decade younger, the arbiter of cool, turns up on Miri's doorstep in that moment. Her photographs were selling. The counter-culture came calling and she was ready.

A handheld camera swings and moves and swoops as the operator gets organized. There are sounds of near rustling as the person—it's a man, I'm sure—arranges himself, and there is distant music. Albert's meticulously stored record albums were organized on slotted shelves near the living room stereo system, scattered by Miri across the carpet without their sleeves or their covers when he wasn't home. It drove him crazy. I grab my phone and open Shazam, which pulses as it absorbs and identifies "Sunday Morning," The Velvet Underground.

I can tell without seeing, by the specific, particular sounds of rustling and rearranging and organizing, that the camera, probably

Albert's prized Kodak Super 8, is held by Ansel. He is preparing to film Miri. The camera moves from her face and angles around, filming the wall, the ceiling, and the floor. There is the sound of a wooden chair—I know the scrape of that kitchen chair—being dragged and situated. Ansel sits across from Miri and finds her face again, from a slight height. Ansel was tall, an inch taller than Henry. He trains the camera on our mother, who shakes her head slightly, slightly bemused.

Their voices.

"Ansel, set up the tripod. You're not holding steady. You're all over the place."

"That's how I want it to be."

"Ah, okay, we're doing Art. Let's get going then."

He loses her when, still out of frame, he bends and reaches. The camera sweeps across the walls of our house. He comes back to her. His voice takes on the manner of someone reading from notes. "Mother . . ."

"Well, that's not very professional. Or fun."

They are playacting an interview. He starts again, and I can hear a tiny smile when he speaks. "Ms. Marx, I want to interview you today about your work."

"Fine. Go for it."

"Are you famous?"

"A little bit. I guess. Ian says I'm infamous."

"What's the difference?"

"Naked kids, apparently."

"Are you going to jail?"

"Don't be silly. Of course not."

"A lot of people are mad at you. They think you committed a crime."

Miri tilts her head and widens her eyes. "Well, if anyone knows that's not true, it should be you."

The camera wavers and shrugs.

She says, "You're not sure? If I'm a criminal?"

The camera stares at Miri. She shifts position in the chair. Crosses her legs. Fiddles with the ties at the neck of her dress. She opens her hands slightly, to question Ansel.

"You make us pose. You take our pictures." His voice is small, younger than seventeen. "Other stuff. People don't think it's art. People don't think it's normal."

"Here we go with the 'normal' nonsense."

"Henry doesn't like it."

"I know that, Ansel. And if Henri doesn't like it, Berenice won't either. I count on you to help me keep us all together. To protect our work. You're the next generation."

A chill crawls over me.

Ansel stands. The video camera rises with him. It judders and loses its subject and finds her again. The camera looks down at her from Ansel's full height. He looms, still completely out of frame. He's close. Miri reaches up, takes the camera to turn it off while it continues to record Ansel. His Levi's fill the frame. They are worn pale at the thighs. There's the Garrison belt with the big buckle. The button fly shows the indentation of the buttons beneath, and bulk behind that. Nothing is boyish.

The voice of Miri says, "Let's do this later. Ian will be here soon. Time to get ready."

The voice of Ansel says, "I'm ready, Mom," and everything cuts to nothing.

I roll my shoulders. I work to unlock my jaw. My brain hurts. My finger hovers. I hit Stop. I hit Escape but I can't, not really. Nothing was boyish. It was that one time, nobody knew. It was hot. I went to my room with my new obsession, a baby doll sent to me by the

Upper East Side Marx grandparents I'd never met. The doll was called Thumbelina, and she had choppy beige synthetic flax for hair, and a chubby body and little clenched fists, and a wooden knob on her back for winding up. To make her move. When she moved, she writhed on her back like a real baby, sort of. I was devoted to Thumbelina, whom I could nurture and protect and pose any way I wanted. I spent hours devising elaborate caregiving scenarios for the two of us, and I took a lot of comfort in comforting the doll the way I never was.

I guess he came in. I guess he flopped on the bed. He said, "Come under the covers." The doll fell to the floor. I probably whined about it. I probably pushed at him, I must have tried. *Don't move.* When it stopped, the heat and the whirring of the Vornado lulled us into sleep. Miri happened upon us and took the picture. *Nap.*

My neck, my chest, my groin, my ass, everything is tight and tensed and clenched. I take a big swallow of wine. I worry about my frown lines; I've been furrowing my brow for hours, play, stop, play. I get up fast and I'm dizzy. I sit back down. I need my phone. I want to call Albert, get an interrogation under way, test his reaction when he hears Ian McNally's name, Miri's nickname, and see if I can hear anything at all in his voice when I mention Ansel. Then I remember. There's no more Albert to ask.

I go to bed and try to sleep. I close my eyes, a little breathless, a little dizzy, awake. I press my hands down on my breasts and I hold myself. They are fine, they are mine, my breasts, part of me, not too big and not too small. I like them. I love them. Firm and resilient, still responsive. I palpate the nipples. I wait for the curl of pleasure. I picture Marcus. I start with his lower back, that's a good start, maybe I'll really commit. Maybe it will chase the ghosts away. I get intensely hot, pulsing hot from my toes to my scalp. I am pinned by the duvet, bound by the sheets, trapped in the bedding, sweating.

Menopause plus insomnia plus anxiety plus grief plus desire. I will never fall asleep, I need to get up, put my feet on the floor, ground myself, but I have an irrational terror of sticking even one toe into the dark. I'm listening hard. Is that the front door? I open my eyes and squint to hear better. Is Echo home? I can't hear. My heart pounds. I hear *boom boom boom*—that's inside me—and then I hear *tick tick tick*. A close presence. Dory jumps and stands directly over my head, tilts hers and stares down into my eyes with all her little-dog energy, and she does her low whine to tell me to get up. I reach my hand to feel her fur, her warmth, to get some love, but she shakes herself and shakes me off. She paws at me and stares at me. There is no time for loving, she wants the walk. I get up and out we go. I appreciate the reality check and I know to be grateful.

Chapter Seventeen

MORNINGS ARE PRECIOUS.

Echo and I have one together. My kitchen is tiny but by New York standards, eat-in is a luxury. The sun streams, NPR is on the radio. We have coffee and toast at my little round table. Dory hops onto Echo's lap. I gear myself up.

"So . . ."

"What? Sounds serious."

"Well, no, not anymore. I mean, it was maybe a little serious. For a few weeks."

"Bea, what? Are you okay?"

My throat goes tight, my face feels hot, my eyes well up at the concern in her voice, concern for me. "Yes! I'm very okay. I was a little bit worried. I had a scare a long time ago. A cancer scare."

"Cancer? What kind of cancer?"

"Breast. But I've been fine. For a long time. A couple of months ago I had a sketchy mammogram, and then another one, and I had to have a PET scan. That's—"

"I know what a PET scan is. Daddy's had them. They aren't fun."

"No, not fun. Anyway, the point is, I got my results and there's nothing going on. I'm fine."

"That's amazing! That's awesome! Why didn't you tell me? We have to celebrate!"

I can't look at her. I'll lose it. She wants to celebrate me. "I didn't want to get everybody all worried until there was something to worry about. There's nothing to worry about. I have a doctor's appointment today. She—Dr. Keswani—wants eyes on me, give me the all-clear in person. Maybe we can go together. Get some lunch or something. Are you around?"

"I'm around!" She high-fives me. She has taught Dory to high-five, so Dory high-fives me too. I'm happy. I shared, and now I'm happier. Also, I love a good plan for the day.

The hospital is like its own little city in the city. The sidewalk is a demolition derby of wheelchairs, strollers, and gurneys, the slow infirm and their supporters, speed-walking nurses and residents, porters and attendants on break, leaning against the building, watching it all. Cabs and cars and vans and Access-A-Rides jam in at the curb, ramps ready, doors ajar, trunks up—every vehicle, every person coming and going, just like us. The halal food cart guys, parked dead center, shout orders and serve street meat to regulars waiting on a long lunch line.

The Madison Avenue entrance offers a run of entry options. The doors marked PULL also have signs that say, USE AUTOMATIC DOOR.

The automatic door's Press Here tile doesn't work. Echo and I bump and cross into each other as we advance and retreat at each portal, along with so many people trying to get in or out of the hospital. The chaos on the sidewalk, the confusing entry options, the ping-pong traffic pattern—it's every woman for herself, so I wait for an opportunity to join the revolving door's spin. Echo seizes the same moment, on purpose, for fun, so we both end up in one quadrant of the revolving door, shuffling and stumbling into each other and laughing.

The lobby has wide terrazzo floors that flatten the noise so even though it's crowded it's kind of quiet. There are expansive sight lines with helpful signage pointing to wings named for the philanthropists who've no doubt had run-ins themselves with cardiology, oncology and all the other specialties that fix whatever might go wrong with a body. The ceiling is a vast skylight and the late-winter light is flattering, even to sick people, and I wonder if the glass is tinted pink. A bronze sculpture sits in the center, a big overflowing female, accessible to all. Doctors, nurses, friends, family, little kids—everybody sits around the bronze thighs, leans against the bronze rump. The pavilion feels like a stage set for a television show about a hospital full of miracles and tragedies and despair and hope and sex and death, with regular life in the background.

We navigate a labyrinth less lovely than the lobby to find the elevator to the Breast Wing. We follow dirty duct tape arrows along the mezzanine walls, take wrong turns by obeying confusing signs, and dodge more gurneys. At one intersection of corridors, it's like bumper cars. Sick men—they all seem to be men—are ferried past janitors with mops and buckets full of gray water, past security guys shooting the breeze, past kids racing down the long corridor, past a candy lady loading Snickers into an open vending machine. The sick men are under thin sheets, nearly exposed, their skin and bones on display. The guys driving them hail each other over their cargo.

Echo whispers to me, "Is it okay for them to be in a public hallway like this? Isn't it really germy?"

I whisper back, "Should a hospital be pushing Snickers?"

We find our way to a waiting room, which is not a waiting room but a long narrow corridor with chairs lined up against the wall. Every twelve feet an old-fashioned box television hangs off a weary-looking bracket. The sets are tuned to bleak news delivered by cheerful people. I'm handed a clipboard holding the many forms I filled out just a week earlier. I politely inform the admin, but she gives me a very effective nod and gestures at the clipboard. "Just bring it to me when you're done."

We sit in small plastic chairs. Echo takes my coat and bag so I can slog through the forms again. She is in all her earnest neo-punk urban regalia today: the carefully distressed inky hair, the pierced nose, the shit-kicker boots, the oversized flannel shirt and ripped jeans. Her skin is delicate and clear, her eyes are clear and eager. We make snarky comments about the television people. The feel of my elbow bumping her elbow, her holding my stuff, our laughing and banter, it's one of those days, everything makes me cry. I can't believe I have her.

Finally, my name is called. "Ms. Seger?"

Echo hangs back but I reach out my hand and say, "Come with me."

A nurse guides us to a small examination room, utilitarian, frigid. She weighs me with all my clothes on, which puts me a full five pounds over the number I like to see on the scale. My nerves fray further. She keeps tapping the Detecto's balance slider to the right.

"That's wrong," I say, blocking Echo's view. "Don't write that down. I have five pounds of clothes on."

"Don't worry about it." The nurse hands me a gown. Easy for her to say. My mother used to smoke to curb her appetite, she drank her calories and I guess I do too.

In the exam room, Echo takes a chair. I pull a curtain around to hide as I change. My teeth chatter and my legs tremble. I don't like taking my clothes off, obviously. I dress in layers head to toe, I like winter clothes best, I cover up as much as I can. I shiver inside the oversized paper gown, with folds and openings that bear little relation to a human body. I keep my boots on, but when Dr. Keswani arrives, she frowns at them. "I'll need to see the ankles, too, Ms. Seger."

Echo comes around and helps me get the boots off. There is self-conscious chuckling and murmuring as we jockey for space in the small room. The paper gown tears every time I change position. I try to hold it closed and make a joke. "I don't mind showing off my ankles. My mother always said, 'The legs are the last to go.'" Miri again, insinuating herself into my good day. I am exposed, so of course she's here, so of course I'm trying to make myself smaller on the scale, I'm trying to hide myself and distract with jokes that aren't funny.

Dr. Keswani to the rescue. Dr. Keswani is beautiful. She has architectural eyebrows and red lips. She wears a white coat with her name embroidered in navy blue, *Prachi Keswani.* Underneath the coat is a form-fitting black dress with an alluring neckline. She's wearing some non-doctorly high heels. I'm perched on the edge of the exam table. She comes close and taps my knees. "Let's have a look." She is so close I can smell minty breath. "Relax, Ms. Seger. Uncross your legs, please. Sit nice and tall and keep still so I can have a good, long listen to your heart and your lungs."

I don't narrate. I don't make jokes. I stay quiet. I concentrate on the ceiling, on Dr. Keswani's eyebrows, on the embroidered name on her coat. Anything but the reality of being nearly naked and told to stay still.

She warms the stethoscope between her palms and listens, first the front, then the back. She instructs me to breathe normally, and that sends me into breathing wrong as I struggle to catch up with the stethoscope moving too rapidly across my chest, my back. I worry that my pounding heart and messed-up breathing are interfering with her ability to hear what she needs to hear.

She says, "Lie back." She opens the gown. I'm shaking with cold and anxiety. I can hear my teeth chattering. In what feels like slow motion, Dr. Keswani probes and presses at my temples, my jaw, my neck. She taps along my collarbone. She walks her fingers along every millimeter of my chest and rib cage. She uses two fingers of both hands to knead my breasts. When she's finished, she takes her hand and sets it firmly across my forehead. She looks down at me. She looks me right in the eye. She says, "You're fine, Bea. Yes?" She presses against my brow, and holds my hand with her other hand. Her hands are warm and strong. I worry she's going to take them away. She's a doctor, but I think she must also be somebody's mother. I take a good long deep breath and yield to the touch and I say yes.

"We will see you in six months." She hands me a manila envelope. "A CD with images, for your files."

I almost laugh. I sure don't need another disc but I take it and that's it. Dr. Keswani is gone. Echo hands me my clothes, article by article, around the curtain. "Okay, I'm decent."

She throws the curtain aside and bends and buckles my boots for me while chattering away. "She was so great! Kind of scary! Don't you think? I totally trust her." Tears gather again, seeing the top of her familiar head as she ministers to me.

I'm trembly. "I just want to get out of here and get some lunch. A cocktail. Let's go." I shrug into my coat, I move to leave, I can't wait to leave. Echo pulls me back by my sleeve. I think she's going to hug me. "I'm sorry." I sniffle. "I'm a mess."

"Don't be silly. Hang on a sec," and she zips my coat. Zips my coat. "It's freezing out there."

I know I'm being mothered all over the place and the irony is, with this other mothering, Miri is gone. For now.

Chapter Eighteen

WE WALK SOUTH from the hospital and east toward the East River.

We window-shop and evaluate restaurant menus posted on store-fronts in search of the right atmosphere. Mondays are iffy for decent day drinking; most places are closed. After twenty-five city blocks, over a mile, I run out of gas. Echo says, "I know a place, next block."

We step out of the bright, sharp winter sun into a dark pub. Costello's is a warren of brown wood nooks and booths, with a long bar and a tiny stage in a far corner. The place has the dank aroma of old beer and cleaning fluid and regret. The walls are lined with smoky etched mirrors, all advertising Guinness. Blackboards are chalked with drink specials.

We sit on stools. The bottles look pretty, doubled in the mirror. Tall draft beer taps stand like soldiers. There are a couple of other patrons, both sitting solo down the length of the bar, reading the tabloids. The bartender cleans and organizes his post. He is inked on all visible skin, except his face. He glances over and does a double take. He lifts his chin in a kind of nod and says to Echo, "You again."

She nods back and shy-smiles in a way I haven't seen. "Total coincidence. We were in the neighborhood. I'm here with my sister. Sort-of sister. Bea, meet Jeremy."

"Hello, sort-of sister." Jeremy shakes my hand. His is warm and dry, a good man hand. He's adorable, reddish hair, peachy, freckled skin alluringly illustrated. I try not to gawk or read his tattoos. We order. When he turns away, I ask her, "Are you a regular?"

Echo gestures to the stage. "Yeah, kind of. It's a big karaoke place. With open-mic nights."

"Who do you come with?"

"Bea, I'm not a freak. I do have friends."

"You do? In the city? I haven't heard you talk about any friends."

"Everyone has friends in New York. Friends from my U Miami days. A lot of them are up here now. People they know. And now I know those people too."

"So is this your hangout?"

"Sometimes. Mostly I hang out downtown. Brooklyn. But Jeremy is here."

"Like, you're a karaoke person? I find that surprising."

She laughs. "No, I do open mic. A lot of people show up. Famous people."

"Like who?"

She shrugs. "Famous to me. Music people. Producers. To find talent."

"Are you a singer? I mean"—I gesture to her clothes—"I know you love music, but I don't think I realized you were a musician. Do you play something?"

Echo turns to look at me. "Well, you haven't asked. But now that you have, I write songs, and I sing and I play guitar. It's why I came to New York. I go to open-mic nights and use tracks I recorded on my phone. I'm saving up for a new guitar. I sold mine to move."

My feelings are hurt. Her musical aspirations seem like information withheld, especially considering it's common ground. But she's right. I heard her tell Clara at Sandy Edge she was thinking about "doing music" and I haven't asked. "Is Jeremy your boyfriend?"

"We've hooked up a few times."

"In the land that time forgot, my day, that meant he was your boyfriend."

She shrugs. "It's not like that anymore."

We watch Jeremy continue to clean and organize the bar. "I don't blame you. I definitely see it."

"Go for it." She leans her head on my shoulder. I tip mine to hers for a little knock.

"Oh, I'm just his elderly type, I'm sure." I say, "Thank you for coming to the doctor with me today." I get misty. We're two drinks in, but they are martinis.

"This is my first," Echo says, and raises the brimming, wide-mouthed glass.

"You're on number two, babe."

"No, I mean, like, in my life. I've never had a martini."

"Well, it is my honor to corrupt you. May it be a lifelong pleasure. Reserved for certain moments, when you're feeling especially adult. You'll have a martini and think of me." I raise my glass to her.

Echo touches her glass carefully to mine. "Let's drink to Daddy."

"To Albert." We drink. I flag Jeremy and he pours again.

"And your good health news." We drink.

"Enough with the toasting." I try to say it in Albert's Brooklyn accent. "I want to know about you. What's your plan? With the music?"

"I don't have much. Like six songs. But enough for a demo. Then I get it out to people."

"A demo, like in a studio? That's expensive, no?"

She says, "Not really. You just need to be obsessive, with the right software. Jeremy's helping me. I watch everything he does. Soon I won't need him anymore."

"Don't you want me to talk to Gary? Gary knows everybody. He can help you. He can snap his fingers and help you."

"I want to do it myself."

My impulse is to insist she take help, but I shut up for a change because, thanks to Echo, I'm learning to listen. "All right, fine. I get that. Can I hear you?"

Jeremy comes over and leans on his sexy illustrated arms and interjects with a cock of his head. "She's good. Really good."

Echo says, "Jer, I told you about Bea. She's a famous songwriter. 'I, Alive' for Chalk Outline." Echo gives my rock-and-roll resumé to Jeremy in greater detail than even I could, without once mentioning the Marx Nudes. Jeremy looks at me in a way that signals I've registered beyond generic older lady.

"I know that song. That's a dope song." He offers his fist for a bump.

"That was lifetimes ago. I'm past tense."

My drunk impulse from long habit is to flirt with Jeremy the bartender. Thank god, I don't. They are young and I'm not. We're at the bar, we're talking music, we're drinking, all the smiling and the back and forth, and I am having an almost out-of-body experience bearing witness to them in the bubble of their early twenties and realizing how far I am from then. I'm sitting on a barstool like a million times before and at the same time I'm looking back over my shoulder from a future they can't know. Shouldn't know.

Echo is inventing herself, giving herself a new name, assembling her image, at the beginning of her story. She is focused. Was I, at her age? I try to picture writing "I, Alive" at twenty-two. What was I wearing? Did I write with a pen or a pencil? In a spiral notebook or a marble composition book? I was married! I curled up on Gary's couch on Third Avenue. I handed my songs to him. Then I lost momentum. I got distracted. I thought that meant I was untalented and unambitious, plain lazy, but now, I think I see: I had always been told to stay still and so I did.

I guess I might be jealous, but maybe I'm just homesick for where I never went. I used to want to be young again but surprise! In Costello's, after Keswani, I am where I am, with the images on the CD in my bag to prove it.

"You need to hear your sister sing. Aah-mazing voice. Come on, get up there." Jeremy nods at the stage. "No one's around. It's totally cool."

I expect her to demur because I would have at her age. She doesn't hesitate. She drinks off the dregs of her third martini and hops off the barstool. She says, "I'll do a cover." To Jeremy, "I don't have a guitar," and he says, "I do," and he calls to the two customers at his bar, "I'm taking five," and there we are, on a Monday afternoon, drunk in an Irish pub, and Echo takes the stage. Jeremy hands her a dinged-up Martin. He says, "Do you want the amp?" and she shakes her head. "A spot?"

She laughs. "God, no," which is absurd, which is a crime, because she is, now that I see her here, breathtaking, made for a spotlight, in her torn jeans and her big shirt with an old-man cardigan on top. Her crazy hair stuffed into a beanie. Her battered boots. Late-afternoon dusty sunlight touches her. I'm nervous for her. I know how it feels to want to be heard.

She bends over the guitar and moves her fingers along the neck, and listens and strums and twists at the tuning pegs, and listens and strums. She stops and adjusts the strap and her hold on the instrument. She takes a deep breath. She closes her eyes. She taps the beat-up boot toe. She thumps the heel of her hand against the body of the Martin, slaps the wood twice and sweeps twice across the strings. I know the song. Even without the dulcimer of the original, the chords revive my own searching questions of a lifetime ago, of today. She presses along the frets to make the small squeaks of the iconic version of this song from the album *Blue*. Her voice starts easy, almost delicate, not unlike the song's creator. As if she doesn't want to scare her lover away with the magnitude of her disappointment. Her skepticism. *"Just before our love got lost . . ."*

Echo raises her chin to open her throat so she can release words, sharp and bright like little bells. The voice gathers something from inside. A realization, a resistance. You can lose yourself in another person. You can deflect yourself away, for love. You need to hold on to yourself. Echo takes "A Case of You" and makes it contemporary. She mixes the song's sweet, urgent, lonely sound with something angry, something cynical. She makes it feminist. She makes it punk. I'm drunk, but I hear the song, a song I listened to obsessively once upon a time, as if for the first time. The audience, all four of us, give Echo a standing ovation. She's a star, I see it. She bows deeply.

Back home, I make us pasta with butter and cheese and salt and pepper. We sit on the sofa and eat from big bowls. We talk about the server job she's decided to take at a downtown restaurant. It's on the West Side so she'll be on the good train line and can save some money by continuing to live with me rent-free. I say, "You can get a guitar."

Echo says, "Yeah, maybe in a couple of months. Jeremy and I took the ferry. To Mandolin Brothers on Staten Island. They're closing. Everything is on sale. I saw an acoustic Martin that felt really good. It fit me."

"Closing? That's terrible! They've been around since I was in high school." I can't stop myself. "You're about to start waiting tables—that place is so trendy, the tips will be great. Let me advance you enough for the guitar before they close. You'll pay me back when you can. You should get it."

"Seriously? I don't know. That's too generous. I'm already living here rent-free. I don't know if I can—"

I wave her hesitation away. "Echo! Don't be silly. You're my little sister. Let me do this."

This day. From Miri-anxiety to the official cancer all-clear. From barstool revelations to sunk-in-the-sofa pasta-eating with my sister. Sister! I almost cap it off by giving her *Carry the Dog* but I'm sober enough to know I'm not that drunk.

Chapter Nineteen

DECISIONS, DECISIONS.

I continue to dodge Bix although he texts daily links and affirmations in support of his vision for *Exposure*, comparing his vision to other visions, invoking women directors with vision, the marketing ideas he envisions for his movie about my mother the visionary. I keep meaning to read everything he sends me and answer, I really do, but to be honest, I hate seeing Bix's name come up on my phone. The movie deal isn't on my mind. I can't stop reliving the horror show of me throwing myself at him to prove the blogosphere maxim that with age comes the having of no fucks left to give. I'm mortified, so apparently I still do have some left.

When Violet calls I pick up immediately because I'm in awe of her, and the power she wields with a phone call eclipses Bix's annoying texting. I tell her what I saw at StoreSpace: rows of shelves, every-thing in place, the labels, the gear, the canvas hood, the archival boxes holding negatives and prints, including *Hideout, Porch Swing, Picnic, Nap,* and *Car*—the lot. I don't tell her about the Ferragamo box with the *Outtasight* tapes. Ian McNally's name has not come up.

She drops a steady beat of *Tentatively* and *We hope* and *If all goes well.* She sketches out a timeline with preliminary approval from the gods of MoMA. I let her lead me along. She progresses the con-versation to *Once we have an agreement in place* and urges an art lawyer's number on me who will bring in an independent adviser, her vaunted museum-world insider contacts. The lawyer will protect me, she promises. "My" lawyer and MoMA will compare notes and cre-ate a master inventory to include every scrap and snip in #201.

I already know, she's already told me several times, but she repeats herself. There is no compensation for my "gift" to MoMA. That's unconditional. MoMA does not pay me, but MoMA is the door through which I must walk in order to access other income streams, the galleries here and in Europe, the increased value of my mother's work. She tells me the tax benefit for art donors is generous; I can confirm that with my "financial adviser." My ears get hot as I pretend I'm listening, I pretend to understand, although my hearing is fuzzy, I literally can't hear, and I have so little confidence that I don't ask for explanations or clarifications. Naturally, I change the subject.

"Does this kind of show get a title? Or just her name?"

"We've been brainstorming a bit. Miriam has been out of the pub-lic eye for a long time. We want to reestablish her."

"Okay. How?"

"Well, I want your thoughts. I'd like to include your insights, quotes for the object labels next to the images. Maybe get you to help with narration for the audio tour. We're talking about a video tour for online, so maybe you'd participate in that, too."

"Me? I don't know anything about photography."

Violet laughs. "Bea, that is not true." I'm flattered. "We're considering *What Mother Saw: The Eye of Miriam Marx*. How does that sound? We'd preview everything with you, all the images, the monograph, the marketing plans. Get your thoughts on how it felt to be 'seen' by your mother, the artist. To be the girl in the photographs. It would confer a stamp of approval, I think, and neutralize the other angle."

Or heat it up again with me right back in the middle. "I don't know. This is a lot. I'm sorry. I'm terrible under pressure. There's so much on the line. The timing and everything. I need to process."

"You've got the lawyer's contact now, he can help you with that, he's waiting for your call. And your husband, can you talk it through with him? He must have an army of advisers."

"Gary's not my husband. He's my ex." The truth is, I don't want Gary near the MoMA deal. It's mine and Henry's, if I find him. When I find him.

It's mid-March, with spring sneaking in, and Dory and I go out early. We walk and walk. The snow and ice are reduced to crunchy slush underfoot. She high-steps purposefully and I watch my own step. Falling is a recent preoccupation, pre-sixty, a fresh signal from the brain reminding me that I am brittle, and that Sensei John has a YouTube channel I promise myself I will not watch.

On this walk, I am either mustering the courage to call Violet's art lawyer or strenuously avoiding making that same call. I am definitely avoiding the memoir file on my laptop. Ten years ago, a lifetime ago, when I was almost fifty, when I was at the end of being young but not yet almost old, when I was still visible, when I still thought I could bang out another life for myself, make myself proud and really write, be a real writer, I naturally thought writing a memoir about being the daughter-subject of Miriam Marx would be cathartic. Like my mother, it was right in front of me. Why not use it for *my* Art? At first, even just the thought—*I'm writing a memoir*—was like a little bit of DIY therapy to complement the self-medicating I've always done with the cigarettes and all the drinking—a healthy, creative project that would save me from the awkward intimacy of sitting across from an actual human therapist. But the story keeps changing. I keep changing. How can I possibly advise MoMA on Miriam Marx?

On Broadway, it's Dory and me and the shopkeepers rolling up their gates or hosing down sidewalks, the truckers making deliveries, the early birds marching to the subway, and leftover night people, everybody holding the first coffees of the day. Sodden trash sticks to sidewalks, dirty snowdrifts block the way, murky runoff banks the curb at every corner. Crossing the street requires fording a stream of sludge. We finally head home. We pass the driveway at the back entrance of our building on Riverside, and the gates are wide open. Marcus is in the courtyard. He hoists and hurls garbage bags to the curb. Something catches my eye. Something catches my attention.

The universe delivers. Marcus is about to close the gates. I call, "Hey, wait," and I step into the concrete yard at the back of the building and pluck the gray-yellow Post-it with Henry's number from a patch of grimy snow. The number is still legible.

The smudged Post-it is now back inside my tote bag. The bag is nearly twenty years old, with studs and long, fringy zipper pulls, very rock-and-roll back when I bought it. I had to have it, I couldn't live without it, and I know it's crazy, I know I'm susceptible—who spends this kind of money on a bag?—but here we are, me and my Balenciaga City tote twenty years later. I pass it now, an old friend slouching on the front hall chair, holding proof of Henry's existence. I feel the Post-it even when I'm in another room. All these years, I've pictured him in San Francisco, a manageable city, living on a steep hill street in a cozy tilted house. An academic or a writer, published under a nice Marx-free pseudonym. I know he started out in journalism, and I know he graduated, but I don't know much more. Or maybe I opted out from knowing more. Maybe Henry believes that *I'm* the one who disappeared into the city, like Albert and Jeanne do. Decades lost, time squandered, all because I based my actions and decisions on assumptions, wrong assumptions.

My brain makes a leap: *Nap.*

He couldn't help himself. He was damaged. I was damaged. Miri pushed us together, positioned us, always too close, always with Henry on the outside edge. I don't remember which photo shoot we had done that day, maybe *Porch*, maybe *Picnic*. I must have pushed him away. I must have said, *No, no, no.* Did I? Didn't I? I never said a word to anyone, including Henry, about what happened because I don't know, not for sure. I do know the memory keeps calling me back, and it must have its reasons.

What did Henry know?

212. I am ten punchable digits and probably not that many blocks away from Henry, the only human left on this earth who speaks Marx-Seger. I imagine us comparing notes, setting each other straight on details, the timing of this or that. We will talk about Grand View, the house Miri wanted so badly—and she was right to want it, it was a pretty house—but we'll agree that by the end, it sagged with sorrow, showed sadness in the set of its shutters, the closed front door, the untended yard, the burnt patch in the woods. Henry can help me with my terrible memory. I can lighten us up now and then with a wisecrack and we might cry too—who wouldn't?—and then we'll consider how

to move on, now that we've spoken the family language, and put family eyes on who we've become, and correct our recollections. We can evaluate MoMA and Hollywood, analyze Violet and Bix together—I don't have to do everything alone—we'll examine the pros and cons of both opportunities. Decide together. Maybe Henry drinks wine, maybe Henry smokes. We will tell the drunk fucking truth to each other, maybe love each other again, help each other be in the world. My Henry will get to know my Gary. My Henry will love our Echo.

Or maybe not. Maybe Henry left because he was done with depravity and death and me and wanted nothing to do with it, and still wants nothing to do with me. I don't know. The fantasy of us coming together and solving our lives is too precious for me to spoil by trying to make it real. The Post-it stays stuck in place for another day and then drifts to the gritty bottom of the bag.

Alone is not necessarily lonely, but Echo is out, Dory's in a deep nap, the apartment is silent and the city is quiet too. I prepare my wine and my cigarette and I do something I have a lot of practice not doing, which is being needy. I tell myself that demonstrating need to someone you love, that loves you, is not "being needy," but I am not sure I believe that. I call Gary anyway.

"What?"

"I miss you, old man."

"You too. What's up?"

"Nothing's up. I'm just calling."

"Bix is working on papers. Maybe you'll have them next week. Sign and celebrate, right?"

"Yeah, maybe."

"What do you mean, maybe?"

"*You* said maybe. I'm agreeing. Maybe. After the lawyers look at it. Right?"

"And after that, signing and celebrating."

"I miss you."

"So you'll come downtown."

"Really? I would love that. I can put Dory in a bag, jump on the train."

"Wait, no. No, Bean. I didn't mean now. Not tonight. Another night."

"Why not tonight?"

He says *Bean* in a familiar tone of voice, ancient and established and weary as an old stone wall on the property line of our crumbled and patched and rebuilt relationship ruins. I'm allowed into his life, but only so far, according to some rock-and-roll man code I'm supposed to honor. That I've never questioned, because it didn't occur to me that I could.

His guard is up, I can hear it. I realize then there's someone else in the room with him, and I picture lithe limbs and long hair, a blur gliding to the kitchen. It's been like this since the beginning, and I've allowed it. Once upon a time, I was the girl. I can't keep blaming Gary for everything.

We have our understanding, we have our arrangement. "I'm sorry." I gulp back hurt feelings and soldier on. I don't want to let him hear how jealous I am. "I've caught you at a bad time. But I wanted to talk to you about a few things. We can do it in person. Go."

"About Bix?"

"Not just Bix."

He lowers his voice, in confidence. "What then? Something about Echo?"

"Echo? No. Why would you say Echo?"

"No, nothing, she's been living with you for a while. I thought maybe you were getting fed up."

"Actually, it's the opposite. She's great. Really great. I'm not supposed to tell you but she's a songwriter. And a singer. I heard her. She's good."

"Why such a secret?"

"You know how it is. She wants to do everything herself. Break into the business."

"Stupid."

"Young." We toss out hollow chuckles. "So that's on the agenda too. When you're free."

Gary says, "Okay. When I'm free."

My heart constricts. I love him more than he loves me. It's another section of the ancient wall I've never tried to breach. He can only love as much as he can. He has himself to consider, first and foremost. I've accepted the boundary. More than that. In some fucked up way, I wanted it there as much as he did. "I really do miss you, Gary. I really do love you."

He says, "Yeah, you too," and by now I should know that saying *I love you* because you need to hear it back is never a good idea.

Chapter Twenty

I GET A Chalk Outline alert.

I'm just about to open it up when Echo shouts, "Bea! Oh my god! Thank you!"

"Thank me for what?" I lean in her doorway. Her bedroom is a wreck. There are clothes everywhere, piled on the bed, the desk, spilling from the open dresser drawers and the open closet door. Considering she showed up with only a backpack and a suitcase, I'm trying to work out how her wardrobe has proliferated, even given how freely she rummages mine. She is sitting on top of a pile on the desk chair. Dory is curled on the bed in another nest of garments and opens an eye in my direction. I pet her and she stretches out long and welcomes my attention. I sit on the bed next to her and stroke her head. She rolls and gives me her silky belly for more. My dog.

Echo waves her phone at me. "The invitation!"

The Greatest Opening Act in Rock and Roll
GARY GOING & CHALK OUTLINE
Tonight 7 p.m.
Bowery Ballroom

Gary's been rumbling about a gig, he needs an infusion of attention and cash and social media presence, and I guess he's pulled it together. I'm not sure how Echo ended up on the list. I'm happy for her: every millennial transplant to New York needs a small-venue rock-and-roll show to feel fully inducted into city life. I'm glad she's excited. It's thoughtful of Gary to include her. I suppress a laugh at the seven o'clock start time—he will play for an hour, party for two, and be in bed by eleven. He is seventy, after all. "Well," I say. "I guess we're going to a rock show."

"I need to find something to wear." She looks at the piles of clothes. I remember being her age, how important it was to dress right for a show or a club, and the impulse is the same for me now, older: How can I look like who I want to be?

I gesture at the closet. "Go through the boxes. There's plenty more."

"Thank you, thank you, thank you!" She is up and consolidating piles to make a staging area for outfit options assessment. "I'll go through this stuff first. I need to try everything on . . ."

"Okay, we have time. We should leave by six o'clock. And straighten up in here. Please."

Echo says, "Bea," and she comes to me. She waves at the room. The new Martin is propped in the corner. "Thank you so much. Really. For everything." She puts her arms around me. She hugs me with all her self. I'm not a good hugger. I never learned how to do it properly. I'm hyperconscious of the bodies, what the bodies feel like, mashed together. When Echo hugs me and hangs on, I start out rigid, but I feel how rigid I am and I don't want to communicate anything other than pleasure at having Echo in my life. I make myself relax. I feel her small breasts against my chest, her flat belly and narrow thighs against my softer belly and thighs, her chin fitted into my neck, her nose in my hair, our wrapped arms, and I let my body fit around hers, all of her; and I think, *Sister*, but I can't help myself, I also think *Daughter*. A hot fullness suffuses my throat and my chest.

I know I'm not her mother. I'm nobody's mother but almost was, and it just never happened for me. For us. Gary and I achieved a few beginnings. We did. Conceptions. The first no-baby was a mutually agreed-upon abortion when I was too young and we were too druggy and drunk and irresponsible to have it be good. Later, after a lot of frustrated old-school "trying," a miscarriage. It was on December 8, 1980, and the reason I am so sure of the date is because I had been all alone, watching the news coverage of the murder of John Lennon outside the Dakota, with no one to hold me and help me process the random, vicious violence. I felt a hard pull and a twist low down in my core. I contracted. I was terrified, cramped over a toilet bowl, and while I could hear what felt like the world—or at least rock and roll—ending in the other room, I was worrying about making a mess. Gary was on tour, openly unfaithful—it had been in the papers—and he called it partying, and I was too stupid to leave him until I wasn't.

Another year, I was seven weeks along, at the beginning of marriage number two. Forty-six years old. It didn't hold, it was a no-take. I didn't stop crying for weeks, and Gary knew nothing. Gary thought it was because of the towers falling down, and I let him think that, and that's my secret, still my secret. I didn't have the nerve to tell him we'd lost another child, and that I wanted to try fertility doctors, and that I was in perpetual mourning for three no-baby babies, all for fear of turning him off and turning him away.

The closer I get to Echo, the less able I am to mute all that loss.

I break the hug. "Six. Be ready."

I assess my own wardrobe. How can I look like who *I* want to be? Aging but easy on the eyes. Sassy but not angry. Alone but not needy. Postmenopausal but not dried up. It's hard to dress all that up, make it rock. I go with the black leather pants and a white silk shirt. I add a jacket for armor, commit to black booties—the amped variation on my usual uniform. I decide to splurge and get my hair blown out at the place around the corner, and I can hide behind that too, for the time being, anyway.

I'm surprised when Echo texts, *Ill meet u @BB,* and, *Do u mind,* which I guess I sort of do. I was looking forward to showing her off, and showing off my old music world to her. Gary's world, now. But I've done this a thousand times, and she's never done it, and she should have the total Echo experience of seeing Chalk Outline at Bowery Ballroom exactly as she wants it to be.

I text, *No problem, see you there,* and she flicks back, *Luv u! C u there!*

I haul myself up the subway steps at the corner of Delancey and the Bowery and emerge into a crowd waiting outside the club for the doors to open. It's a mix of Gen X and boomer white guys, women who stand a little behind them, self-conscious in their rock-show garb, no black people, no Latinos, no gay men—there is a lesbian contingent, curiously—and very few millennials. The men my age are all in puffy down jackets, sagging denim, juvenile concert Ts, bald heads, whiskery jowls and big white sneakers. I try to see them as the boys I once lusted after.

I make my way through to the earpiece-wearing bouncer behind the ubiquitous velvet rope. He doesn't look up from his iPad and I say my name at him and think, *Gary, I'd better be on this list*. The bouncer silently swipes and scrolls for a long time without acknowledging me, not a glance, and I get that anxious feeling because I can't tell, maybe he didn't hear me? I don't want to be pushy. He banters with whoever is in his ear, and his face breaks into the sweetest smile, and he laughs—beautiful teeth, he's gorgeous, really—and still I am invisible to him. How can he even tell I'm too old to bother with if he won't look up? Maybe I no longer give off the whiff of fertility? Is it a chemical thing? I resolve not to google it. The beautiful bouncer finally lifts the rope without a glance at me.

I check my phone. No Echo.

The club is big, the lights are up, and it's still mostly empty so you can see its ceiling's soar and its beaux arts swank. It is, in fact, a ballroom, with a proper stage hung with giant, heavy, fringed brocade drapes. The band's kit is being set up by roadies-for-hire, local guys Gary has used for years. I roam the room. Brass glints. The mezzanine bar is backed by a high arched window at sidewalk level. I drink my wine and poke at my phone for Echo. I could work my way backstage—there's another list, I could watch from the wings—but I want to find her. I want to enjoy her enjoying the preshow and the show and the crowd and the atmosphere. I want to see the Bowery Ballroom through Echo's twenty-two-year-old eyes; I want to hear Chalk Outline through her ears. I am eager to introduce her to Gary. I text and get no reply. The place fills up. I find a good spot on the upper deck, close to the stage and close to a staircase so that when we do connect, Echo can get to me easily.

The canned music gets louder. It's crowd-pleasers for like minds: John Lurie and the Lounge Lizards, Jonathan Richman and the

Modern Lovers, VU, Television, some Talking Heads, plus the familiar factor: Bowie, Stones, Prince. The lights go down to cheers and whistles. The stage goes black. The crowd coalesces into upraised faces with phones at the ready.

Where is Echo? I'm looking for her dark head, her pierced face and narrow frame, but that describes everybody under thirty, basically. Still I scan the crowd, even as it deepens, tightens, presses the stage. I resolve to myself that she is down there somewhere, I'm not going to worry. The place is now packed tight, and the faces turn up for rock and roll, are waiting for rock and roll.

A penlight flares stage right, just below where I'm standing. A disembodied hand, a stagehand, holds back the drape and one by one the boys, probably the third or fourth incarnation of Chalk Outline over the years, saunter or trot out to take their spots. Except for Gary. The crowd pushes farther in and roars for the players. Dennis goes to the drums, Milo to the keyboard, Emma to the bass, and the newest guy goes to lead, and he has a mic, too, next to Gary's. The backup singers step to their mics. Everyone's in adjustment mode: guitar straps, pedals, seat heights, mic heights, water bottles, beer bottles. The crowd applauds and stamps and cheers and shouts. Phones are high. The tuning begins without cuing or synchronization, each person doing what he or she does, and they are all still in their own orbits, getting their own grooves on, before Gary comes out. This goes on for five solid minutes, so that the crowd is whipped up and the chant begins: *Ga-ree, Ga-ree, Ga-ree,* the time-tested, dragged-out pull on his name. It's been going on since Chalk Outline began, because of course, Gary is, was, and always will be rock-and-roll late to a gig.

The curtain is pulled back again, the stagehand's penlight illuminates the path, and the next to emerge from backstage is a girl, thin as a blade, with buzzed, platinum hair, in a black bandage dress—I had one just like it, who didn't—and fishnets and Doc Martens, holding a red Solo cup, and she ducks out and keeps to the side and makes her way down the steps and melts into the crowd. Here comes Gary Going right behind her, taking the stage.

The band's tunings have turned into a slow, out-of-step march to the opening chords of "I, Alive." The crowd is still chanting Gary's name. I can't help smiling at my old rock star in fine form. He is wearing a leopard blazer, so very eighties, cut tight and close, with wide shoulders and narrow lapels. He's got a black shirt underneath, untucked and unbuttoned, so his old-man chest is shown to its best advantage, and he's in the tightest possible custom-made black Nudie Jeans. His nose and chin are beaky and exaggerated by the lighting, and of course, his signature hair. He's had it styled up, and I admit, under the spots, with the sunglasses and the jacket, the shoe-polish black spikes gleam. It looks like iconic rock god hair, a whole lot better than it did at Balthazar.

The band falls in and bumps it up. "I, Alive" goes from noodling tunings to dirge to jazzy to racing rock and roll once Gary raises the mic to his mouth. He sings my song. It's meant to be a woman's lyric, but he gives it the gender bend that turned it into a hit.

Once a week, nothing definite
You steal hours, I make the best of it
Rouge my cheeks, pink my lips
Dance past mirrors, hands on hips
Half past ten, you arrive,
I alive, I alive
Push me down, turn me around
Hands and knees, right now please
You go deep and down we dive
I alive, I alive

The bed's undone, the room smells bad
You're home with her, but I'm still glad
Sneakin' 'round, my best friend's man
One more time, as soon as we can
I alive, I alive, I alive, I alive
I alive, I alive, I alive, I alive

The backup girls cover his weak voice, the new guy shreds the lead, and Gary's stage antics are signature. He used to get on all fours at the "hands and knees" lyric but he's not dropping down anymore. He still moves against the mic stand and mouths the mic, and grabs himself and generally puts the song across so that it sounds dirty, dirty, dirty. The audience knows every line, every pause, and by the end, the whole room is screaming, "I alive! I alive!" and I must admit, I have not heard this song sung live in years and years, and I feel happy. Look at all these people singing my words. The ballroom is bouncing. It's just a sexed-up pop tune, raunchy once upon a time, but I wrote it, me. I'm not thinking about never getting enough credit or money, or storage, or my mother, or the platinum blond with the red Solo cup. I let it wash over me. I make this feeling be enough.

Echo weighs in, finally, with a text. *Amazing!*

I tap back, *Where r u? I'm mezz, stage left, look up, waving!* I start waving wide at the room like Eva Perón on her balcony. I text again—*Do u see me?*—but nothing. To be fair, the band has rolled right into the next song and the next, continuing the fevered pitch and the roaring response and the changing spotlights, the colors revolving around the players onstage. It's rock and roll, the music is the atmosphere, oxygen; it surrounds us and it rises too from beneath us, from under the floor, from the earth—that's what it feels like—it's bouncing my bones. I forget about everything: the phone in my hand, Gary's groupie in the bandage dress, and nothing matters except, as ever, watching my guy rock the Bowery Ballroom. When the lights come back up, only the equipment is left.

I walk the long dim hallway, crammed with fans and wives, their nostalgia-loving sons, and businesspeople and hangers-on. I go into the greenroom of the Bowery Ballroom, which isn't green but wood-paneled, with a long sectional against one wall—not that you can see any of the furniture, it's that crowded. It's loud. The lighting is brutal. I am immediately self-conscious. I find the ladies room and duck in, but I can't get to the mirror. The lineup is dense with young women who look like creatures from an enchanted wood, they are so tall and willowy with parts exaggerated and highlighted, to great effect. The beautiful girls are muscling me out of the way. I make my face sweet, harmless, although I'm raging a little bit inside because why won't they scoot over and let me have a slice of mirror for a minute? I need to see if there's anything crazy-lady going on. Eyebrow hairs go rogue without warning. Mascara flakes and darkens the dark valley under my eyes. My lips go dry and lined, and the lines creep up past my lip line. I can't get to the mirror, so I dab at my lips with Rouge 999, but who knows if my aim is right. I fluff up my hair as if I have the luxury of not caring about my looks.

Gary's holding court in a corner with his back to me. The leopard jacket is off and his black silk shirt sticks to his sweaty body. His Nudie Jeans look good. Young people in a semicircle around him are shiny-eyed.

Micki Lopez, punk legend, occupies another corner of the greenroom. She is the original bisexual rock-and-roll poet, and a painter, and a memoirist, married to a man and partnered with a woman, and they all live together in the city and in the country, with a lot of highly Instagrammable meals and vistas, and multicultural kids, from grandchildren on up to adult children who are famous in their own right.

She is exactly my age. She wears everything oversized and deconstructed, Belgian, and tailored perfectly at the shoulder, the cuff, the ankle, the waist. It costs a fortune to look that good in clown clothes. She's got a mane of gray curls that bounce as she gestures and speaks. She wears no makeup and her skin is beautifully lined. People gather around her. We've met a hundred times, but she never remembers me.

I stop off at a table set up with the red Solo cups, boxes of wine, big bottles of cheap tequila and vodka, mixers in plastic, watery ice. I text Echo: *In greenroom. Micki Lopez is here! Where r u?*

"Bea! Bea!" Micki Lopez is calling my name. Like a cartoon character, I point at my chest and mouth: *Me?* She nods and her hair bounces. The crowd around her parts and I enter her orbit with a big red plastic cup of wine and a tentative smile.

"You. Are. Gorgeous." Micki Lopez takes my hand and kisses it. "I. Am. Honored. To. See. You."

"Micki! Hi! It's great to see you, too! Great! Great show, right?" I realize I've said *great* three times, and that I am exclaiming.

"Bea." The Micki Lopez acolytes are paying reverent attention to every word that comes out of her mouth, and I wonder if she is purposely intoning to keep them on edge. It's like a poetry reading, listening to her speak.

"Yes. Micki." I feel sucked into her weird speech rhythms.

"'I, Alive.' Pop masterpiece."

"Thank you. It's a good song. It's held up."

"I want it. For my label. With someone fresh. May I?"

"May you? May you what? Use it?" I'm trying to follow her.

"Yes. I want to use your song."

I'm not sure where I am in the conversation. A tiny gnome of a man has sidled up, looks at Micki and then at me, and says, "Keith Bakker. The husband." He taps a crystal champagne flute against my

Solo cup and I wonder where the good glassware is hidden. "We'd like to use your song. For Micki's new label. She's assembled some powerhouse young talent."

"I'd love that. That would be brilliant. The thing is, I don't own the song. It's not up to me. Did you speak to Gary?"

I gesture to Gary, who still has his back to me, who is still holding forth, and I know he feels the old husband-wife telepathy-at-a-party thing, because he sidesteps a bit and turns toward me and smiles a too-big smile. I'm immediately suspicious and then I freeze. I am not surprised, he's got the platinum blonde in the bandage dress and fishnets right behind him. I blink hard. I shake my head involuntarily. I start to move toward them but Micki puts a beringed hand on my arm.

"Bea, the song. I want to rerecord. With video. I have thoughts. I need you. To guide it."

I don't know what Micki is envisioning, and it occurs to me that she is very stoned right now, but people a lot more savvy than I am would be paying closer attention to her ideas, which come with healthy paydays and connections to producers who have nothing to do with Gary.

"Oh, okay. Sure. Great! Hey, can you excuse me for a second?" I make a beeline for Gary. Gary and Echo.

"Echo! I've been texting you every five minutes. Where have you been? Why didn't you answer? I thought we were meeting up!"

"Bea, I know, I'm sorry! I got here early. Wasn't it amazing?"

"Your hair!"

"Oh." Echo puts a hand to her head and gives it a rub. "Yeah. I bleached it. And buzzed it. What do you think?"

"You know each other?" I look at Gary. "From tonight? Before tonight?"

Gary shrugs. I say, "What does that mean?"

Echo says, "Gary invited me to come early. We only texted."

The word *only* gives me a chill. I say, "Okay," but I'm confused.

Gary dodges me to join in a conversation with a fan, something he usually takes great pains to avoid. I flash on the moment the curtain was pulled back, the stagehand shined a penlight for a gorgeous young girl to make her way down the steps and into the crowd, with Gary behind her about to take the stage. Her bare skin, cat-eye eyeliner and glossed lips. She doesn't look like some Florida kid obsessively trawling Craigslist with my dog in her lap. She doesn't look like the female Kurt Cobain putting across a killer cover of "A Case of You" in a deserted East Side bar. She looks like a groupie.

I say the most inane thing possible. "How much have you had to drink?"

"It's a special occasion! Chalk Outline reunion!" She tips the red cup to her candy-pink mouth. She's wearing my Doc Martens, my Hervé Léger, my Kamali coat, she's with my Gary. I feel like I've lost my best friend and the only man who will ever want to have mediocre sex with me again, at the same time.

Echo says, "Bea, don't be mad. I didn't mean to blow you off."

"I'm . . . I'm not mad. I need to go home though."

"I might stay for a little while longer. Is that cool? Did you see who's over there? Micki Lopez!"

She seems completely nonchalant about stealing my man. Maybe this is another *It's not like that anymore* thing. I try to relax my face. I try to look not needy, not old, not angry as I make my way through the dense thicket of youth and beauty. I am the storybook hag, the witch, the crone, terrorizing the enchanted wood. I've probably sprouted a wart, or at the very least some fresh hair on my chin.

Micki Lopez shouts, "Bea! I'll reach out!" and I reply, "Great!" again. I make my way down the hallway and realize it doesn't matter one bit what my face is doing: I'm invisible, so invisible that when I pass, no one moves aside for me to leave, but I don't slow down. I know how to push my way through.

Chapter Twenty-One

IN NEW YORK you can get things handled at any hour.

I make the call when I get home at ten-thirty. Ninety minutes and $475 later, the old locksmith hands me new keys. I spend half an hour in the little bedroom throwing everything of hers into garbage bags, including the clothes she borrowed from me. Including the sacred Dolls T-shirt. Including my Trash and Vaudeville motorcycle jacket, bought with my "I, Alive" check. Those old clothes were badges of honor earned when I left Grand View with a rock star, when I stopped being the girl in the photographs, when I became Gary Going's wife and almost a real songwriter. Echo came along, and it gave me pleasure to see her wear my things. What was once cool became cool again, and I foolishly thought that meant me, too. The Doc Martens and the bandage dress, the rest of it, she can keep it.

He's seventy! She's twenty-two!

How could he? How could she? They couldn't possibly. No way. He wouldn't dare, she wouldn't want to. He loves me. She loves me. My father just died! I almost had cancer! In my mind, I play back the phone call I made to Gary the day I was plagued by guilt over keeping secrets. His evasive tone telling me not to come downtown. His laugh, hollow now on replay, when I told him she did not want music business help. Finally, my sense as we spoke that someone was with him. The blur gliding to the kitchen comes into focus. It was Echo.

I pick up the Martin. I sit on the bed—Echo's bed—and Dory struts in with inquiring eyes and bossy shoulders. She takes in the garbage bags, the disarray, me huddling, and she jumps up and settles close. That rips me open. I once thought she hated me. I hug the guitar, I stroke Dory's head, I squeeze my eyes shut to blot out the memory of Gary across the greenroom, with his sweaty silk shirt and tight pants and dyed hair, smiling his cheater's smile in my direction.

Before I know what I'm doing, I'm doing it.

I smash the Martin across the mirror above the dresser. Dory bolts up off the bed and runs for cover. I bash the guitar over and over. My eyes are closed. I smell varnish and my own sweat. I hear cracking wood and cracking glass and fatal twangs. I bash the beautiful guitar into the reflection. Strings spring from the tuning keys. Mirror glass glitters across the top of the dresser and across the floor. Eventually I am breathless and my arms are too heavy to keep swinging. I have pain in my shoulder, and my knee. I stop. I open my eyes and there I am, a crazed slice of me looking back from the only quadrant of glass left on the mirror, gripping a two-by-four section of the guitar's neck. My hair is wild, my eyes are wild, the white silk shirt is torn, my makeup is smeared. I'm dappled with wood chips and slivers of mirror. It's a proper rock-and-roll conclusion to the long, messy jam that's been my relationship with Gary, and the fantasy session I've been playing with Echo who is not my sister and not my daughter.

I work to catch my breath. I put my hands on my breasts: *It's okay, I'm fine.* Dory watches from the doorway. I say, "It's okay," and she joins me on the bed. We look at each other and I say, "Don't worry, we're fine," and she drops her head with a sigh. When I'm ready, I pick up every single shard and splinter and string and key, and I toss the destroyed guitar into the garbage bag on top of the clothes, and I throw in the broken mirror bits for good measure.

I change into an old, limp black Juicy velour tracksuit. I fill my mug with wine and grab the American Spirits. I don't have the big coat to keep me warm so I stay inside; no fire escape tonight. I look around my own serene bedroom, the made bed, a bank of white pillows in silk and linen, textured and smooth, my white dog settling herself in a duvet drift. My desk—Miri's old vanity table, refinished in high-gloss white with brass handles—is uncluttered. Just the laptop and the *Outtasight* interview discs. My limbs quiver from my exertions. I'm so tired. I cry in spasms and heave and hide in my hands. Heavy brow, swollen eyes. I'm low and sinking lower. I finish off the wine and refill it. I light up again. I don't care. I am miserable and ready to wallow, happy to wallow. So of course, I do.

I slide the next disc into the laptop. The first thing I see on my screen is mud.

The camera looks down into it and then looks up. It's handheld, a video recorder. The film quality is what you'd expect: nearly sepia now, spotty audio, and smeared imagery. Filaments scatter across the lens. The camera moves too fast or is fixed in one place for too long, but generally walks along showing me what is unmistakably Woodstock: bare chests and breasts, arms adorned with beads and leather snaking in time to music, bodies huddled under quilts and sleeping bags, flashes of denim and floating fabric and beards and peace-sign fingers flashing the lens, and now and then a sloppy smile, sleepy or stoned or both. The camera pans the sky: morning. The camera pans the mud: epic. The camera shows the kids in the crowd have made friends with the mud, decorated their bodies with it. Here and there naked people are covered in drying clay-mud, like statuary. The camera picks up the labored breathing of the videographer as he walks, and the audio intermittently picks up the mud-sucking sounds of his steps.

The camera follows Miriam Marx. Her thick, dark hair is in a messy braid. She's wearing a white maxi dress that has two straps crisscrossing her back. She is barefoot and on the move. I know that walk, that march. She's working. She's scouting. The bottom six inches of her white dress are sodden, dragging. She keeps trying to detach the hem pasted to her ankles. She turns and says over her shoulder, "This fucking dress," although her mouth doesn't align precisely with the crackling audio. In the background the crowd is calling, "Film me, man, take my picture," or singing, "*Got a revolution, got to revolution.*" Dogs and sirens are in the distance, along with helicopters' chop, and far away, far-out music comes from the stage. I go back and watch again. "This fucking dress."

I can hear Ian McNally more clearly; he's holding the equipment. "I'll help you take it off if you slow down." My mother gives him the finger with a sexy smile, keeps walking. Ian lets the camera look around. The camera shows hippies rising from under quilts or tents or embraces, and standing and stretching, their slow awakening a ripple across the meadow. Smoke billows from breakfast campfires. The boys light up cigarettes and joints, pass to the girls. Tapestries cover the sway of lovers making their morning love. Anybody standing is dancing to Jefferson Airplane.

I watch the camera track Miri up a slight rise. She looks around. She waves to the little freak city from on high like she's its queen. She says, in a voice girlish and fake-British, "My people."

Ian catches up and holds the camera on her face. He says, "Don't stop here."

Miri sweeps her arm over the crowd again to encourage Ian to film it, but the camera stays with my mother. Her brows are dark and bushy; her eyes are black and glittery, all pupil. She is very high. She shines, a warrior for art with her cameras strapped across her breasts like bandoliers, the Leicas, the ones she used for unposed shooting.

Ian says, "The lineup for the rest of the day is incredible. Joe Cocker, Janis, The Band. You have a backstage pass to music history. That's the only art I'm interested in today."

"Everybody will get those pictures. I don't want celebrities. I want real stars. Here they are, right here." She makes unblinking, defiant eye contact with the lens of the camera, ignoring his eyes, looking into mine.

Ian tries to keep it light. "If I remember correctly, my love, it's in the contract. You're shooting the performers. That's what you signed up for."

Her eyes flash, I see it coming but back in 1969, he didn't. She grabs for the video recorder. For a chaotic moment, its eye rolls up and away and shows me a dizzy black-and-white kaleidoscope of sky and bodies and tents and smoke and then Miri aims it down and shows the mud and I can hear her real voice, the voice I know, not the trippy hippie festival voice she's been using. "Ansel? Is he part of the contract, too?"

The video recorder swings slightly over the muddy field. That's the view Miri holds in her hands when the tape stops.

I force myself to breathe so I can think. The film I'm watching was recorded on Sunday morning, the day of Ansel's fire. Miri was on assignment and impossible to reach. She arrived home to the horrible news in the very early Tuesday morning hours, twenty hours after crawling through traffic on her way home from Woodstock. Ansel was dead. Henry, un-twinned, was shocked silent. Albert, the parent on duty, was destroyed. Me? I have no idea. I can't remember.

The video over, I have guitar-smashing adrenaline letdown. I'm queasy from smoking, bleary from watching, rocked by betrayals— Gary and Echo, Miri and Ian. I can't stop thinking. Spinning thoughts and brand-new facts line up. Miri took a lover, a media mogul who could help her fade the stain of the FBI investigation and the child porn allegations by anointing her on the cover of *Outtasight*. A lover who took her son as his lover.

Ansel? Is he part of the contract, too?

The realization blooms from belly to brain. Is this something I once knew but was too young to understand? I couldn't interpret the whispered conversations, the abrupt silences, the odd moods and alliances in our household that summer. It's what I saw but couldn't see on the first CD, what poked at me. Poor Ansel! Albert must have known or guessed.

Four months later, my mother went up to the attic and stood on a chair with the belt from her bathrobe and Albert's bathrobe tied together—her black terry cloth, his plaid flannel; both hung on the back of our bathroom door for my whole childhood—and looped it over a beam and looped it around her neck and kicked the chair away.

The American Spirits pack is empty. I love smoking. I need my loyal cigarette troops standing at the ready. I pile on layers, leash Dory and we go out so I can pick up reinforcements. The streets are lit up and lively. I buy the smokes and walk us to the park. Dory is on alert; we're never out at this hour. She stays close to me. Riverside Park closes at one a.m. but there are no gates, only a small sign with the park's rules, which I find quaint. We enter and walk the curve along the highway. There are couples sitting on benches, watching the traffic. There are fellow dog walkers, fellow smokers. I can breathe a little bit easier now because I'm smoking, and also, the current of the city in the middle of the night pulls us through the dark park. I don't think about anything. It's too much.

When we get home, a whole new Armenian cousin says, "Your sister is locked out, Ms. S. We don't have your new keys."

Echo leans against my door. I say, "Fine. Come in and get your stuff and go."

Dory charges Echo and commences intense, worshipful spinning and yipping.

"Bea! What is going on! Why haven't you been answering your phone! I've texted and called you a thousand times! So has Gary!" She's in jeans and a flannel shirt and some worn-down Vans and my silver Norma, with a scarf wound around her throat. She looks sleepy and blurry, about twelve years old, all cheekbones and deep eyes, the purple commas beneath them intensified by the new platinum hair. She picks up Dory. "You changed the locks. I couldn't get in."

"Of course I changed the locks. You don't live here anymore." Echo follows me. I gesture at what was formerly her room. "Your stuff is in there. In the garbage bags. Just take it." My voice sounds high and strained to my ears. "Leave that coat." I gesture to my Kamali coat.

She unties the bag and inspects the ruins and looks at me with burning eyes. "You're kidding. You smashed the guitar?"

"Not kidding." My voice is so high-pitched it's squeaky. I have to steel myself when I see the broken guitar parts.

"That is so fucked up, Bea. Jesus Christ, I'm not with Gary! This is so not cool!"

"Oh, how tedious for you. I *am* uncool if being cool means my supposed sister can sleep with my husband. Not to mention that he's old enough to be your grandfather. Great-grandfather, in some states." My voice wavers. It pinches my throat. "I shared everything with you. Including Albert. *My* father. Mine."

Echo shakes her head and raises her eyebrows. "That is not fair. You know what? My mother is right! You ignored Albert until you needed him. And for fuck's sakes, I am not fucking Gary, who anyway you keep saying is not your husband. I'm . . ." She hesitates, too young to think fast and lie seamlessly.

I tremble again like a last leaf, brittle and ready to fall, and even though I think it's cheap to do it, I play the senior card. "I can't take this stress. It's not good for my health. Just please go, Hannah. Leave the coat on the bed." I pull Dory from her arms. Echo looks like she's been slapped.

I hide in my room while she packs. I tiptoe around like there's been a death. I did ignore Albert. I needed him but he was lost to me, to himself. So I married Gary Going, now, Gary Gone. I chase an Ambien with a mugful of wine, and then add an Ativan since they work fast. I wait for the tickle at my jaw and the pull of the pills on my eyelids. I go to my bedroom door to listen for Echo. A solid silence tells me she's left. There is one last unwatched *Outtasight* disc sitting on the desk. The circumstances of the fire nag at me. Was it even an accident? Did my brother kill himself? My mother went mad from grief, mad with guilt over Ansel. Did the woods still smell of smoke as Miri drove up our driveway, after her trippy days at Woodstock?

In Grand View, the story of the deaths coalesced into what I came to believe was the truth. But it was not the whole truth. It was a partial truth that drove every subsequent thought and decision—or lack of decision—I faced from then on. I made up what I didn't know.

I'm freezing. My fleece robe hangs on the hook in my bathroom. I'm freezing. The robe is close, right there on the hook. I slip it on. The robe is warm. I pull the belt free from the loops and examine it. I imagine tying this belt to another belt. I drink up, I light up. Alcohol, flames, smoking, suicide, it's in my DNA. I visualize myself doing what my mother did, right here in my bathroom.

That's not me, this I know. I'm an indecisive wallower, thank god. The door bounces against me, and ow, it hurts. The hook hits the back of my head, and I catch myself with a pained grimace in the mirror. It's comical, under the circumstances. At my ankles is Dory, detective dog, who has nosed in to investigate. I sit on the toilet lid. I say, "Up," and she puts her paws on my knees. I pull her on to my lap. She faces me. She examines my face. She reads me with her black eyes. I say, "I'm trying." I push my nose into her fur and I inhale the fragrant mix of her kibble, our street, the park's earth, dog skin, my Dory, my prickly friend. She stands like a sentinel on my thighs. She keeps her legs sturdy, at the ready. I love that. The pills meet up in my bloodstream and play nicely together.

Chapter Twenty-Two

TWELVE HOURS LATER a relentless whine and a steady buzz wake me.

I lurch through rooms to the foyer like the risen dead. Someone's pressing the buzzer and Dory is twirling and whimpering at the door to go out. She can't hold it. She does her business on the sisal rug on cue just as I open the door, liquid and solid both.

It's Patrick and Ronaldo reeking of good health with bright smiles. They don't look like New Yorkers anymore. Their appearance is startling and almost surreal, considering the emotional-Ambien-Ativan-wine-cigarette hangover that grips me.

Patrick says, "You're alive! Did you get our emails? And we've been calling you for days!"

"Not days, just yesterday. And last night," Ronaldo clarifies, and then notices the Dory situation. "Oh, Dory! You bad girl! Look what you did to Bea's rug!"

Dory is beside herself with excitement and guilt. She whines but throws in some happy yips. She twirls in anxiety, but also wiggles her bottom and wags her tail for joy at seeing the men. In between spins she tries to jump up into the arms of her true parents.

I say, "Oh my gosh, no, it's my fault. She's a good girl. I wasn't feeling well. I just woke up. She missed her walk. I'm sorry. It's not her fault." I leave them standing in the doorway. I rush to the kitchen for rubber gloves, paper towels, Clorox bleach spray and a garbage bag. The smell of the disinfectant is like caffeine, and has the added benefit of masking the fumes of my sad last night. I clean uselessly, because I already know that Dory's elimination on the sisal means the rug is trash. No arsenal of products can convince me the braided cords of the rug will be clean.

I try to make small talk as I rub and scrub. "So, you guys are back? Is this a quick stopover? How was . . . where you were?" I know I know these facts, but I can't access and deliver from brain to mouth in time.

"Yes, we're back. It's not a stopover. We're home. Did you get the emails?"

We stand awkwardly in the foyer. I don't invite them in. As if everything about my life isn't bad enough, they're here to take Dory. I gesture and say, "She never has accidents," a weak testimonial. "We're happy," I add. "I love having her and she's learned to tolerate me. And welcome back. And thank you for the Venmos. It's all worked out. I really love her."

Dory squirms in ecstasy in Patrick's tan arms. She's trying to burrow into him. She looks over her shoulder at Ronaldo and her tongue lolls with pure love and her eyes shine. Ronaldo says, "We haven't heard much from you, Bea. We thought you might be sick of her by now."

I can't hold back. "I love her. I've gotten attached to her. I'm going through a hard time." My voice wavers. "My father died. I've been kind of distracted. So it's been great to have her." I want to shout, *She's all I have!* Instead I mumble, "I missed the emails."

I reach and give Dory a little scratch. She offers a polite lick, thanking me for my service, ready to move on. Ronaldo and Patrick exchange glances. Ronaldo says, "Well, why don't we pick her up in a few days? Would that work for you?"

Patrick adds, "It's a good idea for us, too. We have so much to do anyway, to get settled back in." He holds Dory out to me. She paddles the air as if running back to his embrace. Having her for just a few more days seems unbearable and irresponsible, particularly since I missed her morning walk because of a hangover. The generous offer has an inverse effect. I'm about to hit bottom so I might as well keep going, alone.

"No, no. Of course you should take her. She's your dog. If I need her, I'll knock. Haha. I'll look for her clothes. I didn't dress her up much." Or ever. I stuffed the shopping bag full of "clothes" in the back of the coat closet, because she seemed too dignified for dress-up. I bury my nose in the white fur of her neck and inhale and then hand her off and close my door.

Days pass. I am unreachable. The laptop stays closed. I haven't looked at or charged my cell phone since Bowery Ballroom and I don't have a landline. I haven't left the apartment since Patrick and Ronaldo came for Dory, except for just once, in the middle of the night, to put the shopping bag with her clothes outside their door. There's no Dory to take me for a walk. I hear her bark across the hall and each sharp bark cuts me. I hear the elevator arrive and leave, and I picture her righteous resistance until she gives in and hits the streets with her dads. I throw away the dog food, the snacks, the toys, the little beds I've scattered around for her greater comfort. She's gone.

I wear the Juicy tracksuit all day, every day. I sleep in it, with fuzzy socks. I can't look at my hair or my face—not that I'm checking the mirror much, but just in case—so I pull on a fleece beanie that smells like Echo's scalp and wind a scarf neck to nose. I once read that Debbie Harry got so depressed about her aging face that she covered all the mirrors in her home. I don't even have the energy to make that happen. I am congested with sorrow. I haven't showered. Now and then my mind wanders to what steps I'd have to take to have a shower, the first necessary strike to end this siege of me by me, but it's overwhelming.

The cabinets hold enough: canned tuna; crackers; old nuts; fig cookies; pancake mix; two jars of peanut butter which, if I use my finger, can get me through days of meals with no dirty dishes. Canned green beans have been there for years, a constant poke in the eye. The refrigerator has wine and mayo and butter, ancient olives and pickles, half a carton of eggs and a nub of cheese and wilted grapes and exhausted celery and heavy cream I'm afraid to sniff. There's bacon I never wrapped properly, now hard-edged. The freezer is stocked with meats that have frosted over so thoroughly I don't know what they are anymore, and vodka. I have a radio and the full cable package, but even glancing at the remote controls, even considering background noise for "company," reminds me of everything gone, including fucking Mittens.

Before Echo, life was good enough. With Echo, life got sweet. Echo helped me love Albert because she loved him. Echo, young and full of the future, helped me stay in the present and at least reckon with how to leave the past behind. I fell in love again with the idea of family, maybe even a version of my own family, normal-ish, me and Echo and Dory, and Gary downtown. Now, loneliness looms.

To reinforce my misery, I fish out an unread AARP issue from under my stack of unread *New Yorker* issues. There, just what I'm looking for, another article about the dire consequences of loneliness in old age. At this point, it's like sticking a tongue in a bad tooth or picking a scab. The article tells me the Me Generation has become the Lonesome Me Generation. The article says loneliness has the same effect on the immune system as smoking fifteen cigarettes a day, or drinking six drinks. How about all of the above. The article sets free an earworm, "Eleanor Rigby," a Beatles song I despise, have always despised. And now, leather pants notwithstanding, I am Eleanor, with my face in a jar not by the door, but in the bathroom, SPF 30, which I slather on to keep it from turning to dust. "Eleanor Rigby" plays over and over in my head, the violins slice, the violas and cellos slash away.

I confess. I admit. The shame, the horror. I'm an older woman, sad, broke and alone. I'm lonely for everything I had just a few days ago, when my sort-of sister lived here, my sort-of ex-husband loved me, and my sort-of dog cozied up with me in my bed.

Nevertheless, here I am. I do what I do. I move through. As miserable as I am, I manage, to my own surprise, to roll up the sisal rug for the trash. I inventory and organize the cabinets. And the refrigerator. Everything expired goes. On to the medicine cabinet. How much over-the-counter pain reliever does one woman actually need? I tear into my bin full of beauty products and toss anything that says or implies antiaging, all the cures and camouflage, all the powders and gels and paints, brushes and applicators. I keep the pricey creams and serums; I'm not crazy. The radio plays a soothing lady voice interviewing an earnest man voice about being a paraplegic yogi who had to relearn how to be in the body after trauma.

Now I am in the mirror. I unwind the scarf. I take off the beanie, let down my hair. I give my scalp a thorough shakeout and a good, whispery scratch. I bask under the cascading water in the rising steam. I caress myself with my scented soaps. I let the water pound the back of my neck and shoulders. I comb a treatment through my tangled hair. I use a whirring brush on my face. I shave my legs, oppressive old habit I love, making slightly dangerous tracks through foam, revealing smooth skin. I flash on my mother's legs under the muddy hem of the white dress in the field at Woodstock.

A gritty mote of a thought flickers into ember and catches. Are there Miriam Marx photographs of Woodstock? I try to remember the shelves in StoreSpace. I fantasize about posters, music tie-ins, coffee-table books, social media tentacles all released to coincide with the MoMA show, a marketing juggernaut.

What a great thing, showers. I shut the faucet, sweep back the curtain, and there through the fog is *Carry the Dog*. Sister and brother, determined to push on.

If Henry organized the storage unit, he knows exactly what's in it. I move past the fluffy towel, past my clothes. I'm naked and in a hurry to find the Post-it stuck to the bottom of the Balenciaga bag so I can know what he knows.

Chapter Twenty-Three

I'M GOING TO the West 20s on the edge of Flatiron, just east of Chelsea.

The downside is that it's far. The upside is that it's far. I am too agitated for the subway. I can't bear the close quarters of a taxi. Walking will burn off my nerves, theoretically aerate my cells, clear away the funk. Give me time to muster courage. Dialing Henry did not deliver Henry but connected to the generic voicemail of the business's directory.

The weather is fine under a streaming sun with a mild wind. I feel it through my many layers: winter will end. I decide to consider myself lucky—the sun, the wind, the possibility of Henry. I notice a Citibank bike-share rack. People come and go, all ages, taking bikes, replacing bikes. I can't remember the last time I was on a bike. I swipe and navigate to an out-of-the-way spot on the sidewalk to mount, immediately misjudging when and where and how my lady parts meet the seat, and the pain of that reminds me of being a little girl, of learning to ride on the boys' bikes, and once again, I'm laughing at how the past keeps coming back to bite me in the ass, or thereabouts. I'm laughing a little bit at how much I hurt.

I set off south on Broadway, at first on the sidewalk where I feel safe, but pedestrians don't concur. Some jump aside, but most don't— *I'm walking here!*—so I swerve a lot. Someone yells, "Get off the sidewalk!" and I steer to the street and into the bike lane that is totally disrespected by everyone not on a bike. Car doors swing out. People bend into parked vehicles with their rear ends in the way. UPS guys stand and chat, leaning on hand trucks. Runners run. Even a cop car is double-parked, blocking the bike lane. I am afraid to ride wide into traffic, so now and again I stop and walk the bike around the obstacles. It's like a video game.

By Lincoln Center, I've relaxed my ride. I understand the balance, my posture, the way you have to just go and hope for the best and not worry about what might be gaining on you. The plaza's fountain is off—it's technically still winter—but my legs are pumping and there are hardly any tourists. I take two spins around the empty fountain and keep pedaling south. I zip down to Columbus Circle and another dormant fountain, another plaza. Around I go. Look at me, biking through the city. I'm a little bit impressed with myself. I'm a little bit amazed. I resolve to do this again, in the spring, in a dress, with a helmet, without a hangover! I survey up ahead and slow or increase my speed to navigate the chaos. I move along the line of midtown, Hell's Kitchen, the theater district, the garment district, Herald Square. I get to that oddball stretch of Broadway, low 30s, heading south, high

20s, with its mash-up of trendy restaurants and wig shops and glitter phone-case wholesalers and fake flower purveyors alongside the real flower district, and I'm happy to be moving at a steady clip, making my way under my own power. I picture myself: urbane and cool and youthful, like one of those Instagram older ladies, YOLOing. I bite off my glove, I fish in my pocket for my phone. What a great selfie this would make. I can post it and make Echo regret losing me.

A van, double-parked with flashers, suddenly pulls out in front of me. With one free hand, I yank the handlebars hard to the left to avoid rear-ending him. I skid into southbound traffic coming up behind me. I hear it first, the sounds register, tires screeching and steel bending, the thud of me hitting the ground.

I'm flat on my back on Broadway. The van disappears into traffic. The cab driver rushes to me, looks down and admonishes me, barks questions at witnesses, swears his innocence to bystanders. Our smash-up has taken place in front of the Ace Hotel, and hipster tourists stand and smoke and hold their phones high to film my catastrophe.

I blink back tears of shock. I got hit by a cab! I'm wearing a puffer jacket and jeans and gloves and boots, some padding there, and the cab was inching along. I think I'm okay. I lie still and inventory my limbs; I search inside for any screaming pain. My heart is pounding but nothing hurts. I could use a hand getting up and it would be good if the cab driver would stop hollering at me. I mew and extend my hand and the driver's face freezes and softens and he looks stricken by the sudden realization that a human is lying prostrate on the street in front of him, asking for help. He pats my hand and steps behind me and puts his arms under my armpits and kindly, gently—murmuring for me to go slow, to take it easy, to not rush, to ignore the honking bastards in standstill traffic—raises me to my feet. He brushes off my jacket. He reaches and smooths my hair. I say, "Thank you. I'm sorry. It's okay. I'm fine."

He is small and the color of a desert, clothes and hair and skin and eyes. He says, "You fell very well. Very well. Do you need the hospital? I'm calling nine-one-one. I'm calling dispatch."

"Thank you," I say, stupidly flattered and grateful to Sensei John. "But no, no. I'm okay. Really. It was just a shock. I'm fine. Look!" As if I have to prove it, I turn to the hipsters outside the Ace and waggle my hands, my legs, my head, for the videos. "You don't have to call anybody. Don't call nine-one-one. Please. Really."

"May I take you somewhere?" He gestures to the bike beneath the front tire of the yellow cab.

"Oh, wow. That looks bad." I used my debit card when I borrowed the bike uptown, and I'm sure Citibank sensors or drones or something are disappearing dollars from my bank account now, downtown. The cabbie pats my hand and gives an eloquent shrug with sympathetic energy and a furrowed brow. I start to cry again. I say, "I need to meet my brother," and work myself into the next level of crying. I have no idea what to do. A tall, nonbinary human in camo pants and a green army jacket that looks real with a real name patch, Rodriguez, and a brilliant pink wig turns up to wrap an arm around me. Rodriguez surveys the situation and confers with the cabbie. Rodriguez instructs traffic behind the cab to back up, make some room. The cabbie reverses off the Citi Bike, Rodriguez pulls it up and holds it aloft for the Ace Hotel kids to see and they applaud. It is perfectly mangled. The cab driver braves impatient horns and hoots and trots to my side with a business card. He presses it on me. "If you need anything!"

Rodriguez, my pink-wigged support person, guides me to the sidewalk in front of a construction site bordered by a tall wooden wall around a massive hole in the ground. They lean the bike against the wall. I say, "What should I do?" and they nod with a wave and say, "If you can walk, keep walking."

Passersby glance at me with a particular brand of New York curiosity, rabid civic-mindedness mixed with tremendous skepticism. I'm ugly-crying and the Citi Bike is bad, so I rate a conflicted pass—I'm an older woman which works both for me and against me. I figure this is already costing me the most it could possibly cost, which I contractually vowed to pay when I rented the fucking bike, when I hit Agree on the app without even reading it. But I was hit by a cab! They rent these death-cycles without helmets! It's a miracle I'm not concussed.

I do as Rodriguez has advised. I walk. I continue the mission on foot. I can hardly believe I'm not injured and I feel perversely proud of myself, as if I'm not as old and out of shape as I am. I work on restoring equilibrium to my wobbly knees, releasing my clenched stomach. Flakes swirl in front of me. I wonder if it's snowing. I realize my puffer jacket has torn at the shoulder and small feathers are flying. I recall that I was attempting to take a selfie while riding a bike for the first time in decades down Broadway, to spite Echo. I pat my pockets. The phone is gone. I have a vague auditory memory of it skittering across the street when I fell. The sun is still shining. The breeze lifts the feathers. Henry is nearby. I keep going.

And then, here I am. Camerama. The sign boasts: VISUAL EXPERIENCE SOLUTIONS.

I've passed this place a hundred times. It's on a street that was once part of the photo district. An old New York story: Artists—in this case, photographers—needed studios, took over industrial spaces, made them cool. Grocery stores and restaurants and liquor stores and equipment suppliers and processing labs followed. Rundown blocks morphed into a trendy neighborhood its pioneers could no longer afford to live in. Camerama, the legendary photography resource, survived the real estate massacre, and more impressively, the digital apocalypse.

Camerama takes up half the block. The windows are hung with giant photographs—a butterfly in a blurry flutter, a stadium full of fans grimacing together in the agony of defeat, a big crying baby, gnarled old-lady hands. Farther along, the last window is taken up by an enormous video screen and I'm startled—it's me. There's a camera somewhere, and I'm being recorded. I look at myself onscreen. I look pale; my hair is a tangled nest; my neck is short; my shoulders, one sprouting feathers, seem only a couple of inches away from my ears. I realize my hat is gone, another casualty of the accident, and my sunglasses are crooked. I straighten up, I lengthen my neck and drop my shoulders, I adjust my clothes, my hair. I pocket the glasses. I press my fingertips along my tear troughs, I press them to my lids, I tap between my brows, improvised faux-tox. I do my 4-7-8 technique. I collect myself.

To enter, I push when I should pull. I do a shuffle to sidestep a young man who is exiting, but so does he and we end up in an awkward two-step. There's a long, high reception counter. The space behind it is vast. The walls are stark white. A young woman with a cloud of spiral curls and a Camerama hoodie stands up from behind a computer screen obscured by the counter. "Can I help you?"

"Hi, yes. Yes. I'm looking for . . ." I hesitate. "Someone who works here. Henry. Henry Seger? Or maybe Marx-Seger? Hyphenated?" I give too much information too fast. I sound suspicious, even to myself.

"Hmm," the receptionist says. "I don't know the name. Let me look." She turns to a screen, taps at the keyboard. "No. Nope. Do you know what division he's in?"

"Division?"

She laughs a little. "Yeah. We have like fifty different divisions. Also, locations. Around the world." She gestures to a white display map with tiny white lights covering a far wall.

"Oh. Wow. Okay. I'm pretty sure he's here. In New York. I have the phone number. It's 212. I called it, but the voicemail was generic for Camerama." I dig out the Post-it.

She looks encouraged. "I might be able to tell from the number where he works. If he works in this location." She checks her impulse to help and pauses, in acknowledgment of a world full of crazed stalkers and vengeance-seekers. "Who are you again?"

"I'm Bea." I shake her hand, which is totally excessive. "Bea Seger. Henry is my brother."

"Ohhh-kaay. He's your brother but you don't know where he works?"

"We lost touch. I'm hoping to find him. Here. Today." I paste on my benign-elder smile, weary but harmless little me. She takes the Post-it and goes back to the screen and taps. I take a moment to notice where I am and what I'm doing, and my heart starts to pound. Am I really doing this? I feel a little lightheaded. I grip the counter.

The receptionist says, "Are you okay?" and then, "I found someone."

"I didn't eat lunch. I'm fine. You found him?" This is no time for a panic attack, although it literally is.

"I found *someone*," she emphasizes. "In Traditional Printing and Film Processing." She squints at the screen. "But that number goes with a different name. Not a Henry."

"A what then? Who?"

She's a millennial so I forgive her for not recognizing the nickname, a variation from another era on his given name. "There's a Hank? Hank Segretti? Do you know that name?"

Chapter Twenty-Four

I DO KNOW that name.

Behind the reception desk, behind a glass wall, across the open-concept workspace, elevator doors open and Henry steps off.

The girl with the spiral hair and I both turn to watch. She says, "Oh yeah, he's the owner. I'm pretty sure. I'm new."

Henry is the owner of a photography empire that offers "visual experience solutions." He threads through a maze of cubicles with occupants bent over their desks. He is taller than I remember. He lightly taps the back of each chair as he passes. He keeps his head down. He walks beautifully. He walks like Henry. He wears a dark fleece jacket zipped over a black watch plaid button-down over a white T-shirt, and non–dad jeans. He's slim. He has curly gunmetal hair, receding into two graceful curves around a tenacious tuft up front. Once upon a time the tuft refused to be tamed for photographs, to our mother's frustration, and refuses to fully give over to baldness now.

Henry is sixty-two. I had expected, I had braced for, an old man, but he's not.

He is in front of me. It could be Albert thirty years ago, except for the head of hair and the height and the flat belly. He holds back a small smile, but his brown eyes are sharp with something. Anger? He keeps his head at a little tilt, as if he's already listening to me. He takes a long look. My legs have a mind of their own and are shaking uncontrollably. I make myself stay open to his gaze. I tell myself, *Be present for this, this is happening.*

Space and time warp, molecules rearrange, our separate mythological worlds collide. This is happening. It's just us in each other's eyes. The way we used to talk, with our eyes. I'm searching his for love but I see freeze, flight or fight, and the same impulses rise in me in defense. Why did I do this? It's too much. I want to shout, *You left me!* I want to accuse him, force him to acknowledge abandoning me. I want to break eye contact. I stay. I let him see me. This is happening.

Finally he asks, "Berry?" He sounds polite-incredulous, and I worry that I've aged into unrecognizable. The voice is Albert's, too, and talk about old nicknames. Only the twins called me Berry.

"It's me. I swear." I move into his arms, and the scent of him is something I am not prepared for. Up until now, I've tried to conjure the past through photos and film and old song lyrics, and Albert's old stories and my own possessed memories and thoughts, and a brain/warehouse full of negatives never developed to *my* satisfaction. Now, the past stands before me, Henry, his corporeal self, Henry, fully intact. He smells like clean cotton and books and Pears, my mother's soap, and a tree, and vitamins, and faintly, fixatives for photo developing. He smells like everything I know. His scent may as well be paddles pressed against my spent heart. Electricity surges through me and reanimates my love, dark and light and real again. My knees buckle. I nearly swoon. I close my eyes and breathe deeper, take him in, make it last. This brother, Henry. The good brother.

He breathes me back. And then, although nothing changes, molecules shift, he checks himself, the moment powers down. A boundary is established without Henry moving a muscle. He is not unyielding but he has stopped receiving me. He pats my back.

I move away and say, "I got hit by a cab. On the way. I was on a Citi Bike. And I don't have cancer!" Unexpectedly, we both laugh. What else can we do? It is all absurd.

He glances at the receptionist, who is rapt. He takes my elbow and steers me to a white leather couch. "Here, come sit down. Start with the cab."

"I'm okay. I got shaken up. That's why I'm such a mess. Don't look at me. And I lost my phone," as if that explains why I've shown up without warning. "I tried to call you last night." I'm not lying but nothing sounds like the truth.

"Well, you're here now, so let's just . . . You're sure you're okay? I mean, physically? I mean, including not having cancer?" Henry's question is earnest and tentative, he's talking with Albert's voice and the listening tilt to his head and his Henry eyes and I laugh again—really. It's a giggle, a little maniacal, there's a world of hurt in the laughter, and I am mostly laughing but crying, too, and doing the gasping thing. I can't speak. A new customer has entered Camerama, and he and the receptionist are having a hard time minding their own business.

"Berry, shh." Henry takes my hands. I look down and see his. His palms are big and capable, like catcher's mitts. He has Albert's wide, wrinkled knuckles. His fingernails are trimmed and white, so neat. He wears no ring. He uses his big thumbs to stroke my hands. "Berry." He says it in the old way, meaning, *Be reasonable.* "I'm glad you're here. I am. But maybe can we do this another time? I'm at work."

I tap the ring finger. "You're not married?" He shakes his head. I feel relieved, I don't know why. I take a deep breath and count down to the exhale. I concentrate on my skin being stroked. I think about how it must feel under his fingers. I hope not too papery, I hope not too loose. I have a single, faint age spot; I wonder if he sees it, or is that something only another woman would notice?

I'm suddenly self-conscious, disheveled from the bike accident, barefaced with my new no-makeup experiment. "Don't look at me," I say again. "How do I look?"

He says, "The same." He doesn't look up. He concentrates on stroking my hand. His thumbs make little circles. He looks up. "Beautiful." It feels wonderful to hear, like when Albert said, *You still look good.* "But what about cancer? What was it, a scare? Berry, nobody smokes anymore. I can smell it in your hair."

"Yes, it was just a stupid scare. Can you take the rest of the day off? Say it's a family emergency."

He shakes his head. "I don't have to 'say' anything. I'm the boss. But, I don't think I want to do that. I'd rather . . . organize my thoughts. Figure out how to proceed. What's best for both of us."

"What's best is that we're together! I need you! There's so much going on. To do with Miri. All the work in storage. I think there are Woodstock pictures! And MoMA and Hollywood are calling me every five minutes! I don't even know where to start!"

"Let's step outside."

We stand in front of Henry's world, Camerama. I look up into his face. "It's really you. You're in the photography business!"

"I'm aware of that." He ekes out an unhappy smile. His face draws in and now that he looks sad I can see his age. He pulls me to him. We are on the big screen in the big window, on camera, two older people wrapped in each other's arms. I watch us hug. If I were a person who didn't know us, I would know that we are related or maybe a couple who've been together so long, they have come to look alike. So much time apart and yet, we are brother and sister, hurt inside, holding it in, in a way that has imprinted itself on our faces, our gestures, our bodies.

He breaks the hug but keeps an arm around me. "Everything can wait."

I say, "Henry. No. I don't think so. I'm feeling pressure. To sort through everything. I've tried to do it alone. I'm trying. But I can't figure anything out. I can't." I don't want to say it, but I feel like I have to say it to hear it myself, and Henry is as good a listener as I've ever had, so I say it. "I don't think anything can wait anymore. I've waited too long as it is."

He tips his head and presses his forehead to mine, like he used to when we were little. He holds on to me and I'm not expert on being held, but it feels . . . polite. "We will. We will figure it out. I'm sorry. I'm sorry, Berry." He takes out his phone and taps. He says, "There's an Uber, three minutes away. To take you home. Let's give it a little time, just a couple of days. Please."

"An Uber! How do you even know my address? How will you find me? I don't have my phone and I can never remember my own phone number. It's crazy, I have no problem remembering our Grand View number from forty years ago but . . ."

"I know your address and I know your email address and I know your phone number. I got it the same way you got mine. From Albert."

"I had to sneak yours from Alexa, in Daddy's room at Sandy Edge. After he was already dead. I mean later! After he was gone. From the room!" I'm babbling and pleading for him to understand but even I don't know what I'm saying. He searches my face. We're two kids who've lost their father. I burrow into Henry's fleece. I confess, "I gave him a cigarette."

"I heard."

My brain ping-pongs. "You heard?" *Please don't say Echo, please don't say Echo.*

We stand at the curb. Something gloomy has settled over the street at this hour, a dull, grainy flattening of the colors of the afternoon, the time of day my mother loved to shoot us, in the dying light.

"From Carla." Before I can interrogate him further, I'm in the back seat of the Uber. He says, "I'll call you, I will. I promise." He turns away.

Henry never broke a promise to me except the most fundamental one, the one he telegraphed during the photo shoots with his eyes: that whatever came, we'd go through it together. He protected me as best he could, but left me behind as soon as he could. I was a teenaged girl, with a dead brother and a dead mother and a dead-eyed father, and this brother, the good brother, dropped from my life.

I can't demand answers. I can't argue with him. The cab accident plus my pre-Henry nerves plus the physical impact of the past when I smelled him—all the adrenaline drains away, my limbs are flaccid, I give myself over to today's conclusion. I want a good exit so I open the window as the car noses into traffic. "Hank!" I call. He turns back. I scrunch my nose and roll my eyes, to make him laugh, to tease him about his alias. He only waves. He looks at me with the same sharp eyes that he laid upon me fifteen minutes ago, for the first time in decades.

The driver shrugs when I ask if I can smoke. I light up and lower the window. We hit the West Side Highway. Cyclists in fancy attire on fancy bikes speed along the waterway, with proper head protection. Beyond them the Hudson chops and surges and the whitecaps glow through the dusk as the dark crawls in from the east. An icy March wind lashes my face, my hair. Cinders from the tip of the cigarette blow back and sting my skin. The wind is loud and the traffic is loud and I lean into all of it the whole way home and what I think I know, what I do know, what I need to know, it's all obliterated by the wind for a while.

Chapter Twenty-Five

WHAT ARE YOU?

Gary's first words to me from the stage of the Coventry in Queens, New York, on prom night. I still don't have the answer. Berenice or Berry or Bean or Bea? A Marx or a Seger? Runaway or dream chaser? Groupie or wife? Miri's victim or a volunteer? Was I *the* subject, as in the main theme, or *a* subject, as in controlled by the queen-artist-mother who ruled us all? Recognizing the questions is probably progress, although I'm sick of the topic.

The new phone comes. It triggers anxiety: unanswered texts have piled up. Ronaldo inviting me on a Dory walk yesterday; a text from Violet to set up a meeting with the exhibition team at MoMA, ASAP; a text from Bix (*Lunch and contract! When are u available?*). There's a Micki Lopez text that shows multiple beseeching-praying-hands emojis. There are half a dozen texts from Echo, which I close out fast so I don't see the content. Let her beg. Nothing from Gary, nothing from Henry.

But Henry exists. That is something. I saw him, the actual walking-talking delicious-smelling Henry. We stood on a street in Flatiron, two adults in the world, out of old photographs, far away from the woods, flesh and blood. There's been a shift in my brain, that disorganized, disordered unit. Like I cleared part of a path.

I pack all the *Outtasight interview* CDs back in the Ferragamo box, including the one I haven't watched, and stand on a chair to stow the box on the top shelf of the closet in Echo's old room. There's another unmarked box way back that's also been taped up for years, same intense duct-taping, but this one was taped by me. I guess I'm my father's daughter. I know what it is. I take it down. I cut through the tape.

The notebook covers are warped, the pages are slightly yellowed. I wrote by hand in medium blue Flair felt-tip, now not blue, now mauve with age. Short paragraphs like diary entries, a lot of swooning or agonizing over my relationship with Gary. With some regularity, I would burst through with a long run of pages of songwriting attempts, jotted phrases, lines from poems, lyrics from real songwriters. I knew nothing about composing music but I was obsessed with words and writing words in search of a melody. Bernie Taupin wrote that way, and he'd send his pages to Elton John. To inspire myself, to feel how real songs flowed from brain to fingers to page, I painstakingly wrote out the lyrics to half a dozen of their hits.

I'd forgotten how much I wrote, and how diligently I revised. I slashed and redirected with long curved arrows. I wrote *no* or *save* or *bridge* or *chorus*. I drew hearts next to verses. I changed a word and tested options in the margin; I reverted to the original word. I doodled sad faces or scrawled *Sucks!* or made big Xs across a page. There are song titles: "*Little Sis*," "*Pose*," "*The Woods*," "*Naked Nude*," "*I, Alive*." So many starts and stops, and seeking, and reaching, and retreating, do-overs—everything hot with effort, and then the effort dissolves. Aggressive circles trap a phrase, demanding attention; exclamation points and question marks score the page; a word is underlined many times. In some cases, a good line stops midsentence. After a while, lines dangle without notes.

I've never done it—it never occurred to me, which is crazy—but I google my name plus *Chalk Outline*. The screen fills with some, not many, vintage Chalk Outline studio session images, and there's Gary, and other guys whose names I forget, and there I am, blurry in the background, lolling on a sofa, standing near a door, avoiding the camera. I'm in a uniform of skin-tight jeans, flimsy belly shirt, no bra. My hair is wild. Anyone looking at these pictures would think, *Ah, the groupie*. They might not notice the notebook and pen I held.

I made the work in these books. It's beginner's work, trying to be worthy. The pages vibrate with something unruly and dynamic and insistent and unique. "*I, Alive*" started on one of these pages. "*I, Alive*," the achievement I never enjoyed for a second—until Bowery Ballroom, and then that got ruined, too—without the tuneless accompaniment of financial and legal conflicts. My marriage staggered under the weight of it, and it was a different time, and I wanted the marriage more than my own success. When we broke up, I kept waiting. I told myself I was waiting for recognition, for the money I was owed. For fresh creative inspiration. But no.

I was waiting for Gary. That was my role. For Gary to finish work, for Gary to turn to me, for Gary to listen to my lyrics, for Gary to hear my voice, for Gary to give me the melody, for Gary to marry me, twice. For Gary to stop "slipping" with other women. For Gary to see me clearly so I could be me. It's on the pages: energy siphoned—from me, by me—to Gary's needs. My deference to a "real" artist. I had been in the foreground from the age of three. Once I left home, I retreated to the safe background.

When Miri was the age I was when I wrote these songs, she had already had a photograph published in *Life*, she was earning an income from Manhattan Moments. She'd met Albert and had twin boys. She was developing her creative vision, and fiercely protecting it. At all costs. I think about Echo and the way she found me and secured a home base in New York, and within weeks found her musical tribe and then seized the moment to emerge from behind the curtain at Bowery Ballroom, transformed, Gary behind her. The ambition it took to betray me.

My preferred coping mechanism is to pile on, so I let my thoughts flow into the stream of sub-worry: money. The breakup with Gary might mean—and maybe should mean—a breakup with the monthly subsidy. There's no contract binding him to that old agreement. My email has been distressingly free of queries or prospects for new work. I peek at savings and checking, my tiny money market account, my modest IRA. I review outstanding invoices—there aren't many—and I'm owed a few thousand dollars. If I say yes to MoMA, any money from collateral events and exhibitions will take a long time to materialize. If I go with Bix for a fast check, I will—along with defying gut instinct—be stuck in Gary's—and Echo's—orbit for a long time.

I go back to my phone and see a Google alert, *Miriam Marx*, and for a second my heart thumps. But the linked article is not about her; she's only briefly mentioned. After a long and influential career in media, after having interviewed rock stars and politicians and artists of all kinds, and winning a National Magazine Award, Ian McNally, founder and publisher of *Outtasight*, is dead at the age of seventy-eight, after long-managed HIV manifested as full-blown AIDS. The article mentions that McNally is survived by his wife, Nora, who gave him her inheritance to start the magazine so many years ago. I read the obituary on my phone and before I know how to feel—oh, too bad; oh, good riddance—a new text arrives and stays suspended at the top of the screen. I can't not see it, so I see it, and it's from Echo and the words swim and my eyes go hot.

Now I know why she's been trying to reach me. Another man down: Gary has had a stroke.

Chapter Twenty-Six

I'M LATE TO the party.

He's been here two days. Flowers, balloons, cards, and unwrapped gifts are set around the private room that overlooks Central Park, all attesting to how beloved he is. He is alone when I enter, dozing, or so it seems. His head is wrapped in dull gauze, I don't want to imagine why. His crazy black hair stands straight up. He wears a thin hospital gown, gray with a navy blue fleur de lis pattern. It's lost its life after too many industrial launderings and barely covers him. Same for the sad, once-white blanket and white sheets. Gary's body is slack on the left side. His left leg is uncovered, which disturbs me because he's a burrower; he hates any part of himself out from under the covers. He's dozing with the little oxygen plugs in his nostrils, and tubes coming out from the short sleeves of his gown, and also at the neckline, and judging from the outline, at the groin too. A monitor at his bedside reads his vital signs: blood pressure, heart rate, oxygen in the blood, respiration, and temperature. I don't exactly know what I'm looking at, but the lines and flashes and soft beeps are rhythmic and consistent, which seems good. Gary's room is across from the hub of the hospital floor, the central station where personnel gather and confer, or grab charts, or enter information into computers, and that's good too. Being in a VIP location surely makes him happy. It pains me to see him here. I make a note to myself to bring him pajamas and his fleece jacket and socks, the crocheted blanket his mother made, some comforts of home, some dignity.

He's not asleep. His eyelids are tense. I say, "Gary." He turns his head away. I sit on the bed, on the left side of him, the bad side. I lift his exposed leg to get it under the blanket, and it's heavy and pale, dead weight. It doesn't feel like Gary's leg. I tuck the bedding. I take his left hand. It's too cool. It doesn't hold mine back. His lips get taut and his cheek twitches slightly. "Old man," I whisper. "Look who's here."

A tear pushes out into the corner of his eye and slow-rolls down. I wipe it with the edge of my sleeve. "It's okay." He moves his head slightly. It's not okay.

But it will be. "Look how close you are to all the experts." I gesture to the hub. "They've got their eye on you. Can you open your eyes? Let me see you. I missed you." It's true. We haven't been apart long, but the breach felt fatal and then he was struck down, and I wasn't there for him. I warm his cold hand between mine. He opens his eyes. He glares at me, I think, but it's lopsided. The left side of his face sags: the eyebrow, the eye, the cheek, half his mouth, all have slid off grid. Maybe the teardrop wasn't relief at my presence, maybe he was just leaking. It's the mouth that's most disturbing. Even with the dislocation of half his features, he looks furious with me.

"You're mad at *me*? I'm the injured party. I mean, aside from your medical condition." I'm trying to stay light. This is no time for ancient recriminations with a contemporary twist: Echo. "This stroke is your dramatic attempt to try to get me back, isn't it?" He tilts his head to the right. He opens his mouth and the corners are dry and crusty. I bring a water bottle from the bedside table to his lips and help him close them around the straw. He does his best, he really does. I use my sleeve to wipe him up. I make another note to myself: bring a washcloth, bring the aloe.

He tilts his head to the right again and I realize he's trying to shake it. *No.*

I say, "No what?" and I shouldn't but then I say, "No, you didn't cheat on me with my own sister? It's a *Jerry Springer* episode." It's wrong of me, but I'm hurt.

His voice is weak. "Did not." He speaks out of the right corner his mouth, like a gangster in an old movie.

"I saw her backstage. I saw how she was. How you were."

"No." He burns a look into me. Even the droopy left eye gets into the act.

I laugh to de-escalate, but it's forced. "Are you seriously arguing with me right now? You might want to conserve your energy. Keep your conscience clean." I mean it to be funny but it's not funny at all. He's half dead and I'm teasing him about dying.

He does the tilt again. "Did not."

"You understand why that's hard for me to believe."

He rasps, "Did. Not."

I search his eyes. He does not look away. How could he be lying right now, so weak and sick? He hasn't bothered to lie about women in the past. He always assumed I would understand that cheating, his slipups, went with the territory. It's the Echo part that makes it unforgivable, that is making me mean. I don't know what pisses me off more, their affair or the terrible karmic injustice of seeing Gary Going in a flimsy hospital gown with no control over the left side of his wonderful body.

"Let's forget it. We can argue about it when you're better. Something to look forward to."

The tiny hairs on the back of my neck prickle. I feel her over my shoulder. She leans in the doorway, presumably not wanting to interrupt. She has a backpack. I turn and Echo says, "You got the texts. I'm glad you're here."

Gary shuts his eyes. *Let the womenfolk sort it out.* Echo comes close and unpacks the bag: Gary's pajamas, his favorite fleece jacket, his socks, a washcloth, his mother's blanket. "You forgot aloe," I say. "What does the doctor say?"

"Oh, yeah, aloe. That's a good idea." She moves around the room, arranging Gary's things. "The doctor says he's had a stroke. He was complaining of a stiff neck. And then a headache. And then, I don't know. He fell in the middle of the night and hit his head. He got stitches but it's minor. Anyway. We got here fast. That's in his favor."

"You're living at the loft?" I can't say his name to her. We are in dangerous territory.

"You kicked me out. Gary offered."

I wait until I am in control of my voice and say, "And?"

"And they don't know yet. It's too soon to tell. He could recover, with therapy. But because of his age, they say not to expect anything. A full recovery might not happen."

"Will he play again? Did you ask that?"

Echo says, "I didn't ask," and I realize how young she is. How much she's had to handle, Albert and now Gary, and how overwhelming it must be.

There is a slight exhale like a sigh from Gary, and I answer, "Don't think like that. Don't be negative! You will!" The atmosphere in the room gets muffled as he sinks into the no-man's-land of sleep, where the brain heals itself.

Echo says, "I miss you."

"It's been a week."

"I don't mean time. I mean you. And Dory."

"Well, I'm sure there will be lots of new and exciting people to fill the gap left by me." She shakes her head and starts to speak but I'm on a mission to hurt her back. "Dory's gone, by the way. Back to her real parents."

She looks shocked. "Oh, Bea, that's—"

I wave her off. "It's okay. She's just across the hall. She was too much work for me anyway."

"Bea, you're wrong. What you think. About me and Gary."

I'm not going to help her by engaging or drawing her out. I stonewall.

"It's true that we met before the reunion show. A couple of weeks before. It was right after Daddy died. At first, I thought you knew. But then in Costello's when you offered to introduce us, I realized you didn't."

"Okay, fine, I was wrong. You were fucking him on a different timeline." I wince. I wish I had chosen a different word. *Fucking* sounds more profane in the hospital room.

"Not fucking." Echo lowers her voice. She closes the door to the room. She comes to me with her phone. I stand up from the bed, where Gary rumbles and snores unevenly. "I got his number from your contacts. He promised he would tell you." She holds the screen up for me to see. "We're not fucking. We're working." She taps her finger to the arrow on the phone's screen.

There she is, at the loft. There's a photographer's backdrop cloth behind her and studio lights. It's before she buzzed her hair. She's in the flannel shirt, the jeans and sneakers; it's the version of Echo that she was in Costello's. She's holding Gary's Silvertone, the one he pretended to play at Bowery Ballroom. The roadie—it's Jeremy and that hurts—plugs her in to a small amp. It looks ad hoc, but there's a professional quality to every move. It's fully realized. It's a Gary production, without a doubt.

"Whatever it is, I don't want to see it."

Echo says, "Just watch," and then it's too late, I can't not watch. She's strumming the intro and she clears her throat and smiles with her wolf eyes at the camera's eye and moves to the mic and does my song, unplugged, raunchy and slow and girly, like smoke, exactly as I heard "*I, Alive*" in my own head so many years ago, before Gary took it from me. I mean, before I gave it away. It's so owned by Echo, it's like a new song.

"So? Why are you showing me this? To rub it in? Another version, without my knowledge or my input or my permission. Great," I say, without the least bit of sincerity. "Is this all over YouTube already? I hope not, because I am finally going to take everybody's advice and get a lawyer."

"Bea, no. This is just a demo. He wants to produce an album. My album. This is only one track. There's more to do. I'm writing."

"Demo? This looks finished."

"No, it's not. Gary made this version for you. For your input, your permission. To pitch the idea to you. Get your blessing. He doesn't have much more than this yet." She looks shy. She says, "We, I guess. I'm coproducer."

Gary's sputtered denial and Echo's steady denial are truth. They were not fucking. I wonder, *Is this worse?* This might be worse. They met, they worked, they planned behind my back. On the other hand, maybe I'm being invited in. Maybe I am not being left behind. Instead of defaulting to being hurt, I take a deep, deep breath. I look into Echo's eyes. She holds steady in my gaze. I like the song. I can't deny it.

"I thought you didn't want his help."

She glances at the bed. "He is relentless, isn't he? He convinced me that this is how it happens. One voice catches one ear. It felt stupid to turn it down. One of those opportunities I'd always regret not taking."

I say, "Echo, I am getting a lawyer. Everything on my terms."

She puts her arms around me and I'm hugging, being hugged, I'm doing it right.

I mumble into her neck, "I'm really sorry about the Martin."

Her voice is close to my ear. "Yes, for sure, a lawyer. Gary promised me. I won't leave him alone about it. And he has a fucking wall full of guitars; I got to pick my favorite."

I laugh and cry. I say, "I know about all the guitars."

Echo presses the arrow again, to show it again. She's so proud of herself, and I'm so proud of her too, and before the intro starts I say, "Come home. I have some stuff I know you can use." I correct myself. "I know *we* can use."

Chapter Twenty-Seven

HE PICKS ME up out front.

The weekend Armenian holds the car door open for me, and makes his eyebrows jump lasciviously as I get in. I fumble with my seat belt, and the Armenian leans in and does it for me and jokes to Henry, "Have her home early," because I'm an older woman heading out on a date, and that's a universally acceptable topic of ridicule. I try to feel aggrieved but I don't. I appreciate the joke and I like the attention. It's spring.

I've dressed carefully: broken-in jeans and sneakers, chunky sweater, a scarf and my favorite sunglasses. This morning, because it's my day with Henry, I considered my stripped-down makeup bin in search of a little shine, but got distracted and never did do my face. Why highlight what isn't there anymore? I'm getting used to the uneven skin. I'm wearing my hair in the side braid, and as I braided it in the mirror it felt like the hair of someone else, a woman living out in the country, not the city.

Henry's car is a brand-new Volvo. I say, "What, no Prius?"

"I know. It was a dilemma. When I hit sixty, I felt like I should be able to have whatever car I wanted."

"I'll be sixty at the end of this year." I find it endearing and very Henry that he chose the safest car on the road. I say, "I have only driven a dozen times since high school."

"Neither of those things can be true."

"Both true. I will definitely be sixty, unless fate has other ideas. I've driven a little, but mostly Gary does the driving. Or did, before the stroke. We'll see."

"How is he?"

"Home. He's got a team, speech therapist, occupational therapist, massage therapist. Even his therapist-therapist is making house calls to see him. Echo is staying with him for now. To help."

"Echo. I know her as Hannah. I met her at Sandy Edge. She was just a kid."

I warm to the subject. "Well, you'll have to get acquainted with the new version. She's very cool. A musician. We're working together. Some music stuff. She's fun. And funny."

Henry knows where he is going. We head north on the parkway along the Hudson River, toward the George Washington Bridge and the Palisades beyond. It's the same route Gary and I took in the Uber back in winter, the day I fell apart, what seems like so long ago.

We make first-date small talk. No, never married, no kids, but he has had partners. He's alone now. He started as a stock boy at Camerama when he was at Columbia, and used the same modest pile of estate proceeds from Albert to buy an equity stake. Eventually, he outlasted the other guys and bought it all. He lives in Chelsea and walks to work. He has a summer place in the untrendy part of the east end of Long Island.

It is both strange and familiar to be in such close quarters with Henry. I am remembering and memorizing my brother's profile as he talks and drives. I can see the worried boy and the tightly wound teenager and now, this older man Henry.

"Henry." I am trying it out, testing his presence. He nods. I say it again. "Henry."

He laughs. "I'm Hank in my real life. I've gotten used to it."

"I can't call you Hank. Did Albert call you Hank?"

His top lip tightens. "Albert called me 'Son.'"

It makes a kind of sense. "Did he forget which twin you were?"

"After Ansel . . . and then Mom, I think he just couldn't bring himself to say my name."

This is a tiny aperture that could open further on to the topic of everything, all of it. I can't do it. Not yet. "I'm surprised to hear you were in contact with Albert all these years. Were you visiting him regularly? Why weren't you at the memorial thing at Sandy Edge?"

"I was at a conference in Berlin. Also"—he pauses—"I knew you were down there. It seemed best to let you have him all to yourself. I was always in contact with Dad, Berry. You were the one who stayed away."

"I keep hearing that. That's what Jeanne said, too. Albert thought the same thing." I look at Henry, my Henry. "That's not how it felt to me."

"You took off with Gary."

"Only after everybody left." I look away and out my window. "I stayed after they died. After you went to school."

The road takes us farther north. We ride in silence for many miles. Every gesture he makes feels like my own—his grasp to adjust the mirror, the flick of his finger on the blinker, the roll of his shoulders when he's held one position too long. He extends his neck and tilts his head to check his blind spot, and I have to stop myself from doing that too.

I say, "When was the last time you were up here?"

He shakes his head. "StoreSpace? I've never been to StoreSpace."

"You've never been there? Who did all the work?"

"I hired people. Photography nerds from Camerama, some Columbia students, for the most part."

"You haven't looked at any of it? I assumed you'd gone through it all. I mean, there's a lot. I've looked at a few things. And . . . there are some tapes. Of Miri. With Ian McNally." I pause, but push ahead. "Ansel, too."

A serious silence descends. When he speaks, his voice is sharp. "I hired help. The contents are documented on spreadsheets. I'd say, exhaustively documented. I gave all that a pass, Berry. I left it behind."

"I noticed. You gave me a pass, too."

"I went away to school, like I was supposed to. That was always the plan."

"Ansel and Miri fucked up the plan, Henry. Maybe the plan should have been amended, considering? You called me, what, three times? You hardly wrote to me or invited me to visit or anything. Twenty miles away." My heart is pounding, my breath is choppy. I don't like this, I can't stop myself, this is too soon. Words rush out that have been trapped inside me for a long time. I can't hold them back but I don't want to fight with Henry. I try to calm down. I watch the landscape, accusing the trees and the sky and the river as we rush past. I feel queasy. I don't know where my eyes should focus or what they should follow. "I needed you. You could have stayed home. Until January. Deferred admission, or whatever they call it."

"It seemed like the best decision for everybody."

"There was no everybody. There was just me."

"The best decision for you, then. To be away from me."

"What does that mean?"

He doesn't answer. How can he have believed that breaking all contact with me was the best decision? But recriminations now might be dangerous. We are too new. We're strangers, in a way. "Can I ask you a question, Henry?"

"You can ask. Whether I answer is a different story. I'm trying to pace myself with all of this. I'm trying to pace you, too." He waves a hand in my direction. "It's a lot."

Meaning, I'm a lot.

I feel let down. What can I do? Getting older means accommodating disappointment. I have to put it aside inside myself to appreciate the day we finally have. "Well, I'm glad someone is slowing me from hurtling myself into the abyss of our childhood."

We exchange similar tight smiles, grimaces, our long-standing levees built against trauma. We sit with it for a few miles. "What's your question?"

"So much happened. The way we grew up. Was it, I don't know, pornography? Were we, like, abused? I go back and forth. She was a feminist before it was a thing. We were what she had to work with. It's silly to expect some kind of television mom standing at the stove in an apron. But she was also our mother. Did she just not realize what she was doing? What about Albert? How could he allow it?"

"That's more than one question." There's a long silence. "Are you in therapy? Hasn't that helped you with all this? It's helped me. With this part."

"Therapy? No. Therapy hasn't helped. I've gone a few times over the years. Not anymore. It's too expensive. I couldn't really connect. I made too many jokes. One shrink said, 'Once you're done entertaining me we might get somewhere.' And then years would go by where

I thought, *Who cares? I'm okay, I'll muddle through.* I can't imagine sitting down with a stranger and explaining everything. What's the point? I always feel like I'm, I don't know, making up stories about the past. Things that I only sort of remember. Things I can't do anything about anyway."

He nods. "I thought that in the beginning too. Until I found a good fit. Once I got the backstory out of the way, it helped. Not to cure the past, but to deal with the present. I still fuck up. I haven't done so well in the relationship department."

"Me neither. I have Gary but only sort of. Gary only goes so far. Gary has his own agenda. I don't blame him. The truth is, I wanted him to carry me so he carried me, and then I was mad at him for carrying me, and then I was mad at him for putting me down and mad at myself most of all. It might be too late, but I'm working on being less . . . dependent."

Henry says the nicest thing. "It's not too late."

"I've tried—I'm trying—to write about it. Like, a memoir." I've never admitted it out loud.

He nods. "Ambitious. Not to say you couldn't do it. You're a writer."

"I am? Is that how you think of me? I feel like I lost that version of me somewhere along the way." I correct myself. "Not lost, let go. I was young, with Gary, and I just stopped. When the songwriting thing got complicated, I didn't fight for it. I could hardly say it to myself, that I wanted what I wanted, let alone to the rest of the world."

"Doesn't writing a memoir count as doing something about things you can't do anything about?" He's sly, my brother.

"Yes. No. I've been writing it for ten years and I've made zero progress. I hate doing it." I realize I mean it. "Henry, I'm curious . . . Are you gay?"

He raises his eyebrows. "Is that your theory?"

"I'm trying really hard to be done with theories. I am wrong a lot. I'm especially terrible at theories about sexual orientation. Anyway, it doesn't matter."

"You're right, it doesn't matter. For the record, I've been with women and men."

Nothing is surprising. "That seems sensible. It really does."

We're witnesses. We're testifying to each other, the only two people who speak the same lost language of the ancient Marx-Seger civilization. We are together again, and I realize my breathing is good and my heart feels right. We are talking to each other. We are listening to each other.

I say, "We probably have PTSD. Depression. Or anxiety. One of those. All of those. Is that what your therapist says? I see the effects. I've been stuck my whole life. I don't have a family of my own. Or a real career. I've never accomplished anything. I can't make a decision. I live alone and I'm sort of broke with no clue as to how to take care of myself financially. Half the time I feel like I'm invisible to the world and the other half I am disappearing myself, smoking, drinking, hiding. Where is all the bad stuff lurking? In my head? StoreSpace? I want to exorcise it all."

Henry takes his hand from the steering wheel and puts his palm flat against my sternum. The heat and weight of his hand presses where the cancer I no longer have grew years ago. It sends a jolt from my breast to my heart to my brain.

I nod. "Everything is inside us." I've just said things out loud that I've only ever kept to myself. I think about smoking. I realize I haven't had a cigarette in days.

He keeps his eyes on the road but gives an Albert shrug. "We're doing this, today, together. A little progress. For me too."

"That's true. And I'm not wearing makeup and I think I quit smoking. I might cut my hair."

"You think you quit smoking? You're not sure?" He laughs. "Well, I guess it's good to leave a little wiggle room." He tugs my braid. "This is too much like Mom's." He moves his palm to the side of my face. "Your face is exactly how it's supposed to be. Anyway, this is how I know you now."

We're at StoreSpace in under an hour. The blue-gray hangar-like structure is nestled in leafy green trees that were bare the last time I was here. Jeff sits in his dreary office. He registers that I am with a man who is not Gary Going this time, and he seems a bit miffed. He says, "You know how to get to 201?" and I do. I don't notice the birds.

Chapter Twenty-Eight

"WELCOME TO THE abyss."

"Wow."

"That seems to be the consensus."

I lead my brother. Henry taps the labels and bins and equipment, the books and crates, just as he tapped each office chair when he walked off the elevator and toward me in Camerama. He says, "I guess I got my money's worth with the nerds. I was expecting—"

"I know. *Hoarders.*"

"Look at these. First editions." He strokes Miri's books. He looks around. "Wow."

I want him to be less awestruck. I thought he was the expert on unit #201, but he only knows it via a spreadsheet. He has to help me figure out what to do, which is totally irrational of me considering my own first trip here nearly caused a breakdown. Henry is my partner in this enterprise now, whatever it becomes. I need to let him help me, without bickering, without criticizing him, without micromanaging, without expecting everything to be done my way.

I want to have, like, a meeting. I pull out a crate and empty its contents without really noticing them—old manila folders and composition notebooks—and turn the crate over so I can sit and address my new partner. "We should talk about what to do."

Henry is nimbler than Gary. He lowers himself easily and leans back against a tall shelf. "What you were talking about in Camerama? MoMA and Hollywood?"

"Yes." I launch into an account of the dueling decisions. I leave out my paralyzing stress, but do include my very amusing, if I do say so myself, profile of Bix and the tale of unrequited love. "I don't know what to do. Or maybe I do nothing. I don't know."

He nods. "I've expected this for years. I'm only surprised it took this long." Henry puts his elbows on his knees and his head in his hands. His eyes are closed and I take that to mean he's listening, so I keep going. "To be honest, it's kind of a gold mine. For me. I mean us. You too, of course. My income is so unpredictable. I can't keep hustling for projects anymore. I'd like to have enough money to pay for healthcare and food and stay in my apartment and maybe get out of the city now and then. Maybe rent a little cottage for a couple of weeks out east. Near you. But not too close, don't worry." I give him a crooked smile, which he does not return. "I'm trying to take care of myself, without Gary. I need the money."

"Okay," he says. "But I don't."

"You don't? You don't what?"

"Need the money."

That stings. I struggle to keep my voice even. "Well, that's great for you. Really great. But, I'm not in that position. And all this stuff . . . Maybe we can make it pay off. For both of us."

He says, "And Woodstock? You mentioned Woodstock in Camerama. How does that figure in?"

His voice holds the weight of his grief over Ansel. I go slow. "Albert kept a few videotapes. Footage of Miri being interviewed. Footage from Woodstock. Taken by Ian McNally. They had a contract for her to shoot there."

"Berry, I know that. She was at Woodstock on assignment." He is trying to rein in his exasperation.

"No, I know. But with all the . . . all that happened that weekend, and then at the end of that year, did anyone, Albert or you or your nerds, locate Woodstock pictures? Are they on your spreadsheet? I've never seen any." I take a deep, shaky breath and forge on. "Did she hand them over to *Outtasight*? McNally wanted her to take rock star photographs, photojournalism stuff. She wanted to take artsy pictures of the crowd, the . . . generation. It was a point of contention between them." I pause. "Another point of contention."

"So? Woodstock. Yeah, there might have been Woodstock on the spreadsheet. But there are millions of photographs of Woodstock out in the world. Why is this a big deal?"

"Maybe Bix or Violet will be excited for them. Maybe it's a revenue stream? I know how that sounds, but it's all just sitting here! Hipsters are dying for cool, new stuff. I at least want a look! Not to mention, they're the last images she took, and we're not in them. It's a new ending to the nightmare. It's not us . . . entwined. Can we please just look?"

He takes one row, I take another. We check each bin's label. I see a bin, high up. I can't make out the label but it might be what I'm hoping for. I direct and Henry climbs. I say, "Be careful, be careful." He strains to reach. I hold my breath. "Be careful!"

He leans and reads, "August 1969," and I get goose bumps.

"That's it! Can you get it down? Do we need a ladder?" It's too late, he's pulled at the bin and it crashes down and bounces off my shoulder. Number 201 is still trying to kill me. The lid pops off and the contents scatter, dozens of contact sheets and cellulose negatives and a few eight-by-tens, printing experiments, wild colors, and they are most definitely of Woodstock.

We look at images and at each other. They are of little kids at the festival. The work is surprising, not very Miri, and I don't associate little kids with Woodstock, but of course it was its own small city. They kept saying that on the news, here's the proof. Miri shot kids in mud pools, hanging off the back of a straggly-haired father or mother, wrapped in quilts, sleeping like angels in tents, tricked out in miniature hippie gear, long dresses, dungarees, or naked except for sneakers. Some make funny faces, some blow bubbles. So much unexpected sweetness. We pass them back and forth. Henry holds negatives up to the light. We point at our favorites on the contact sheets. We say, *Look at this one, how cute is that? Little hippies!* It's my mother looking at children through another lens and finding another light. Nearly normal.

Henry packs *August 1969* back in the bin and finds a logical spot to shelve it. He slides back down and covers his entire face with his hands. "Meanwhile, Ansel was on fire."

I sit back down on the crate and reach to him and pull his hands down. "Henry, look at me." It takes him a long time but he lowers his hands. I say, "These pictures are the end of all of it, that terrible time. It's"—I gesture at the bin—"joyful. Maybe we can hold on to that. Give ourselves a better ending."

He looks at me. I wait. I use my eyes to reassure him, *We're a team,* but the longer I look back, the more he seems like a stranger. I don't really know him, and he doesn't know me. I want to convince him. "*Outtasight* never published the Woodstock photographs. There was a lot going on. With Miri and McNally. And . . . other stuff. Henry, I'm just asking you to think all this through with me."

He laughs. It's derisive. "Think it through? You're asking me to think it through? You really are something." He sighs, and it's a mighty one. "The interview. In *Outtasight.* Berry, did you know it was supposed to run in October of '69, a couple of months after Woodstock? Ian spiked it, maybe because she delivered something he didn't want, maybe because of what happened to Ansel. And then there she was on the cover in February of 1970, sitting naked on the stool, with a black banner around the edge of the issue with her interview. *Miriam Marx, 1932 to 1969.*" He shakes his head. "Six weeks after she hanged herself. Ian used her suicide to sell his fucking magazine."

I don't like the way he says *Ian.* His grasp of the timeline, his read on McNally, he's way ahead of me. I've just started paying attention, revising as I go, but I realize Henry has been analyzing and interpreting all of it for years. On the drive, he said he doesn't think about it, but I can hear in his angry voice that he's always thinking about it, and he's lived his whole life trying to manage the thoughts. I have mastered compartmentalizing and denial, but Henry's grief is right there, spread out, a second skin just below the surface. We share loss but I can see that Henry lost more. He became un-twinned. The death of Ansel enlarged the twin-shaped shadow that lived inside Henry, that was cast across his identity from the moment they were born.

I try to edge us back to common ground. "This is what I'm trying to say. There was so much we didn't understand."

He lashes out. "*You! You* didn't understand! And you want to drag it all up again. For money!"

"Yes! For money! And to empty out this tomb. It gets worse. The tapes. She was sleeping with Ian McNally. But McNally was interested in Ansel. Meaning, like sexually. I saw it. It was undeniable. I think poor Ansel was being molested by Ian. I think Miri knew."

"I thought you were so completely done with theories."

"Woodstock was the horrible end of our fucked-up childhoods. Don't you want to finish it? Finally?"

"I *was* finished. Then you showed up."

This hurts me but I still have his hands in my hands. I press his fingers to my lips. I inhale his skin. I bring his hands to the sides of my face and lace my fingers between his and hold them there, warm to warm. "There's more." I look into Henry's eyes, to anchor him, to anchor myself, to anchor us right here. "I know they wanted us to believe the fire was an accident. But I don't think it was. I think Ansel was tormented about McNally. And everything. I think maybe he killed himself. He was trying to escape! Like we all were! Miri too! So she did! I understand why you left me. It doesn't matter. We're here now. We will figure it out together."

Henry probes me with his look. "You *think* you understand."

I pretend not to hear that. "We'll blow off the Hollywood thing. Let MoMA have her. We can write the monograph together—Violet will go crazy when she hears it's the two of us—and then, once it's behind us, we'll be done with it. Miri will get what she always wanted. We can stop wishing she'd been a normal mother."

My brother takes his hands back and, standing up, shoves them deep into the front pockets of his jeans. He shakes his head. "Berry," he says. His eyes are hooded and cloudy.

"What," I say. "What? You're scaring me. What is it?" I move toward him. He steps back.

"For fuck's sake, Berry."

"What? Just say it."

"It wasn't only Ansel."

"What wasn't only Ansel?" *What?* I squeeze my eyes shut to not see what he's trying to show me. The foundation shifts, the myth twists, the narrative snakes away again.

"Everything. All of it."

I can't speak. I want to shut him down, stop what I've started, refute him. I begin, but I can't. I can't not hear him. Whatever is coming rumbles from inside me, where it has always lived.

"Ansel didn't kill himself in the woods and it wasn't an accident. Not really. He was furious that he didn't get to go to Woodstock with them. I couldn't understand that. I wanted him to feel like I felt. Happy they were gone. I wanted them to never come back. McNally had been interviewing Miri all summer. I couldn't understand why Ansel didn't hate them like I did. He was okay with it. With Ian. With Miri knowing that Ian had been with . . . us." His eyes slide along the shelves, taking it all in. "Both of us."

He takes a deep, shaky breath. "We had stashed a thermos. We'd been drinking. And arguing. I lit a match. I tossed it into the pile of branches and leaves where Ansel was sitting, smoking and drinking. The thermos had tipped over. Grain alcohol. I just wanted him to shut up. I was sick of him. Sick of myself."

My ears roar. "No. That's not right. You were in town. Or at the river with your friends. Albert told the police."

Henry laughs a dead laugh. "None of us *had* friends." He hangs his head. "Ian went after Miri first. It didn't take long for him to come after us. I hated him. Them. All three of them."

"Are you saying you set the fire? To hurt Ansel? On purpose?"

"No, not on purpose. Or yes. I don't know. I just wanted him to stop being someone I didn't know. We were twins." He pauses and peers at me, intent. "I told Dad."

"Don't say anything else! Don't! I don't want to know." I put my hands over my ears but I'm listening hard. I have to hear him. I've wanted the truth and I saw it coming the day I breathed his scent in Camerama. The past is no optical illusion. The past is almost here.

"You said you wanted to know. I'm telling you. I told Dad. He slammed me against the dining room wall. He made me promise not to say anything. To never talk about Ansel. He let the fire department and the cops draw their conclusions. He was protecting me. But also Miri. One of us dead, one of us in jail—he thought it would kill her."

"It killed her anyway!"

"Listen to me, Berry. I told Dad everything. Everything. About you, too. About *Nap*. He put his hand over my mouth and he told me to keep it shut. He made me promise to go to school. He made me promise to stay away from you. I promised. That's it. I promised."

"Wait. What? *Nap*? The photograph? What do you mean? What about it?" Of course, I'm not really confused, I'm only acting confused. As soon as he said "*Nap*," I knew he knew.

Henry says nothing.

"Henry! What are you saying? No wonder Albert couldn't look at me ever again! Did Ansel tell you something happened? Nothing happened! It was one time. I never even said anything. Because I don't know anything! Brothers mess around, they do. I bet it happens a lot more than—"

"No, Berry, they don't. Brothers don't do that." Henry comes to me. He encircles me and holds me tight. His arms. I am inside his scent again and the pressure he exerts, the long form of him, against me, chest to belly to groin to thigh, the very thrum and hum of his alive self and mine. His voice and breath in my ear, near my neck, his whisper. "I ruined everything. I had to leave. I'm sorry."

I let Henry's whisper in. I let his scent do its work. In my mind's eye, I recall a brother, shoulders and sheets and shadows. The bed-covers are lifted. In my mind, I hear the doll drop to the floor, I hear the fan. Sometimes even I couldn't tell them apart. In my mind's eye I look, I try to see. I try another way, I try to see what Miri saw, stand-ing in the doorway. Who she saw.

I just decide, I just choose. "It doesn't matter," I say. "I have to get out of here."

I pack things back into the crate I was sitting on, and I notice its contents, the yellowed files and the composition books. I register my mother's penmanship, small and careful. The white subject field on the black marbled cover says *Miriam July 1940*. I lift the crate and it's heavy, and Henry tries to take it, to carry it for me, but I pull away and carry the crate myself.

We walk down Hilltop, past River Place and Woods Road and Boundary Avenue, past other people's lifelong secrets. I'm floating, I'm fluttering, I'm a feathery thing. I could lift and join the birds on the ceiling. Something hard inside me has dissolved and dispersed into a brew of anxiety and clarity. I'm younger and older. I can't yet tell if it's a good feeling or a bad feeling but it's a new feeling.

I concentrate on carrying the crate. The crate is ballast. I have to make conversation, I have to use my voice to retake reality. "Look at the birds. They live here. Up there. They must wish they had a normal sky." The birds fly and dip and caw softly. They seem smaller and far-ther away now than my first time here.

Henry looks. "Maybe the ceiling is the only sky they know."

We go to the car. Henry rests his head on the steering wheel. He looks older and exhausted and the receding tuft of curls at his hairline

looks lank and thin and grayer. I touch his back. His shirt is damp
with sweat. "It doesn't matter." The spring sun warms away the chill
of StoreSpace. I say, "You made a life. I made a life. Despite all this.
Because of all this. We got through."

"There's more to say."

"Oh, no, Henry. Not today."

He holds out a shaky hand. "I don't think I can drive." He looks
at me. I shake my head but he's already getting out from behind the
wheel. "Yes," he says. "You drive."

I adjust all mirrors so I can see what's going on behind me. I pull
the seat belt across and buckle up. Henry's legs are longer than mine,
so I have to bring the seat forward. I test the blinkers and wipers and
climate buttons; I don't want to have to figure anything out while
we're moving. I start it up and put it in gear and back up, and he puts
a hand on my arm and says, "Whoa. Wait a minute," and I am so
startled, I hit the brake too hard.

"I heard correctly back there? You said Violet? Violet at MoMA.
Right?"

"Yes. Violet Yeun. Dr. Yeun. She has a PhD in our mother."

"Yeun? That's not the name I knew her by. But there can't be more
than one Violet in the photography department at MoMA."

"You know her?"

I forget to worry about driving. Henry tells me about the Violet he
knew at school, obsessed with Miriam Marx, who offered to him to
help with the archives a few years later, when she was doing her post-
doc at Yale. I just drive. He talks and I hear the past's pull in his voice.
I can tell he's holding something back. I am astonished by everything.
Nothing is what it seems, including Henry. We've only just met, kind
of, and I may not know him, but I am fluent in his language, including
interpreting what I am not hearing.

I drive us all the way home to the city. I'm shaky too, and shy now. I can't meet Henry's eye but I can feel him looking at me, trying to see where I am with all of it.

Henry is shy too. He opens the back door of the car for the crate. I put up my hand. "It's okay," and he steps back and plunges hands in pockets. The weekend Armenian comes to help me. I say, "What's your name? Are you Artur's cousin?" I extend my hand. He's called Alex. Alex pulls the crate from the car and somehow—men can be so kind, so dear—he knows something has gone awry with my "date," and he is completely on my team. Nice to meet you, Alex. I'm Bea.

Henry drives off.

I'm finished for today. Against all odds and fuzzy facts, despite all thoughts, known and not, alongside ambiguity and uncertainty, in the midst of confronting too much truth and opting to back away, for now or forever, I am no longer terrified. I am angry and hurt, I'm rebooting my brain to make room, but I'm not afraid. My only thought is: *I'm dying for a cigarette.* The problem is, I threw them away and made the guy at the corner store promise not to sell me any, and I know he is a man of his word.

Chapter Twenty-Nine

THE EYE IS a lens even when it's closed.

It was Labor Day weekend, the Saturday, I think. Such a pleasure it was, lying inert for hours on my bed, sweating and reading—what I'd done all that summer, which was the summer I began menstruating and also what the newspapers were calling the Summer of Love—and anticipating the oscillating fan's turn to me. The whir, the creak of its neck, the wave of cool relief, gave rhythm to the long afternoons. I was inhaling library books that I'd pretended to check out for my mother, which the town librarian surely did not believe since Miriam Marx would never step foot in Grand View's little library, nor any other shop or bank or gathering place where she might have to act like a neighbor. I read *Rosemary's Baby* in sheer terror. I read *The Valley of the Dolls* in a haze of tittilated confusion. I retreated to my Agatha Christies to relax.

I had used my pocket money to buy *Seventeen* magazine's annual back-to-school issue on one of the trips to town with my brothers. Twiggy was on the cover, nubile in pink, lush-lashed, braless under a coat, captured in a mod moment with a pixie haircut I coveted. I wanted desperately to cut my hair; I was obsessed with the idea. Miri would never allow it, let alone bring me to a salon. I went so far as to get the good scissors and face the mirror with the magazine's cover held up next to me. I had the big eyes and the pale skin, but my mass of unruly hair was nothing like Twiggy's sleek look, and I was too afraid to make a cut.

I studied the magazine's contents. So many of the advertisements, previously a mystery to me, now made sense. I understood the black-and-white Kotex ad—"Remember how simple life used to be?"—with the childlike drawing of a bashful girl. I was still a bashful girl in a way but I had a rough-and-tumble side because of the twins and I was trying, I think, to see how to put myself together like the girls in the magazine. With this issue, I felt inducted.

I no longer tried to keep up with the boys. Instead, I starred in my own daily sleuth adventure, spying on them. I tracked them on their forays into the woods. I hid and watched them build their forts, light cigarettes, duke it out, walk the woods with arms slung over shoulders, boost each other into trees. Henry and Ansel, nearly identical, often only distinguished by tone of voice and flow of certain gestures. Naturally, they read each other's thoughts. They approached the world each in his own way, but each was in the other's head.

By the end of that summer, the boys were fourteen, almost fifteen, more man than boy. I was eleven, but my body was already changing. I sat in the bathtub in my Levi's, much to my father's horror, to make sure they shrunk and stuck to my curves. I went from training bra to no bra at all. I was thrumming with the intensity of my reading list, and of course, music. I had a phonograph in a light-blue vinyl suitcase, and I listened to 45s. I was obsessed with "Ode to Billie Joe" by Bobbie Gentry. The song told the tale of a humid Southern love affair with a mysterious tragic ending. I played it again and again to try to crack the code of the lyrics. The boys' records reverberated through the ceiling from their attic bedroom, equally mysterious, sex instead of romance. The Doors rumbled like stormy weather from above.

It was my time of the month for only the second time. When I went to Miri white-faced with my bloody pajama bottoms back in July, thinking I was dying, she handed me a box of tampons and said, "Read the directions, don't worry about it." I had no friend or sister with whom I could consult. I did what my mother told me to do. I read the directions, I tried not to worry. The tampon was meant to be worn internally so you wouldn't feel it, but I could. It felt lumpy and big inside me. I'd scrubbed myself nearly raw with a washcloth to stay clean, but my panties were always dappled red-brown, because the tampon didn't stay put. I wasn't secure or confident or poised in the least, the way the ad promised. I felt disgusting.

I had fallen asleep with a book on the bed. I remember waking up with a start and a feeling of dread, and there was my mother. "Berenice, we're waiting. It's after four o'clock. Come on out." I was already late, which drove my brothers crazy. I slouched out and sat on the porch step. I wore a pajama top and baggy dungarees, and a sour look on my face, I'm sure of that.

Miri's gear for the shoot was set up in the driveway. The camera pointed toward the Chrysler. Albert was probably somewhere in the house—it was a long holiday weekend—but in my memory, he's far away. My mother wore her uniform, his old shirt with the sleeves rolled above her elbow, black Bermuda shorts, black Keds. Ansel had a new SuperBall, and he and Henry bounced it between them. It was small and black and hard. I hated it because I'd been "accidentally" dinged with it more than once and had the bruises to prove it. I flinched every time it bounced close.

Miri looked up from her adjustments and said what she always said. "Okay, kids, let's go." The boys pulled off their shirts and stepped out of their shorts.

I couldn't take my clothes off. I pulsed with shame and sweat. "Miri, I can't."

Ansel bounced the SuperBall in my direction, so hard that my arm went up in defense. He shot me a look that said, *Don't stall, let's get this over with.*

My mother was dismissive, impatient. "Yes, you can, Berenice. I don't have all afternoon. I need this light."

"No, Mom, really, I can't." I tried to impart secret female urgency into my plea. "I really can't."

She came to me. "Now what?"

"I have . . . my friend." I don't know where I picked up the euphemism, probably *Seventeen* or girls at school, but my brothers were staring so it seemed like the right time to use it. Miri did not do euphemisms.

She looked at me blankly. "Your friend? You mean you're menstruating? Bleeding?"

My face went red, hot. I nodded. In my peripheral vision, I could see the boys, their body language. Ansel leaned in slightly, attuned to this new development. Henry pulled back with the typical reticence of a boy confronted by the femaleness of his little sister, and at the same time, his face tensed with my distress.

"You're wearing the tampon, right? Just get undressed. It doesn't matter. I'm not shooting close. You'll be in the car."

I always come back to this moment, this question: Why didn't I say no? I was a cranky menstruating preteen girl. I could have run to my room and slammed the door. That must have been my impulse.

Why didn't I say no? In the interview about *Car*, Ian McNally asked Miri: "Isn't it possible they do it because it's what they've always had to do?"

We climbed in, without our clothes. I went first. Henry was in the back seat and Ansel, the driver's seat. I was closest to the camera, near the window on the passenger side, which was open a couple of inches. Ansel bounced the SuperBall against the seats and dashboard and windows. The boys horsed around, shoving each other. I was used to my brothers roughhousing but this time was different. The longer we were shut up in the hot car, the stronger the rank smells, including body odors, including alcohol. They'd been drinking.

Ansel pointed at me and laughed. He was incredulous. "Berry has big boobies! Berry has big boobies!" It was true, they were newly swollen and sore.

Henry pushed at Ansel from the back seat. "Shut up, you ass."

"Don't fucking tell me to shut up. You're an ass! You're a fucking ass!"

I was pressing myself against the car window to get away from them. The tampon had shifted down, heavy with too much blood. I was clenching my thighs to keep it inside. I needed to get out of the car. I was frantic. I tried to pull the lock tab sunk into the side of the door but I couldn't get hold of it, I couldn't open the door. I pounded the window for Miri. I grabbed the edge of the window and shouted out the open two inches. "We need to stop! I need to get out!" I was light-headed, I was hyperventilating. I couldn't breathe.

The SuperBall shot past me like a bullet and hit the window. Henry shoved Ansel. With a hard, grim tone, one I'd never heard, he said, "Leave her alone. Freak."

Ansel shoved him back, harder. "Fuck off, freak. You love her. You fucking love her. We should all just screw and get it over with."

A fuse, lit. The photo shoots, and the too-soon sexuality we'd been subjected to and were subjects of, what was always between us, never uttered, ignited in the hot car. I heard Ansel's invective, and deep within it was some wrong thing I'd known but never understood.

Henry threw the punch at Ansel's right ear. Ansel's head bounced against the driver's side window. I was so shocked—I'd never seen Henry be violent, even his roughhousing was half-hearted—that I burst into tears. I felt fluid, the tears, the sweat, the blood. The windows clouded over with condensation. I could see my mother out there under her hood, shooting away. Ansel held his injured ear. Henry said in a quiet growl, "You fucking touch her again, I will kill you."

Ansel lunged. They fought across the seat of the car. Limbs flew. I cried, "Stop, stop, stop, please, stop, stop, stop."

A sudden stillness descended. The boys were frozen. They looked at me in horror and pity. Henry said, "Berry . . . ," Ansel said, "Oh, gross . . . ," and I looked down and the tampon was on the seat of the car, thick with black-red blood, and red blood shined sticky on the inside of both of my thighs. I pressed my naked self against the car window, crying in shame, howling to be let out, with the boys behind me. Miri got the shot, of course, before the light was lost, before I stopped complaining.

Car 1967.

Chapter Thirty

IT WAS ALL predicted, long before I was born.

I don't need a shrink to know, trauma takes up a lot of space, and it can overtake the space—meaning me—unless I take continuous inventory, count the back stock, organize it in my mind. Not to fix it, not so everything is all la-di-da, but so I can make room for the present. Just like Henry said.

Here are Miri's notebooks and manila files from the crate off the shelf in #201. Marbled composition books, the experiences of a young girl in the early 1940s. She detailed what she had for breakfast, who said what in a conversation at school, each purchase and dollar spent after Saks or Bonwit shopping trips with her mother. In 1943, she makes a list of book titles. Had she read them or planned to? *A Tree Grows in Brooklyn, Johnny Tremain, The Robe, Little*

House on the Prairie, Being and Nothingness. She was eleven, caught between *A Tree Grows in Brooklyn* and *Being and Nothingness*. She wrote a movie review of *Shadow of a Doubt*. Neatly, she capitalized the letters of the director's name, A. HITCHCOCK. She found the plot implausible, but the movie made an impact on her. She noticed how the camera moved, how angles created tension. She noticed that music provoked and amplified her own reactions. She saw shadows and light that hid and revealed life in the film's cozy family home. She recognized that what she saw was packaged in a certain way by the director. The only memory I have of my mother hugging me is in a movie theater during a Hitchcock film. I smell cigarette smoke and musk as I read Miri's review.

About her own mother, all complaints. Too strict, too boring, too bourgeois. Too—her word—*obedient*. There is nothing about her father. Something is alive in that omission. Brief mentions of Stanley, never more than a few sentences, her penmanship stitched tight around the words. *Stanley snores. Stanley shaves now. I want to die when his feet touch me.* And, scored with exclamation marks: *SM leaves for France with his class! Magnifique!*

In another notebook, Miri was twelve, close to the age I was when my humiliation was captured for *Car 1967*. She went to libraries to read and write. She ate a sandwich, liverwurst with mustard and lettuce on a kaiser roll, on the steps of the Metropolitan Museum of Art. She recorded the duration of her visits: 1.5 hours; 2 hours, ten minutes. With her pocket money, she bought tabloid newspapers. Her favorite was a New York weekly, *PM*. She made a list titled *Look Up,* presumably those photographers and writers for *PM* whom she admired: Weegee, Margaret Bourke-White, Helen Levitt, Ernest Hemingway, Dorothy Parker, Irving Haberman. There are check marks next to each name but I don't know what they mean.

I stop to clean my glasses.

I take out yellowed pages from a manila folder. The onionskin is stiff and dry, crackling and cracking. Letters. I see the salutation: *Dear Mimi,* the pet name. I brace myself. Truth comes hard. Truth hurts. I don't need the faded signature but there it is, there you have it. These are love letters from her brother. A horrible accumulation of years of letters, Stanley at camp, Stanley in Paris, Stanley at college. He wrote explicitly. He was relentless.

My face goes hot. I shut my eyes, but the eye is a lens even when it's closed, and on the inside of my eyelids, I see desolate fields of color with two **X**s, figures in what I first thought was a dance, but now I see is a hunt, one in pursuit and one fleeing. *Marx Xs the Spot.*

In an interview, Diane Arbus said: "A photograph is a secret about a secret."

When Miri sat squinting through cigarette smoke while we bickered through awkward dinners in Grand View, she was envisioning what tomorrow's tableau would be. Ansel and Henry, two aspects of "brother." Me, the little sister, in distress. How she would pose us, prop us, use us. I thought she created ugly scenes because what she saw was that *we*—her children—had something ugly inside. But no. By staging the photographs, Miri was trying to obliterate—to shoot— the ugliness inside herself after the violence done to her by Stanley. Who stole her girlhood, who altered her identity and made her what she became. An artist, for better or worse. Now I realize: what Miri saw through her lens was Miri. Always Miri. She was trying to process her trauma by staging the scenes over and over, with me as the little girl and Henry as the good brother and Ansel as the bad brother. I'm not saying she was justified, I'm saying she had a reason.

What I *am* saying is I was no collaborator. I was Berenice the complainer, the only defense I had.

Albert wasn't sacrificing us to protect Miri's artistic nature. He was protecting her violated body and damaged soul from something even uglier than the Marx Nudes. I'm about to search for my own duct tape to seal Miri's words away, stow the bin and Albert's box in the basement of my building. I remember, there's one more CD left.

What can I do but watch.

My mother is in the distant dining room, reading at the table. We are in the foreground. Albert sits in Miri's chair, singing along with Sinatra. The home movie shakes and jitters and shows his bare feet on the ottoman, the same mustard yellow field where black-and-white zebras run for their lives from flying arrows. Henry is cross-legged on the floor next to him, leaning against the chair, in plaid pajama bottoms and a T-shirt. Our father has his hand on Henry's head, lightly tapping his son's dark brown cap of curls in time to the song. I'm lying on my stomach in a long, flowered flannel nightgown, fuzzy slippers dangling from my feet. We are watching *Frank Sinatra: A Man and His Music II* on television, in living color. I google it: 1966. The square film is faded and grainy. Fuzzy black borders frame our living room, the new television. The film flickers and the subjects move slightly slow or too quick, it's hard to tell. The sound is distorted and doesn't sync. It's Ansel with the Super 8.

I don't think of our household as filled with song. Albert has a good voice. I'd forgotten that. He does all the gestures, mirroring Frank's: the hands go up and down and over and out, the fingers snap, they point up again, back on top. Henry nods along, and Ansel's camera nods too. We know the song, obviously—our father must have had the album, must have played it many times, judging by the television special. When Nelson Riddle cues the orchestra to hit it, and tuxedoed Sinatra stays out in front of the horns, we four chime in. We shout the tongue-twister: *puppet, pauper, pirate, poet, pawn and a king,* and dissolve in laughter, and Albert says, "Shh, shh, the next part," and then he sings out with great strength, pumping his fist along with the words, *"pick myself up . . . get back in the race!"* Just before Ansel stops filming, he zooms in on Albert laughing and wiping his eyes.

I watch again. We are a family. Do I have to say it? Normal. The last CD was stacked with the others in the Ferragamo belt box, possibly by mistake. But maybe not. By that time, my father had been transformed by massive, incomprehensible loss. I don't know. What I do know is somehow, the remaining Marx-Segers did pick themselves up. We did. I wish we could have helped each other more. Maybe we did in ways I can't yet see. I hope so.

What I do know is I have it, here it is, my father's voice, and he's singing.

Chapter Thirty-One

THEY SAY THE legs are the last to go.

At any rate, I never wear dresses, like, never. I should wear dresses more. I do admire women who wear them as if, *No big deal, I'm going to the market, let me throw on this frock*, but I feel vulnerable in a dress. Mass transit means running for the shuttle or the bus, climbing stairs with pervs taking up-skirt pics with their phones, bumping up against a lot of foul poles and people, sitting in just-vacated seats, having puddle scum splash my legs. So no.

But now I have a bike, so today, I'm breaking out my wonder dress. It's a Versace I got at Charivari, Columbus and 72nd Street, early eighties. Simple cut, close to the body, hugs the curves, my natural waist, with a wide boatneck that falls off the shoulders. It has long sleeves and hits at my knee, and my knees are still pretty good.

The dress is a riot of flowers in many colors, and it's sneaky stretch mesh—you can almost see right through, and underneath it's obvious I'm wearing a black bra and black panties, if someone were looking closely. Which I hope he will.

The fantasy when I rode the Citi Bike to Camerama before the crash was to pedal through Manhattan in a dress in springtime. Here I am, on my new bike wearing my old—I mean vintage—sexy dress. I have been practicing diligently in the park, and up and down Riverside Drive. It's the season, and I can tell you, I am the only person in New York City who uses hand signals. I find them helpful. Henry had this sweet yellow ride with matching helmet delivered a couple of weeks ago. It has a basket, too. My theory—can't stop, won't stop with the theories—is that Henry gave me the bike to keep me moving, but also to keep him in my thoughts. It's kind of a peace offering, and I accept it.

I wheel the bike into the elevator and ride up from the building's basement storage. Marcus and Artur hang out on the street in front of the building. Artur smiles and points at me and shakes his head as if I'm a piece of work, now with a bike. I delude myself that Marcus gives me and my underwear the once-over, which is faux-inappropriate since that's not what he's doing, but that's why I put it there, so it's much appreciated.

I hop on, no problem. I'm wearing sneakers, I'm not crazy. I hitch the skirt of my dress together and tuck it between my legs and sit on the fabric a little, so it won't catch in the chain. I stuff the Balenciaga bag in the basket. Dory in the basket would be the perfect Instagram image, but the reality is I would have had to MacGyver some kind of seat belt, I would have been nervous she'd jump—she has a lot of her own ideas and I've had one near-death experience 'gramming myself on a bike. I've seen Dory around with her dads and she greets me like we're related which makes me feel good and bad. And yes, I'm perusing Petfinder again.

I'm taking my new bike and my new skills on the road, to the East Side. My route is south, slow and careful to 72nd Street, where I'll enter Central Park and loop back north, a little bit out of the way up to 89th but I want to zip past the Guggenheim, just because I can, and then I will go back south and east.

What a day, a Tuesday in May. The sun, the blue sky. I ride along, a model cycling citizen, using hand signals nobody's noticing. I'm doing my best, staying steady, and when I get to Central Park, I join the loop, I go with the flow, I'm part of the crowd—strollers and walkers and runners and scooters and skaters and cyclists, and those recumbent guys, always men, and wheelchairs and Jazzies, and we're all out here, navigating the paths in the park. I steer around obstacles and veer off and retake the path. Of course unexpected things happen and I course-correct and continue, and once or twice I stop and step off and muster my resolve and then move along the loop again to get where I'm going.

I arrive alive. I did it. It's a little victory all my own. I wrestle the bike up the curb and find a place to pull myself together. I fix my dress. I retie my sneakers. I take off my helmet and catch a reflection. The more gray—or as I like to say, silver—I have, the frizzier my hair gets. My hair is not cooperating with my new helmet-wearing lifestyle. It doesn't look like Miri's anymore, but it doesn't look like mine, either. Victory and defeat, a win and a loss, both inside a moment. I take out the Dior Rouge and do my mouth. I'm not dead yet.

I don't want to leave the bike outside. So, another door, another struggle. I get stuck halfway in, halfway out of Costello's, trying to get the bike over the threshold. My dress gets caught on the pedal. I'm in a bit of a pickle, trying to enter, and Jeremy appears, wiping his hands on a bar towel. He flicks it over his shoulder and unsticks my dress and opens the door wide with one hand, then lifts the bike with the other. He parks it and hangs my helmet and says, "Martini?"

"Cranberry juice and seltzer. With a lime. Please."

"On the wagon?"

"More like on the bike. Also, I'm taking a break."

He gives me a concerned look. "You okay?"

"Yes, I am. Let's change the subject before I lose my willpower. Do you mind?"

He's a sensitive millennial, of course he doesn't mind. "Well, you look great."

Considering my age, I'll take it. I'm needy and shameless. I turn for him. "I do? Really? The dress? It's okay?"

He gives a long, slow whistle to indicate his approval. A wolf whistle! Women don't need a man's approval, certainly not on appearance, that's reprehensible. Still, I haven't been on the receiving end of a whistle in years, and we're in Costello's, there's nobody around, and I'm a hypocrite and a half-assed feminist, and he's just being nice.

Jeremy says, "I've been practicing whistling. This seemed like the right moment to road test it. The right recipient."

"*To Have and Have Not*! Bogart and Bacall! The legendary whistle scene!"

Jeremy takes out his phone, makes a note of the movie title. "Never heard of it."

I die a little inside. He goes behind the bar; I take the same barstool from my afternoon with Echo. It's just Jeremy and me, on another afternoon, no other patrons, no music, sunlight streaming in, illuminating my bike in the corner. I say, "When are we getting together again? Next work session?"

He shrugs. "Ask your sister. She's the boss. Even Gary defers to her."

"And you two? You and Echo? Personally?"

"You mean are we banging?"

I'm so old I blush. He's really good-looking. He's wearing an X T-shirt he probably got at Anthropologie but I can't hold that against him. At least he picked a good band. "I guess so. I can't figure out what you two have going on."

"I love Echo. Like, like-love. As a friend. Sometimes, too many drinks or other substances, we get together. I'm not sure of anything other than that. She is very focused on her career. She's not letting anything—any*one*—get in her way. We hook up. I'm allowed to say that, right? I mean, you're not her mom or anything."

"No, I am not her mom but I *am* her sister. And I love-love her, as a sister *and* as a friend. I'm being nosy. I want her to be happy. I'm looking out for her. Things are so different. When I was your age . . ." I put my hands up in surrender. "Okay. Whoa. I promised myself those words would never escape me. Let's just say, I'm keeping an eye on your intentions."

Jeremy grabs the soda gun from its holster behind the bar. He leans in and squirts more seltzer into my glass and tops it off with cranberry juice, which I find sexy, so sue me. "That dress makes me think *I* should be wondering about *your* intentions. What are you doing here?" He tips his head and raises his eyebrows and he's flirting harmlessly and it's gratifying and, also, bittersweet.

"I'm meeting someone. I wanted an easy place to—"

On cue, the door opens. Bix has arrived. He looks around, sees me and laughs. "A dive bar. I see I should have picked better the first time."

"Be nice, Bix. This is Jeremy, he takes a lot of pride in his place of work. Jeremy, this is Malcolm Bix."

The men shake hands, but Bix says, "Martini," instead of hello to Jeremy. I've seen him boss service people around already, I'm not surprised. He takes both of my hands and stands me up. He says, "Let me guess. Versace?"

I say, "You really are gay."

We sit shoulder to shoulder. His tangy woodsy scent becomes my atmosphere. He's in a light tweed jacket, a white T-shirt, expensive skinny jeans, and those cool Italian shoes with the straps across the instep that Gary refuses to try. His hair is the exact same, the facial scruff is the same. His cologne is still divine.

He nods. "I am. Gay and married."

"I'll say it again: I'm an idiot. I misread things that afternoon at your place. Or you misrepresented things." I have promised myself I would not apologize for being taken in by Bix's manipulation of me via reckless cross-orientation flirting.

"I was interested in you, Bea. Things aren't always so black and white, right? My instincts kicked in and you responded and I was flattered. Misrepresentation is a bit aggressive, don't you think?"

"Not if you and your fancy husband collect Miriam Marx."

He gets his martini and we toast. He says, "What are you drinking? A Cape Codder?"

"Yes, without the vodka. Less drinking, no smoking. It's tragic." I bump his shoulder with my shoulder. "We have business to discuss, Bix."

"Danilo and I collect photography. We got interested in Miriam's work while he was writing your uncle's biography. The whole crazy story, it seemed like a natural for film. Dani wanted to try the screenplay. I knew Gary from *Opening Act* and that you two were close. I felt like there was an opportunity for you. For us too. That's it."

"If you'd said all that up front in Balthazar, instead of handling me, we might be having a different conversation."

"That's fair. I get that. You might be right." Bix is a smart man.

"I've been back to storage. I mean, the archives. We—my brother Henry and I—really dug in. It's all inventoried." I give a dramatic eyeroll to incite his curiosity, to taunt him just a little. He must be dying to know what I've found.

He takes a deep sip of his icy martini. After a long pause, he says, "Let me ask you a question, Bea."

"Fire away, Malcolm." He smiles because I've used his name, a little dig. I'm sharper when I'm sober.

"Have you read Danilo's book? Your uncle's biography?"

"No. You recommend it? I didn't know my uncle. He and my mother didn't speak."

He takes a long drink. He tilts his head and gestures with his glass in my direction, very confident. "Yes, I recommend it. Very informative. You might learn something. I'll send you a copy."

There is a moment between us that clarifies what we know: we might not be suited for each other in one way, but we are well matched.

"You know what? Don't bother. I don't need it. I have Miri's notebooks, from years and years. From her childhood. Also very informative. Very enlightening." *And you are not getting near them, Mr. Stock Photo Lumberjack.*

"I'll bet." He smiles and places his drink carefully on the bar. He takes out a hundred-dollar bill and slides it under his glass. "I'm sorry we couldn't work together. I really am."

Bix exits and leaves a dark, choppy wake. The light in Costello's changes. He wanted me to read the biography to learn what I already know about Stanley and Miri. To hurt me. Because he didn't get what he wanted. Jeremy comes down to my end of the bar. "You wore the dress for that guy? You get that he's gay, right?"

"Well, of course, I'm not totally clueless." I sigh because I was, but I'm only partially clueless now. "I've got to get out of here. I'm about to fall off the wagon. Do you know if I can put the bike in an Uber?"

Chapter Thirty-Two

"BEA! YOU LOOK amazing. What's different?"

Sure, I have gotten some sleep, I'm okay but *she* looks amazing. She is wearing a white poplin button-down shirt with rolled sleeves, and a voluminous black tulle skirt. She's got a skillful head wrap in a graphic black-and-white print tied in a knot like a bloom right in the front. She wears the shoulder-grazing gold tassel earrings. Her lips are my favorite plum.

I say, "Violet, I have to know. How old are you?"

She laughs. "Why? I love a turban but maybe it's aging me."

"No, just the opposite. You could be thirty-five or fifty-five. I absolutely can't tell."

She says, "I just had a big birthday. Sixty."

"Sixty? Really? We're almost the same age. I'll be sixty soon." We take a new look at each other. We give each other the once-over. We laugh. She's ordered champagne but I stick with mineral water. We are at a good table at the Modern in the Museum of Modern Art, overlooking the sculpture garden, in bloom. In the garden, couples stroll, seniors sit on benches, children run. The trees are bright green. Huge sculptures placed around the garden are hard to understand, but I like looking at them. Abstract forms in neon colors next to giant bronze action figures, as tall as the trees, made to look like partially melted plastic. It's otherworldly, through the glass.

"Let's have lunch and then we can go upstairs. You'll meet your team. We are all very excited to get started, Bea."

I've rehearsed. I've had this conversation in my head but my mouth is dry. The champagne bottle sits in its bucket tableside. My mouth waters but I cover my empty flute when the waiter comes by.

Violet gestures to my dark blazer, my folded hands, the empty champagne flute. "Very professional today."

"I'm not sure I'd go that far. I'm working on it. We'll see." I take a long drink of water. "I've been back to storage. I had an adviser this time."

She lifts her eyebrows—*Oh, really?* She also flashes a glint of curiosity, a twinkle in the eye I've noticed with some women our age, the ones who seem like they know how to be older. The twinkle says, *It's all messy, bring it on, we'll figure it out.*

"Bea, what are you trying to say? Speak freely, please."

"I want to thank you, Violet. Seriously. First of all, you're so impressive. You make me want to dress better and take up more space in the world and be confident. I'm not kidding. But also, you've helped me. You really have. If it weren't for you, I'd never have gone to StoreSpace in the first place. You made me realize that there was . . . hidden value. Beyond the Marx Nudes."

"Are you talking about additional Miriam Marx photography in existence? I mean, I hoped that was the case."

She doesn't just hope, she knows. She knows exactly what's in there. I don't want to overplay my hand because I have a girl-crush on Violet. We're like Sondheim lunching ladies in our nice New York clothes, sipping from crystal, waiting for our fancy food. I want to be friends with her. But we have business. "I went to the storage unit with Henry."

She doesn't seem surprised. "Aahn-ree," she says, with the Parisian spin. "You've reunited."

"Yes. And the value, for me, has less to do with the work and more to do with dealing with it all. With help. From my brother. That kind of value. Which is invaluable." I drink my water to slow myself down. "Where do you get a skirt like that? I could never pull that off. The older I get, the more manly my clothes get. Like Georgia O'Keeffe. You met Henry at Columbia, right?"

She doesn't flinch. "He was a few years ahead. My first. Believe it or not."

"You were Henry's favorite photography nerd, all those years ago. You know unit 201 better than anybody."

She takes her time. She butters her bread. "It took a long time for him to tell me about the photographs. The circumstances. He was hard to be with. He never really let me in. I ended it with Henry, but I got very interested in your mother's work. I stayed in love with Miriam, I guess, as a baby feminist and as an art historian. A few years later, he put out a call for help with the archives. I was at Yale. I kept my distance from Henry but I couldn't resist getting in there. I was ambitious. *Am* ambitious."

"Why didn't you tell me? Why hide it? It seems weird. Stalkerish."

She gives a rueful smile. "Well, maybe a little stalkerish. I didn't want you to think I had ulterior motives or designs on the work. I genuinely want your support for the project. Yes, I organized the space. I bought a combination lock and I had a key, before it changed over to digital. After that, I didn't have the code so I stopped going. But in the beginning? Going through the boxes? It was a shrine. I wrote a lot of my dissertation sitting on the floor of that storage unit."

"A shrine. That's interesting. I described it to my brother as a tomb."

She nods. We sit with it. She says, "How is he? He's the head guy at Camerama now, right?"

"Yes. He has an alias. Hank. Hank Segretti. Albert's name, before Seger. He's very neat. Drives a Volvo. Good hair. How is it that your paths have never crossed?"

"I had a different last name back then, too. An early marriage, when I was naive enough to take someone else's surname. I went up to StoreSpace every few months, and one of the other students sent the Excel reports. I followed your brother's career over the years, but I have no idea if he followed mine. You Marx kids are pretty good at blocking stuff out, I've noticed."

"He was surprised to hear your name, that you were my MoMA contact. Surprised, but not shocked. I could tell there was more to the story of the two of you. And it explained so much about how the work was stored. I didn't push him. We've been apart for a long time. We're taking it slow."

She shrugs. Big matte black plates arrive with artisanal arrangements of spring's bounty, fragrant herbs, lamb and duck and beef, lavender and mint, and precious peas and spring onions and sorrel and pears. "This is lovely, Violet. You might be wasting your VIP mojo on me, though."

"Please don't say that, Bea. We're scheduled upstairs in under an hour. There's no sinister plot. I knew more than I let on. I shouldn't have kept that from you."

"You've mentioned a few times what else might be in storage. Your hope. Undiscovered work. What else is in there?"

She is authentic and straightforward even though she's been caught out. She looks me in the eye. "There are more nudes. There are negatives and prints in several bins labeled *Cuts*. I've been through them many times. Most of the images are good. Some very good, with the anguish your mother liked to expose."

"Instigate is more like it. Go on."

"Out of all the cuts, probably a dozen more align with her work at the time of the Marx Nudes. They are very powerful. The most valuable are the ones she printed herself, of course, but we have experts who'd faithfully print any worthy negatives. The path through the woods. The porch. The staircase inside the house. I haven't gone into detail about them to anyone here. My thought was to let you see first and decide."

"I appreciate that. What else."

"The personal items. Notebooks, papers. They will definitely give context to her work. There was nothing explicit but much implied. Why she chose to focus the way she did. We can set aside an area for a display case, show the notebooks, some of the pages."

I say, "And Woodstock? Henry and I saw those pictures."

"Yes. Woodstock. A lot of negatives and contact sheets and a few dozen prints."

"The weekend my brother died."

Violet puts her hand on mine, brown skin, white skin, and she holds on. Her nails are long and almond-shaped and varnished pale purple. "It was horrific. Truly terrible for you all. For her, too. So much loss."

She is sincere but I take my hand back. I can't give in to sentimentality. I have to be a businessperson. Businesswoman. "What about those pictures? From an expert's perspective. Is there value? Are they worth anything?"

"Look, everything is worth something. The Woodstock photographs are beautiful, but interesting more from an artist's career arc perspective."

I stay quiet for a change. I let her fill in the blanks. I'm learning.

"They show that your mother was moving away from the Marx Nudes. The Woodstock photographs feel like a different Miriam Marx. On the whole, they don't really add to the value of her brand, if you're inclined to think of her work that way. They're sweet, and collectors are not looking for sweet from your mother. That's not to say there aren't plenty of lesser venues who'd want them. Beyond the . . . auspices of MoMA. In other words"—she waves at our exquisite surroundings—"let us do our job. We will do it properly. I promise you that."

I have Henry's outraged *"For money?"* in my mind. In his question, I hear his un-twinned self, full of self-loathing because of a violent impulse and the devastating consequences, and then the banishment by Albert. Albert's mortification and shame, which he had to box and tape the hell out of and stow away so he could have a life. Neither my brother nor my father had the strength to set foot in that storage unit. But I did.

I did. I came along and forced it open. For money. "Violet, do you remember a box? A Ferragamo belt box? Duct-taped like crazy? Labeled *Outtasight Interview?*"

She nods. "I do. I shook it and it rattled and I thought *Eureka! Tapes!* I've been curious for years. Obviously, I've read that interview a hundred times but to hear the whole thing in her voice, unedited. I wanted to open the box but the way it was sealed—so methodical, it seemed almost personal—I resisted the impulse to cut through."

"I didn't resist. I did cut through." Our plates are empty. Dessert and digestif menus arrive. We shake our heads, no thank you. We're both done. Violet plays with a teaspoon. She organizes whatever is left on the table. She uses her index finger to corral crumbs. It must be excruciating to have to wait for this puzzle piece, but she waits.

I let her wait. For a change, I don't speak. I sit with my lips pressed shut. I keep it all to myself to protect us, to honor us, Ansel and Henry and me. I'm possessive. Our trauma is ours. My refusal to share more with her—because really, Violet is not one of us, no matter how closely she has studied the Marx Nudes under the boom light— makes me resolute. I hadn't really, until this moment, decided what to do. I put my coat—vintage Burberry trench from a consignment store—over my shoulders. "I think you should cancel the meeting. For now." I practice not apologizing. I say, "I hope it works out for you. That you're not in trouble with your boss or somebody. The art gods."

We stand and face each other. Violet grips my upper arms and looks at me dead on. She flashes a twinkle again that confirms what we know: disappointment is a given, but the way it plays out, the sur- prises and coincidences, the unpredictability of who or what you think you know, the not knowing much at all, the unexpected outcomes and fuck-ups—it no longer represents a terrifying loss of control. Watching the messy narrative of life make its way—bearing witness, being present—is its own pleasure. After a certain age, it might not be fun, but it's too fascinating to fear. It's what I—we, because Violet understands—couldn't have appreciated before now.

Violet says, "I am disappointed, but I'll survive, and the art gods will survive, too. I haven't gotten what I want, but the journey has been interesting. Getting to know you. Let's not close this door." She holds my gaze and I hers, and she gives me what might be a sexy wink. "I don't give up."

"That's fair. One last question. Echo is dying to know. Did you write Miri's Wikipedia entry?"

She shrugs in an artsy French manner, which means, I assume, *oui*. We hug goodbye. I'm still practicing, and of course, she is great at it.

I decide to walk all the way home, from 53rd Street to 103rd Street, up to the park then Broadway all the way. This time I bounce to the mantra, *I'm on Broadway, I'm walking myself home*. I make it a song. I'm proud of myself. On top of all my action items—StoreSpace? check; Henry? check; Bix? check; Violet? check—and even though I'm totally gun-shy on theories, my assumptions are outdated and my gaydar is vintage—but damn, I could swear Violet was flirting with me. I'm a little bit fed up with art at the moment, but you never know.

Chapter Thirty-Three

I THOUGHT, I assumed, I wondered. I forgot and I remembered.

I drank and smoked, drifted and dozed, tossed and turned. I felt everything, even when I pretended not to. I compartmentalized and denied and that worked for a while, and then I went to the warehouse and punched in the code and stepped into the scary fairy tale.

I opened boxes and bins, I scissored through tape, I slipped the discs in. I looked into everybody's eyes, heard the voices, including my own. I tried to bring to the surface what was known to me but unthought by me. I tried to separate the new known from my long-held wrong assumptions. I didn't want to but I had to challenge the many misty, water-colored memory varieties my brain conjured. I had to resist the mercies of memory. Memory, what the fuck *is* that? I picture the whole mess like DNA strands, so hard-wired and twisted, so deep-core.

I tried and I tried. Not to pat myself on the back but I got here. Not to brag, but I had to be brave, at least in flashes, at least in fleeting moments, and I'll have to be brave again. It's the job description at sixty. Happy birthday to me.

Of course I'm sick of the subject—meaning, the subject in the photographs. That little girl still lives inside me but she's . . . little. She's a faraway little girl in a faraway place, one aspect of the landscape of me. She can stay where she is; that real estate is hers. There's plenty of room. I remember saying to Jeremy in Costello's: *I'm past tense.* That's just not true. I picture myself as Bea on a balance beam, not looking over my shoulder, using my night vision, putting one foot in front of the other. If I fall—I mean, when I fall— I'm going to tumble until I find myself in the sun at the sandy edge of the ocean, which might just be me on my fire escape, listening to the tidal flow of traffic on the highway.

God, I slept well last night. The insomnia isn't gone, but it was gone last night. Mornings are precious. I sit for twenty minutes on a cushion in my new office/meditation zone, Echo's old room; she moved downtown. I do an inner third-eye thing as best I can, although I'm like, *Ugh, who needs a third eye?* I use the same old mantra, *I'm on Broadway, I'm walking myself home. I'm on Broadway, I'm walking myself home.* I do the probiotic and the smoothie, and then an espresso. Dory is here; Patrick and Ronaldo have had a death in the family and are away for a week and I'm the doggo-grandma. So Dory and I, we walk. The park, the trees, the Armenians, the shopkeepers. My neighborhood. My new hobby is hollering at cars and trucks creeping into the crosswalk. I death-stare them and shout, "I'm walkin' heah!" like Ratso Rizzo in *Midnight Cowboy*, and Dory barks like mad to support me. We proceed.

I no longer smoke. I still drink but never alone.

It's such a cliché, but another goddamned AARP article advises that as you get older, you need to make a conscious choice to stop and honor the big five, really see, hear, smell, taste, touch. This conscious practice actually lowers your blood pressure, manages your hypertension, helps with insomnia. And the world is more vivid when I remember, especially now that I'm not as fogged over by alcohol or cigarette smoke.

AARP didn't mention the legitimate sixth sense: proprioception. It doesn't fit the single-syllable singsong recitation, and yet it's in our genes. The awareness of where the body is in space. Little-girl me knew how my body was arranged was wrong, but I couldn't physically move away so I adapted. I moved my mind away. From the age of three. That required subconscious heroism and that effort took up so much of me that it hurt, and it's not okay. But that's what happened. I'm fine. Mostly fine.

Echo is here. Gary is here. He's traveled all the way uptown to my place, to my home, which is a first. I'm indulging him as usual. We drank champagne and now I am sitting on the closed lid of the toilet bowl in my bathroom, with a white towel around my shoulders. The towel and my lap and the floor are strewn with skeins and coils of black and silver, there it goes, my magnificent hair, at last. Gary shuffles around me with sharp scissors and a comb, lifting sections, slicing at them, stepping back to evaluate his work, stepping in to cut again. He has no special talent for haircutting, but he thinks it's "in his blood." Mr. Goldbaum, Gary's dad, owned a wildly popular chain of hair salons in the early seventies, Hair Today, when hippies made unisex a thing and beauty parlors became uncool. Gary did the sweeping up, and eventually the shampooing, and my theory is, this is when he learned to become irresistible to women. He was so good at my braid, and he is very good at head rubs. He's not in perfect shape, he's got weakness on the left side from the stroke, so this whole situation is dicey, but he is getting a terrific kick out of it and it's making Echo laugh. I'm happy to share my anxious ambivalence regarding Gary's work with them.

He presses the scissor blades against my newly exposed nape and trims with great delicacy. He is close. His breath teases my ear. He smells like coffee with cream and sugar chased by a Life Saver, and Kiehl's aftershave and champagne. I shiver, not exactly desire, not exactly no desire. His Einstein eyebrows are nuts. He's let his hair go. It's still styled sharp and spiky, it's coming in gray-white now, hardly any black. The onstage part of his career is over, but now he is patron saint of Echo's career. And maybe Jeremy's too. I hook my finger into the belt loop of his jeans. I look up into his face, which I have always loved and will love forever, no matter how tired and wrinkled and droopy-on-the-left it has gotten. I am not his first love, I am not his big love, but he loves me as much as he can, and it's Gary who has kept us together, and duration counts for a lot.

Echo sits on the floor with her phone, alternately taking videos and pictures. She calls Gary Gary, but now and then when she's trying to get her way, she calls him Dadish. Adorable. She calls me Bea, just Bea, and with the three of us each at our ages, laughing together in my tiny New York bathroom, my no-babies crowd in with me too. I've never discussed this grief with Gary. I've always blamed him for not being wired for the conversation, but let me amend that. Let me do better. I'm not really wired for it either. I used to rant to myself, *Why do I have to bring it up? Why is it my responsibility?* The answer is, because I can. Gary can't. I can guide us safely through the sorrow. We need to talk. I promise myself I will bring it up soon, just not today.

My old man says, "You know, I once cut Exene Cervenka's hair in the kitchen of a restaurant on Spring Street with an eight-inch chef's knife. True story." He pronounces it *Egg-sheen Sherfenga* and *Shpring Shtreet* and *Too shtory* because his lip still droops.

I am trying to practice my newfound power of keeping my mouth shut, unsuccessfully. "Is your hand shaking? I think I need the salon for this."

"Why spend that money. Trust me, haircutting is in my blood. My father—"

"No. Absolutely not. Do not start with the father."

"Stop talking. I'm trying to keep it even. Now the bangs."

"Gary, god help me, no. I don't want bangs. No bangs." I look at Echo who has a pained *eek* expression on her face. Her hair is still buzzed, still platinum, and honestly, I can't imagine it any other way. She is wearing massive jeans that droop to show off her flat stomach and her hipbones, and a big plaid bathrobe over my old Patti Smith T-shirt, the one with Patti in the white shirt, the loose tie, the slung jacket, from the cover of *Horses*. Taken by Robert Mapplethorpe. I say to her, "You can't have that shirt."

Gary says, "By the way, Bean. Your boyfriend, Bix. What did you do to him?"

I laugh. "It's the new me." I say to Echo, "I kind of kicked ass with the Hollywood guy. He rejected me and then I rejected him harder." I point at her T-shirt and start to give her Bix's backstory, but I wave it away. She can discover Mapplethorpe for herself.

Echo watches us and records us and whistles, some tune I don't know. I beam at her. "That's good whistling. Did Jeremy teach you that?"

She gets coy and says, "Maybe." As old-fashioned and stupid-romantic and not-like-that-anymore they keep telling me things are, I have hopes for them.

Gary keeps talking as if our sidebar hadn't occurred. "He's got a script. He's going to change the names, do it anyway. His own money."

I shrug. "I don't care. What will be, will be. I can't control Bix."

"He's after me to be a producer. He likes the proximity to you. Wants to keep the door open."

I'm practicing everything. Hugs, not apologizing, listening better, fewer words, more action, looking out for myself. "Gary. Let me be direct: Do not work on Bix's movie. I would be upset. Upset enough to yank my work and my Echo from your projects and your world. She's mine." She is my person. I wink at her. "I haven't signed anything yet, old man. My lawyer still has the papers. I could change my mind and transfer the notebooks and all my lyrics—my intellectual property, my publishing deal—over to Micki Lopez, who would love to have Echo on her roster. Our roster, now that I'm Micki's . . ." I look to Echo. "What am I, again?"

"Creative development . . . person? Something like that?"

"Right, creative development person. Something like that. You know the name of Micki's new label, right? NoBAM. No Boys Allowed Music. You are lucky, Gary, that I have a soft spot for you."

"Jesus Christ, don't get excited. I'm trying to finish up." He comes at me with the scissors.

"I'm not excited. You told me to get a lawyer. I got a lawyer. From now on, he will get excited for me."

"Look at you. Threatening me. All this empowerment, it's a pain in the ass."

Echo and I both laugh. She provides color commentary as she records. "Folks, that is the sound of the dying patriarchy."

He grumbles, "Nobody's griping about the patriarchy when it's time to write the checks."

I sigh. "That is an excellent point. I'm working on it. Sincerely. Your investment in me may be amortized at some point. Now that 'I, Alive' is back from the dead again. Now that I have"—I make a dreamy smile—"income. And the possibility of revenue streams."

I deleted *Exposed/Exposure*. I couldn't write it anyway. The story kept changing. Keeps changing. I'm not ready to draw any conclusions. Of course there's more to it, but I am done deepening the Marx

Nudes groove for a while. I don't know Henry's thinking on this and I'm open, I'm available, but only to a point. We communicate by text and email and FaceTime. It's not the way I pictured it, and I'm a little disappointed about that, but also, it's the way it ought to be. It's the way *I* want it to be. For now. Henry and I don't know each other. I'm just starting to recognize myself in reflections. I don't need any old, rogue chemicals screwing up my development process.

It's my narrative and I'm sticking to it.

Of course I had the fantasy that I would ambush ninety-one-year-old Stanley Marx, sunning himself in Sagaponack. I would introduce myself and . . . What? Accuse him? Beat him up? I also daydreamed about going back to StoreSpace and hauling everything out to the parking lot and throwing a match and walking away, cool and casual with a giant conflagration behind me. But that's the Hollywood ending.

Instead I got Jeff to reprogram the keypad for unit #201 and send Henry the new code in an email. I've put the *Outtasight* CDs back into the Ferragamo box and duct-taped the hell out of it again, and I tossed it into a crate with Miri's notebooks and the fucked-up love letters. I took the crate down to the basement, to the little storage cage that comes with apartment #12D. My plan is to give it to Henry at some point. What Henry does with all of it is up to him. I kept the CD of Albert singing Frank, and used a black Sharpie to label it: THAT's LIFE. I made a copy for Echo. I like to imagine her watching that old piece of music history in her shoebox studio apartment, considering a punk cover of Sinatra, like Sid Vicious and "*My Way*."

Gary says, "All done."

He rubs my head and the last clippings flutter down around me. The amount of hair on the towel and my lap and the floor is astonishing. He uses a washcloth to clear cuttings from my face and neck. The damp cloth and cool air on my bare neck is delicious. I feel lighter. I say, "Can I look?"

"There's your mirror. Who's stopping you?"

Echo says, "It's rad."

"Okay. Let me look." I step to the bathroom mirror. I see myself best here. The light is right. My color is good. My eyes are clear. My skin is lined from living in it, from laughing, from squinting and crying, from surprise, from thinking hard, from figuring things out or being absolutely unable to do so. So much black hair has been cut away, what's left is gunmetal gray and the streak at my widow's peak is bright white. I have a long neck. My eyes look bigger. I look boyish. I have my pixie haircut.

Echo and Gary drift away. She walks Dory. He makes alarming noises in my kitchen, trying to set the table for lunch. I'm starving. This morning I was ambitious. I made a dressing from olive oil, smashed-up anchovies, garlic and lemon juice. I washed green leaves and toasted pine nuts. I boiled eggs and plated pickles and olives and I sliced turkey and rolled salami and cheese. The plate is covered with a cloth, sitting in the refrigerator, waiting for us. At lunch, I plan to float the idea of taking a trip to Italy, a belated birthday celebration, we three and maybe Henry plus a container of Albert dust, and Jeanne and Deborah too, to the town the Segrettis came from. When I get back, I'm getting my own damn dog.

My apartment rests in afternoon light. I keep looking in the mirror. There I am. I stretch and then I bring my hands down together, namaste-style. I say, "*Thank you, Bea*," out loud. I picked that up from a gratitude video on YouTube and at first I felt stupid doing it, but it actually does help me stop and reset rather than reach for a cigarette.

I read something recently about microchimerism. Micro, "tiny." Chimera, "fire-breathing hybrid monster," from Greek mythology. Genetically different cells can be found in mothers, meaning she has retained their cells in her body after her children are born. Those tiny monsters colonize her. Bits of her babies stay inside for her lifetime. And it goes both ways. Mother has colonized her children, too, and bits of her can be found inside them. So when the greeting cards or advertisements remind us that our mothers are always with us, it's not just Hallmark, it's science. Scientists can also see the trauma of the Holocaust in the DNA of family members two and three generations after that event. Trauma is alive inside. My mother, the artist, she's there, her wounded self and her warped vision and her remote parents and her brother the rapist. My brothers, the idols of my girlhood, fighting for scraps of love from Albert, trying to hide from Miri's lens, trying to extinguish desire, they're there; and my father, of course, duct-taping a box full of darkness, his gift to me, along with sending me my Echo. Gary is in there, too, naturally, in the wayward cells of our three no-babies. Speaking of cells, I still surf waves of worry over cancer. How could I not? I promise myself I'm going to talk with Gary about this too, my health, because happiness shared expands, and fear shared is cut down to size. My fingers are crossed for luck. More luck.

Age is not just a number. I'm all my ages, and I'm all my names. I'm Berenice and Berry and Bean and Bea. Everything and everyone is inside me. I don't need to exorcise anything. I have plenty of space. I just need to keep storing and sorting as I uncover and discover. There is no alternative, there is only getting in there and doing the job, and then doing it again if I need more room, and then again. When I can.

I don't feel cursed, I feel blessed.

I take one last look. I'm framed by the mirror. I'm new with my new hair but I see the old young me. I see behind me to the black-and-white past, where the girl is stopped in time and caught by light, but it's a photograph, just a photograph, and any viewer would know that in the very next moment the girl moves into her real life. I really love it. I might give it to Echo as a gift to celebrate an accomplishment, or I might keep it. I don't know.

Acknowledgments

THANKS TO CHUCK Adams, Amanda Dissinger, Betsy Gleick, Brunson Hoole, Debra Linn, Abby Muller, Elisabeth Scharlatt, Sue Wilkins, and the entire team at Algonquin. Thanks to Stephen Brayda and Cathy Schott for the thoughtful cover design.

Thank you for much more than agenting to Jane Berkey, Andrea Cirillio, Meg Ruley; also to Jessica Errera, Chris Prestia, and the staff of Jane Rotrosen Agency.

Thanks is not enough but thank you, most especially, to Sophia Hoffman and Grace Dover Hoffman; and Neil Lester; and Melissa Glassman; Catherine Heraty, Sarah Key, and Beth Ann Maliner; also Fareeda Ahmed, Blair Breard, Emily Doyle, Celia Fogel, Joseph Krongold, John Morris, Julia Race, Tracy Rhine, Hillary Richard, Kent Shell, Sue Stoffel, Anastasia Zankowsky.

Thanks to the Leopardi Writing Conference for recognition and resources: founders Thomas Cooney and Lain Hart; my teachers and colleagues in Recanati, Italy, especially Lou Berney, Anthony Franze, Lynn Freed, Jennifer Robinson, Charlie Schroder, Lynn Swanson.

Thank you to Jennifer Gilmore and Caroline Leavitt.

Thank you to Hanna Irie, Ann Patty, Elena Seibert, Dina Seiden, Karen and Dan Stewart, and Bess Weatherman, each of whom knows why. Thanks to Nina Lorez Collins and the women of the Woolfer community for their voices.

Thanks to my parents, Marie and Tom, who taught me to find the fun; my daughters, Sophie and Grace, who taught me how to joy; and Enzo, who, to be honest, did most of the carrying.

CARRY THE DOG

What Really Happened
An Essay by Stephanie Gangi

Questions for Discussion

What Really Happened
An Essay by Stephanie Gangi

CARRY THE DOG is not an autobiographical novel. I did use some of my own memories as I wrote it, even though aging has worked its disappearing trick and I've forgotten so much. I filled in the gaps with hazy assumptions and wobbly conclusions in order to create a narrative of me. Basically, I made stuff up.

The whole darned concept—memory—is only tangentially connected to what *really* happened. What really happened lives deeper than the story we tell ourselves about who we were, who we are.

When I'm reclined, eyes closed, in the endodontist's chair, the bright operatory light angled on me like my personal sun as I wait for the root canal, I call up "that day at the beach when the kids were little" to steady myself in the spin of anxiety. As a young mother I reclined in a summer-striped beach chair with my eyes closed under the actual sun, skin sprayed by the crashing surf while my toes sifted sand and I listened to the kids' laughter on the wind. Thirty years later, I clean out a cabinet and toss an old bottle of suntan lotion, get some goop on my finger and smell that scent, and—*bam*. On that beach day so long ago, I was imprinted with happiness to infinity, so much so that I use that memory like kryptonite to repel dental pain.

Just before I drop the lotion into the trash, sorrow sneaks in too: that day was a couple of blurry weeks after the death of my mother, who would typically have been with us. I was a young mother with a mother who died too young. What a cascade of past happy/sad selves, all in a moment, in a scent, years later. I wanted *Carry the Dog* to show Bea's deep dive into memory to find a truer narrative than the one she's been telling herself, so she can figure out how to be Bea going forward.

I make the quest hard. She's on the brink of sixty with a dark childhood, stalled ambitions, collapsing beliefs about herself and her family, plus she drinks and smokes too much. It's time—with less time ahead than has gone before—for her to take stock of the past in order to move into her future. She needs to know what really happened. She needs *to want* to know.

In the novel, Bea tells Echo, her half sister, about going to a punk show on prom night lifetimes ago. Like Bea, I went to my high school prom in a cornflower-blue quasi-Victorian gown, and afterwards to a club to see the New York Dolls. I was mesmerized by the lead singer's long legs in jeans, his platform shoes, his snarl and sweat, signifiers of some subculture I hadn't known existed. David Johansen, now seventy-plus, was noted and processed by my seventeen-year-old neural pathways; many years later I conjured Gary Going, aging rock star and Bea's ex-husband, one of my favorite characters to write. Without giving anything away, Bea finally examines the myth of their meeting and gains insight into complex relationships. More than four decades later, I think my memory served its purpose for Bea.

Speaking of complex relationships, I was left with the contents of a post-divorce home that had to be moved into storage and then sat for years waiting for me to deal with it. It took up a lot of psychic space. And so, I burdened Bea with a storage unit too. For me, finally unpacking and sorting brought mostly sentimental recollections and mild aha moments, but I don't come from a family full of secrets. Bea does. She knows that stepping into unit #201 won't be a skip down memory lane.

She discovers some of the same items I did when I opened bins and boxes. In the olden days, my father was obsessed with a new slide projector, the one Don Draper famously brands in *Mad Men*. My dad spent hours organizing slides, setting up the screen, adjusting the height of the projector. I'd forgotten about the Carousel until I opened a box and there it was—with sleeves of slides, a scent distant and dusty, my father risen like a genie from a bottle who could not grant my wish, which was for him to still be around. But here he was, sort of, so, wish granted?

In the boxes, too, were journals, big black sketchbooks for writing and drawing and into which I taped ticket stubs and matchbooks and fortune cookie predictions. On one page I taped something I wrote for a young man. I was secretly dallying with him, the on-again, off-again beau of a friend of mine. We were shameless, moths/flame. I wrote a song about him in a bar, on a napkin, called "I, Alive." There it was, in the old notebook. I gave it in its entirety to Bea, who has lost track of her dream of being a lyricist. I thanked my twenty-two-year-old self!

Another bin holds photographs, snapshots and Polaroids of every size, various and odd-shaped, black-and-white or faded. One stack became another catalyst for *Carry the Dog*. My mother—nothing like

Miriam, Bea's mother—had taken pictures of me in the den of our split-level wearing a Wes Anderson-esque succession of sixties outfits and tortured facial expressions. I was a gangly twelve-year-old; my guess is my fashion magazine–wielding mother guilted me into "modeling," posing me in a pleated tent dress with a psychedelic swirl print, a black-and-white-striped vinyl raincoat with a matching newsboy cap, and oh yes, a white bikini that looks like underwear. In the tragic bikini shot, my arms are crossed to hide my body and it appears I'm about to cry.

I'm not suggesting anything more here than what it was: my bored, formerly glamorous mother stuck in the suburbs with a camera and a daughter and the haul from a shopping spree. But coming upon those images blasted open so much for me, particularly what it was like to be an introverted girl with an extroverted mother (and I know I'm lucky that that's the most I had to endure). How a mother can—in my own case, innocently; in Bea's case, not—hijack a child's body and identity in order to make themselves make sense. I literally shake the snapshots to try to free my young self from my mother's gaze. For Bea, the stakes are much higher, the gaze much darker. She must step out of the frozen past and her mother's vision to be free.

Bea's quest, my quest, maybe anyone's quest, is to accept that memory is unreliable. It's a hologram, purposely shape-shifting as the light hits it. As we gain wisdom—hey, as we age—we see angles and shadows, blur and glare. It all serves to show us who we were and who we might be next. Bea is not me but is not *not* me. I'll give the protagonist of my new novel-in-progress the gift of my faulty memory, too. I'm in the process now, again, of making up what really happened.

Questions for Discussion

1. The first line of *Carry the Dog* is "I'm in the dark, I can't see." What do these words reveal about Bea? How does this reverberate through the rest of the book?

2. The philosopher Soren Kierkegaard said, "Life must be understood backwards but lived forwards." Bea is fifty-nine years old and has done the latter without dealing with the former. Why has it taken her so long to look at the past? Why now?

3. In what ways does Bea resist the cliché of "older woman"?

4. As Bea is confronted with new truths about her family, she realizes that her own faulty memory, wrong assumptions, and impulse to

compartmentalize have all contributed to her being "stuck." How do these traits of Bea's play out in the novel in terms of her relationships? Her career? In addition to the ways they've held her back, have they also helped her become more resilient?

5. Bea is a baby boomer, and the novel's backdrops—photography and rock and roll—are, for her, twin pillars of her generation's culture. What else in the novel do you associate with boomers? How does Bea's boomer identity shape the way she looks at Echo's world?

6. The past is alive for Bea in many ways, in particular through storage unit #201 at StoreSpace. Have you ever found yourself unexpectedly confronted with physical reminders of the past? How did you react?

7. *Carry the Dog* is a book full of brand names and fashion and objects. How many can you remember? How do Bea's belongings help ground her? Which of your "everyday things" help ground you?

8. ". . . Miri's photographs showed that childhood is dark, innocence is a myth, motherhood is a trap, and art—Art—will set you free." This is Dr. Yeun's perception of Miri's work. She believes that although making art took its toll on the Marx family, it was a higher calling than motherhood; Miri was obligated to honor it because of her unique voice and talent. What do you think?

9. The reader learns that Miri's own secret trauma fueled her art. While this knowledge doesn't exonerate her mother, it gives Bea context for the Marx Nudes that is easier to live with. Does the context make a difference to you as a reader in your perception of Miri?

10. Names are significant in this book. Bea herself has many: hyphenated and unhyphenated names, nicknames, pet names. Other characters, too, have names that are evocative and meaningful. What meanings can you identify?

11. Four key relationships define Bea's reality: Gary, Dory, Echo, and Henry. With each, Bea gives and receives great love, but she mistrusts the love that's returned. She is always on the lookout for disloyalty, betrayal, and abandonment. Why? What does she learn?

12. Echo represents many things to Bea: motherhood, sisterhood, daughterhood, friendship, her younger self, her freer self, her lost ambition, her late-blooming feminism. What scenes and events in the novel evoke each of these for you?

13. Bea has a conflicted relationship with Albert and a similar relationship with Gary. The two men are insensitive, misogynistic, living in the past, and self-absorbed, but they are also funny and loving and abiding. Do you let them off the hook, as Bea does?

14. Malcolm Bix offers the lure of fame and fortune, while Dr. Violet Yeun offers an artistic legitimization of Miri's work. Bea is conflicted. What do you think of her ultimate decision?

15. In the initial draft of *Carry the Dog*, Bea and Henry grow close and even decide to live together. Stephanie Gangi made the big change to that relationship's arc late in the editing stage because the neatness of the ending didn't feel organic to Bea's own arc. What do you think of the author's decision?

16. What is the last sentence of the novel? Why do you think the author chose it to end Bea's journey?

© ELENA SEIBERT

STEPHANIE GANGI is a poet, essayist, and fiction writer. Her acclaimed debut novel, *The Next*, was published when she was sixty. Her shorter work has appeared in *New Ohio Review*, *Arts & Letters*, *Literary Hub*, *Catapult*, the *Woolfer*, *Bust*, and *NextTribe*. She lives in New York City.